LOVE AFFAIR

At her door Desirée said, "I enjoyed tonight, Austin. Thank you."

"I'm glad you had a good time."

Desirée unlocked the door. "I don't think we'll have a problem fooling anyone with our little charade. We get along well enough to give the appearance that we've known each other for years." She flipped on the foyer light, stepped inside, and turned to him. "Thanks again, Austin. I'll see you Sunday afternoon."

"Good night, Desirée." Spontaneously Austin bent and kissed her soft cheek.

She saw the action coming and thrust her chin upward so he wouldn't have to bend so far. Her body tensed slightly when Austin's fingertips grazed her chin. A gentle but firm pressure turned her face toward his, as his warm, moist lips moved along a diagonal trail to her mouth.

She gasped. This was the last thing she had expected from Austin Hughes, her *boss* . . .

His fingers still held her chin, and a fingertip moved to stroke the corner of her lips. With his other hand he cupped her shoulder in an attempt to bring her closer. Desirée spread her palms on his chest, not to stop him, but in an effort to prevent the kiss from getting too intimate.

Instinctively she knew it was about to end. Austin's hand slowly fell away from her chin and their lips gently broke apart.

She stared at him expectantly, not knowing what to say.

"That probably shouldn't have happened," he said, his voice low with embarrassment. "But I think it had to, and I can't say I'm sorry it did."

Love Affair

Bettye Griffin

BET Publications, LLC
www.bet.com
www.arabesquebooks.com

ARABESQUE BOOKS are published by

BET Publications, LLC
c/o BET BOOKS
One BET Plaza
1900 W Place NE
Washington, D.C. 20018-1211

All Kensington Titles, Imprints, and Distributed Lines are available at special quantity discounts for bulk purchases for sales promotion, premiums, fund-raising, and educational or institutional use. Special book excerpts or customized printings can also be created to fit specific needs. For details, write or phone the office of the Kensington special sales manager: Kensington Publishing Corp., 850 Third Avenue, New York, NY 10022, attn: Special Sales Department, Phone: 1-800-221-2647.

First Printing: February 2001

10 9 8 7 6 5 4 3 2 1
Printed in the United States of America

This book is dedicated to the
Smith "Coughdrop" sisters of Yonkers, NY:
Mrs. Juanita "Weenie" Smith Morton
Mrs. Eva Mae "Bettye" Smith Griffin
and the Coughdrop Sisters' little sister,
Mrs. Marguerite "Micki" Smith Morris

ACKNOWLEDGMENTS

A big mm-wah to all of the following for your assistance and support:

The Indianapolis/Bloomington connection: Katrina and Aaron Underwood; Gary, Robin, Eva and Gabriel Griffin; Mrs. Cornelia Golden; and the staffs of the Doubleday Book Shop at Circle Center and Waldenbooks at Lafayette Square.

The New York connection, both direct and secondary intention: Ray Baer, Alisha Griffin Baez, grand nieces (and future readers!) Melody Stokes-Baez, Nidia and Serenity Baez; Marshall Ballard (who agreed I could use that neat name of his for a future hero), Mrs. Peggy Black, Cheryl McFadden Charles, Evelyn Davis, James "Jimmy Dee" DeRosario, Gail Sullivan Forrest, Mrs. Dorothy Gill, Dianne Griffin, Bea Hardy, Dorothy Hicks, Sharon McDaniel Hollis, Gwen and Wilbur Holt and daughter Tonya, who in just three short years (gasp!) will be old enough to read my books; Joy Jarvis, Sharon Julius, Pat Kasper, Helen McCoy, Mr. and Mrs. Chester Morris, Alicia Morton, Mrs. Juanita Morton, Dawn Babak Mytych, Lori Babak Siudym, Wade Smith, Lana Thomas, Rhonda McDaniel Tirfagnehu, Sheila Tyler, Lillian Morton Walton and especially the Alexander Reading Group and my girl Carol Jankowski.

The Internet connection: Ruth Bridges of the Atlantic Bookpost, avid readers and reviewers Brenda Woodbury and Sean Young, and, fellow MTs Vickie Herndon (and daughter Kimberley Hartley,) Janice Morningstar, Rae Morrill, Christine Myers, Joy Rademacher, Torrey Shannon and Becky Woodford for taking time out to help me come up with a new title (back to work, girls!).

And, closest to my heart, the Jacksonville connection: Bernard Underwood, Timothy Underwood, my mom, Thomas and Beverly Love, Griffin Love, Lorna Love and Erica Griffin.

A special thank you to The Bard Society, including Frank, Jeffrey, Lee, Steve, Beth and Tom.

I hope I haven't left anyone out, but if I have please be assured that even if my brain overlooked you, you're in my heart.

Prologue

Austin put the signed contract on his desk. He leaned back in his chair, closed his eyes and enjoyed a rush of exhilaration as he savored what this piece of paper meant for Wallace and Hughes, the consulting company he co-owned.

In the midst of his triumph he took a moment to be grateful that Elaine, his secretary, had closed the door to his office on her way out, after she handed him the fax. He wouldn't want any of his employees to see him now, sitting with his eyes closed, grinning like a fool.

After just a few moments of quiet satisfaction and anticipation, he reached for the phone. He was anxious to make the announcement to the others in the office, but before he could do that he had to inform his partner, Phil Wallace, who headed their firm's operations in Boulder, Colorado.

"We got the Accolade Group," Austin said without preamble as soon as Phil came on the line. Grinning broadly, he held the receiver away from his ear as Phil shouted in jubilation.

"Oh, man," Phil said in a normal tone after he had calmed down, although his breathing was still coming in short spurts. "I can't believe this. What did Collins say when you took him to dinner last night?"

"He didn't say a word about signing, but this morning

Federal Express dropped off an envelope from their New York office. I opened it, and out fell a letter requesting a one-year contract for semiannual surveys of all their properties. I drew up the contract and faxed it over to him, and the signed copy just came back. I don't know what swayed him. You of all people know you can never tell what makes a client decide, Phil. Maybe he just liked the restaurant I took him to. I got him on the phone as soon as his fax came in, and he's anxious to get started. Just think: two full surveys of every Accolade Hotel around the world! They're on every continent except Antarctica. And get this—he wants us to do one-time limited surveys of the Salud Hotels as well, at least the ones with locations in the same cities as the Accolades."

"Their competition?"

"Hell, it won't be the first time we've been asked to shop someone's rival. But we stand to make a fortune from them, even doing the Saluds only once. I've got to get a second contract drawn up for that part of the deal, but Collins assures me he'll sign it while he's in town if I can get it over to him before he returns to London. Elaine made an inquiry to the Saluds, and they're sending us an updated property list, which we'll use to determine which cities have both a Salud and an Accolade."

"Oh, man, this is great, just great. It looks like our little venture is truly global now. You done good, Jack," Phil added, using the grammatically incorrect phrase they had favored ever since their college days.

"Doggone right I did," Austin replied, grinning.

They spent a few more minutes discussing the wishes of their newest client, agreeing that October was the soonest they could begin.

After their conversation ended Austin leaned back in his high-backed leather chair, his hands clasped and comfortably tucked behind his head, again thinking about what this latest contract meant for Wallace and Hughes's standing in their field of quality control in the hospitality industry. Then he impulsively lowered his hands, reached for the phone and tapped out a number with the pad of his index finger. He waited patiently while the line rang and was answered by a voice mail recorded message in Monique Oliver's carefully clipped tones. She knew when it was appropriate to project competence and efficiency and when it was all right to let her hair down.

They had met over a year earlier and had clicked from the start, but despite common interests their relationship had not blossomed. Austin was surprised Monique hadn't dumped him by now in favor of someone who was around more often; his constant traveling made it difficult to sustain a relationship. Not that he and Monique really had a *relationship;* they were more like two really good friends who shared a bed whenever the mood struck, which was fairly often. It was comfortable, even if there was no future in it. If it was okay with her, it was okay with him. It wasn't like there were any other prospects on the scene for him.

"Hey there," he greeted at the prompt. "Just wanted to say hello and let you know I've got a few local surveys coming up next month. I hope you can join me. After these dog days of August we can celebrate autumn in New York. See you, sweetness." He hung up and leaned back in his chair, his head resting against his palms. Yes, he thought, things couldn't be better.

Austin stared openmouthed at Phyllis Thomas. "You're leaving? *Now?"*

"I know it comes as a shock, Ozzie, but we have to move quickly. Eddie didn't expect to be transferred. He wants me to go with him, and the only way I'll go is if we get married first. And the bank wants him down in Charlotte ASAP."

"But you know we've got the African surveys coming up. They want a married couple. You're the only one I can bring, Phyllis. I can't show up with Julie or Fran; I doubt the clients would appreciate the controversy of an interracial pairing. Besides, we're supposed to be inconspicuous, not stand out like Shaquille O'Neal among a group of munchkins. Can't you put the wedding on hold until after we cover Africa? It would mean a lot to me."

Phyllis shook her head, her distress at the situation obvious by her pained expression. "Ozzie, I really wish there was some way I could handle this that would make everyone happy. I know how important the company is to you, but my personal life has to come first. No one wants to see Africa more than I do, but I've been hoping Eddie would propose for nearly a year. Now it's happened, and as it is there's barely enough time to organize a ceremony and reception before we relocate. But I'm not exactly leaving you high and dry. You've got that new girl in Boulder; she's black."

"I know. She's doing the Phoenix resorts with Mickey. It's her first survey," he added pointedly.

Phyllis sighed. "I know she's new, but I hear she's really good, and she speaks French and everything. And there should still be time to shuffle the schedule. I'm sure they haven't even gotten the airline tickets for October this far in advance."

Austin assumed the classic pose of the thinker, his chin resting on his closed fist. "I guess she's a possibility, but I would much rather bring a more experienced agent. This is too important to leave to someone brand new."

"I really am sorry, Ozzie," Phyllis repeated softly. "I hate to leave you in the lurch. But you can always send Julie or Fran with one of the senior guys. Or send Paul and Marianne. At least they're already married and won't have to pretend."

Austin frowned. That had occurred to him as well, but he wanted to go too badly. He'd never been to the land of his ancestors. The whole time he was courting John Collins of the Accolade Group to sign on the dotted line, he vowed that if they came aboard he'd be the first to shop their hotels on the African continent. If he didn't make it this time, he'd have to wait six months, until the second survey. He simply didn't want to wait.

He placed his hands palms down on the desk, then rose and approached his employee and frequent work partner. "I'm the one who should be apologizing to *you.* Here it is, the happiest time of your life, and I'm so wrapped up in business I didn't even congratulate you." He bent to kiss her cheek. "I'm really very happy for you, Phyllis. I'm going to miss hearing you carry on over Eddie."

"Oh, come now; I never carried on. I just talked about him a little, that's all."

"You talked about him, all right. All around the world," he teased, putting an affectionate arm around her shoulders. "And I certainly hope I'll be invited to the wedding."

"Of course you will be, silly."

Austin's smile faded the moment Phyllis left his office. His thoughts immediately turned to the new junior quality control agent. Donna, Dorothy, Denise . . . he couldn't even remember her name. She had started working for Wallace and Hughes just two weeks before and was on her very first survey. It was hard to believe that someone so new to the company was about to be handed the weighty responsibility of surveying the finest hotels in West Africa, but if he wanted to go he had no choice. Still, it was far from an ideal situation. He'd never even met the woman, which in itself would make pulling off the married couple scenario difficult at best. What if they had no chemistry?

He reached for the agent schedule. Her name was Desirée, Desirée Mack. At least he remembered it started with a *D.* She was presently on assignment at a resort in Scottsdale, Arizona. He'd call Mickey, the senior agent on the site, and have him break the news to her. At the same time he'd find out if Mickey thought she could handle it. And she could always refuse to go. In that case he'd have no choice but to hand over the Africa assignments to one of the senior agents.

For a moment he considered asking Monique to take a leave of absence to accompany him. She'd surely jump at the opportunity, and of course no one would doubt *they* were a couple. They wouldn't even need a suite; they could share a bed like a real married couple. But Monique didn't know the first thing about the work involved. There was no justification for bringing an unqualified person along; what counted most was that they do a good job for their new client. Desirée at least had undergone extensive training by Mickey, who was one of the best. No, Austin would have to forget Monique, cross his fingers and hope like hell it all worked out with Desirée.

It was asking an awful lot for a woman to leave her home for over a month. The majority of Wallace and Hughes's agents were unmarried, and many of the female agents had cited the lack of time spent at home in handing in their resignations. Travel was glamorous and exciting, but the frequent flying to this destination or that didn't give them time to cultivate relationships, they complained. How could he ask Desirée to put her life on hold and travel with him just because it was what he desired?

He looked at her name on the printed page and noticed her name was the word desire with an *e* at the end. Maybe it was an omen.

He held on to that hope as he reached for the phone once more.

Desirée leaned back in the lounge chair and sipped the tall, orange-red fruity concoction the bartender had made her. She gazed at the azure water of the lagoon-style pool. If this wasn't heaven on earth, it was as close as she'd probably ever get to it.

She and Michael "Mickey" Spivey were on the first of a series of appraisals of resort hotels in the Phoenix-Scottsdale area. The management here had very little to be concerned about. So far their staff couldn't have been nicer or more efficient.

This was the perfect way to start off her new position as a junior quality control agent for Wallace and Hughes. It was their job to register at hotels and make a complete report of how efficient the service was and how they were treated as guests, as well as other observations requested by the powers who had retained their services.

One of the biggest challenges facing the agents was trying to project the image of a typical business or pleasure traveler, which was difficult to do. Conducting a survey required a constant presence at the hotel, which could give them away if not handled delicately. But this resort was all-inclusive, with every imaginable activity, a variety of restaurants and even boutique shopping right on site. It was not unusual for guests not to leave the hotel grounds during their stay, except, perhaps, for forays into the exclusive shopping areas of Scottsdale and Sedona, or to take a tour of the desert—out here they called it the Valley of the Moon—either by Jeep or hot-air balloon. Knowing she wasn't being eyed with suspicion by hotel employees made Desirée feel a lot more comfortable and therefore more efficient.

The most difficult part of the job, besides making a

record of even minute details that would interest the general manager, was checking the hotel's restaurants. It wasn't uncommon for Desirée to order six meals a day. She couldn't possibly eat them all, so she carried a large purse lined with a four-gallon trash bag to help her dispose of the excess. There was a trick to that. She'd load her fork with food and discreetly lower it until it was out of sight, then dump the contents into the bag, repeating the action until most of the food was gone.

At six she arrived at one of the resort's restaurants, where she was meeting her supervising agent. At smaller hotels agents never allowed themselves to be seen together in public, but this resort was large enough for them to be inconspicuous.

The female hostess greeted her pleasantly with a hint of expectation, as if she had been waiting for her. Desirée noted the woman's name tag, which she would need for her report. "I'm Denise Miller," Desirée said, giving the pseudonym under which her room had been reserved. She even had been provided with a corporate credit card reflecting the false name, which she would use for six months, until it was time to change her alias. "I'm meeting someone."

"Yes, Miss Miller. Your dinner companion is here already. Won't you follow me?"

"Certainly." As they walked single file toward Mickey's table, Desirée mentally recited the observation she would record when she returned to her room. *The agent was cordially greeted by "Jenny," who correctly guessed the agent's identity immediately after the agent stated she was meeting someone and offered to guide the agent to her companion's table.*

Mickey was sitting in the rear, always the agents' preferred location because it made their observations less obvious. She giggled at the sight of him wearing a black cowboy hat. He had a commanding presence even bare-headed, tall, broad-shouldered and handsome, with wavy textured black hair, a deep golden-brown complexion and green eyes. He had, Desirée thought, the slightly cocky air of someone who knew he was good-looking. For that reason she had no worries about their working relationship moving into other territory, especially considering the close proximity their jobs required. She preferred a little humility in her men.

"You look kinda cute there, dude," she said as she slipped into the seat opposite him.

"Thanks, dudette." He lowered his voice. "Desirée, we need to talk."

She tensed. "Did I do something wrong?"

"No, you're doing great. But the New York office called today."

She spoke equally softly. "Isn't that unusual while you're on a job? I mean, don't you worry that an operator may be listening in?"

"You're right; it is unusual. They use a code name when they call, so the hotel doesn't get tipped off. Then I return the call from a pay phone off property."

"So what'd they want?"

Mickey cleared his throat. "There's a problem. It seems that Austin Hughes's junior agent caught him off guard by submitting her resignation."

Desirée shrugged. "So? What does that have to do with you?"

"Nothing. Austin wanted me to tell *you* that they want you to go with him on the surveys of the Accolade and Salud hotels in Africa in October, since Phyllis is leaving."

"Me?"

"The client specified he'd like a married couple; apparently it fits the mold of their typical American tourists. I don't know if anybody told you, but Austin is a brother."

"No, all I knew was, he's the other partner out of New York." Desirée sighed. "I don't feel comfortable with this. How can I pretend to be married to someone I've never even met?" She drew in her breath. "Wait a minute. How can we possibly pretend to be married? Married couples share rooms and beds, Mickey. No way *that's* in my job description!"

"All your accommodations will be suites. Knowing Austin, you'll stay in the bedroom while he sleeps on the couch."

"Oh. Well, that sounds like the gentlemanly thing to do."

"If it was me, we'd flip a coin, baby." Mickey flashed the devilish grin she had become accustomed to since they'd been working together.

"I would expect that of you. You're no gentleman, Mickey," she said, playfully rolling her eyes. "But I still don't like the sound of this."

"Austin and Phyllis did it every now and then. It's all very respectable. It just comes down to putting on a good front for the client."

"But Mickey . . . he's the boss. I wouldn't feel any more comfortable on a survey with him than I would if I was on a survey with Phil, and Phil I've met." Phil Wallace was the one who had hired her just a few weeks earlier, after a preliminary interview by Mickey.

"He a real nice guy. Relax. You're getting to go to Africa. If you ask me, that's a great stroke of luck for somebody who just came on board two weeks ago. Hell, it'll be six months before I get there."

"That's because you're going to Brazil next month, remember?" she reminded him. "You said yourself Bahia is just Africa on the other side of the Atlantic . . . and we all know how anxious you are to get to Ipanema Beach in Rio." She fell silent, trying to come up with a way out of this unwelcome situation. "You don't suppose they could send you to Africa instead? At least I've spent enough time with you that I could pose convincingly as your wife . . . sort of."

"Much as I'd like the idea of going to Africa next month, I know Austin would never consider switching with me. He and Phil grab all the best surveys. Phil and his wife are doing the major European cities: Paris, Rome, Madrid. It's one of the advantages of being a partner."

"I suppose. And no black woman is a senior agent?"

"Phyllis is the only black female agent we have other than you, and she'll be gone soon. There are two other women, plus Phil's wife, who gets back on the payroll if Phil has nabbed an especially nice assignment. She used to work for us before they got married. But no woman has ever made senior agent."

"That figures." *There's probably a lawsuit in there somewhere.* Desirée sighed heavily. The whole thing was so bizarre. She had serious doubts about being able to pretend to be the wife of a man she had never even seen . . . and a partner in the company at that—yet she knew how important this was. The Accolade Group was a major client for Wallace and Hughes, bringing with it hundreds of thousands of dollars in revenues. Everyone had been jubilant when the announcement was made. While on one hand it was challenging to be given the responsibility to make a good impression on a new client, she would only be kidding herself if she believed it was because management thought well of her. This had nothing to do with her ability. The only reason she had been chosen was because her complexion fit. What if she muffed it? Word got around quickly in this industry. She'd be a laughingstock, labeled unemployable.

"You'll be okay, Desirée. I even told Austin as much."

Mickey picked up his menu. "Come on, let's get our orders in."

But she had lost her appetite.

One

"Is y'all ready?" came the female voice through the drive-through speaker, heavily laced with impatience.

Desirée groaned. Only at this particular fast-food chicken restaurant did the help routinely keep the customers waiting without acknowledgment, then ask if they were ready to order in an annoyed tone that suggested the customer had been keeping *them* waiting. They were the same way at every location she had been to. Perhaps rudeness was a job requirement for them. Despite palate-pleasing chicken, this rudeness was a little hard to take after being catered to at resorts in the Arizona desert and, if not fussed over, at least treated politely at urban hotels in the Pacific Northwest.

She recited her order, having decided what she wanted early in the long wait.

"It'll take four to five minutes for a chicken sandwich," the voice informed her flatly.

"Four to five . . ." This was ridiculous. Desirée decided these people were taking advantage of her good nature. No chicken in the world was worth all this aggravation. She drove off, not bothering to respond, thinking that it shouldn't take any more than four or five minutes for them to figure out she'd gone.

She'd stop somewhere and get a burger, somewhere quick. She had a lot to do and very little time. She would be leaving for New York the next morning, and she had several errands to run before that. She had decided to sublet her apartment to a college student for the semester and had to stop at the office of the real-estate management firm handling the rental. She wouldn't be away that long, of course, but when she returned she could stay with her mother until Christmas. That way she would come out ahead financially, and she had her mother's assurance that she was welcome to stay as long as she wished.

Before she saw the realtor Desiré had to go up to the Wallace and Hughes offices in Boulder and see Eve Brown, the travel agent, and Bill Sampson, the controller, as well as Mickey.

"Hi, Maddie," she said when she entered through the front door. "Please tell me everybody's back from lunch."

"It depends. Who're you looking for?"

"Eve, Bill and Mickey."

"I don't think Mickey's back yet, but the others arc here."

"Thanks."

"You all ready for Africa?"

"Oh, sure," she said. After she passed Maddie's desk she rolled her eyes, not as a gesture to the friendly secretary but to the unknown and mysterious Austin Hughes, who at this time tomorrow would no longer be unknown . . . though probably still just as mysterious. How was she supposed to make like a wife to a man she didn't even know? she wondered for the hundredth time.

Eve had someone in her office, a middle-aged woman Desirée didn't recognize. "Oh, excuse me," she said.

"Have a good trip, and please come by if I can help you with any other reservations," Eve was saying, handing the woman a business card.

"Thank you, Eve."

"You're welcome, Mrs. Jacobs."

The woman exited through an outside door Desirée hadn't noticed before.

"Hi, Desirée. I've got your itinerary," Eve said.

"Thanks. I didn't know you could go directly outside from your office."

"Oh, yes. I'm open to the public, not just for Wallace and Hughes. It was part of the deal I made with Phil." Eve reached for a folder and began thumbing through the white pages. "Ah, here it is, all stapled together. You have your passport ready?"

"All set."

"Get your shots?"

"Yup."

"You know, you really lucked out."

Desirée responded with a dubious stare. She doubted any of the agents other than Mickey were anxious to go to West Africa. "Why do you say that?" she asked.

"Because you're a new agent and will be traveling with one of the bosses. This is a great opportunity to get noticed, show him what you can do. Most agents are here for a long time before they get paired with Phil or Austin."

"Probably because the partners don't want to deal with novices."

"I heard you were a meeting planner for a big pharmaceutical company before this," Eve remarked tentatively, in a tone that suggested Desirée would be crazy to leave such a cushy position to work for Wallace and Hughes as a junior agent.

"I was a meeting planner, but not for a big company. It was a relatively small outfit. They were bought out by one of the giants and my job was eliminated, or at least it was going to be. I was lucky to get hired here."

"How'd you like Phoenix?" Eve asked.

"It was beautiful. I'd like to go back on vacation."

Desirée laughed. "Where do QC agents go on vacation, anyway?"

"Anywhere they want, but I'll bet wherever they go, they make notes about how the service was. Can you imagine how full their comment cards must be?"

They laughed, and Desirée noticed there was a certain glow to Eve's rather plain face. "You're looking really good, Eve. You look like you've lost weight."

"Ten pounds. I eat so much salad, I'm afraid I'm going to turn into a rabbit."

"That means you're motivated. What's your secret?" Desirée asked.

"Well, I'll tell you." Eve lowered her voice and spoke in a whisper. "I'm in love."

"That'll do it," Desirée said enviously. "And I'll bet the object of your affections appreciates the low restaurant tabs from all those salads."

"We don't see each other that often. He lives in the East. New York."

"New York! Wow. How'd you meet him?"

"I took a trip there in June. I met him then. We haven't been able to see each other, but we talk all the time. I was just talking to him a little while ago."

"Isn't it hard having a long-distance relationship?"

"It's the pits, but so far it's working. I'll be going to New York again in October for a long weekend. You'll be in Africa then."

"Well, have a good time."

"Yes, you too."

Karen Bowman was in the conference room, inserting candles into a sheet cake. "Ooh, are we having a party?" Desirée asked.

"Hi, there! Yes, it's Bill Sampson's birthday. I'm just getting ready."

"It looks delicious. Where did you get it from?"

"I made it."

"You did? It looks so professional."

"When you've got a seven-year-old and a nine-year-old you *are* a professional. Every time I turn around one of my kids is asking me to bake a cake for their friends, for bake sales at school or at church, you name it."

Desirée was impressed. The chocolate-iced cake was trimmed with yellow and green flowers and borders. *Happy birthday, Bill* was written across it in yellow script. It looked as good as any cake Desirée had seen in a bakery. Of course, without tasting it she couldn't know if Karen could bake worth two cents, but she certainly had a knack for cake decorating. Mickey had filled her in on most of the office staff while he was training her, and she knew from him that Karen, a model-tall, leggy brunette of about thirty, had an active social life. She hadn't known Karen had children. However did she balance it all?

"Can I do anything to help you?" she asked. "I was just on my way to see Bill, but I've got a few minutes if you need me."

"You can keep Bill occupied for about five minutes. I'm going to take the ice cream out of the freezer so it can soften up a little."

"Will do. See you in a bit."

The accountant's office was in the back of the suite. Papers were everywhere, stacked on his desk and along the top of his credenza. Desirée wondered how he managed to keep track of it all. Maybe she should ask Maddie to double-check and make sure her direct notice of deposit was mailed to the New York sales office. It would be highly upsetting to go to an ATM machine, only to learn there were no funds available.

Bill Sampson had never been particularly personable, but this afternoon he didn't even smile when she greeted him. "I've got a check for you somewhere. I'm just trying to remember what I did with it. . . ."

"Oh, take your time. If I don't get to the bank this afternoon, I'll go tomorrow morning." Office gossip had it that he was in the middle of a divorce—his second. Had his work habits suffered because of the stress, or had he always been scatterbrained? She didn't know him well enough to know.

The click of an intercom sounded. "Bill? You there?"

"Yeah, what is it, Maddie?"

"Doug McClellan from the bank on Two."

Bill immediately picked up the phone. "Doug. Bill here."

Their conversation lasted about two minutes, during which time Bill managed to locate Desirée's paycheck. "You'll get one more paycheck before you take off, but I'll be sending you an advance along with it because you'll be out of the country so long. I'll take it from your net over the next couple of paychecks following that."

"That's fine. You did activate my direct deposit, didn't you?"

"Yes. It'll be in effect with your next pay."

"All right. Thanks." Desirée decided to double-check with Maddie after she was in New York. Bill looked like he had too much on his mind, and she wasn't about to go to another continent without any money in her pocket just because he was going through a hard time. Credit cards were all right, but there was nothing like cash money, especially when there was an exchange rate to be calculated.

Desirée ran into Mickey as the staff gathered in the conference room to sing happy birthday to Bill. He greeted her jovially, and they carried their plates of ice cream and cake back to his office.

"Wow, this tastes as good as it looks," Desirée said, swallowing her first bite of cake.

"Oh, yeah. That Karen can really bake. She makes everyone's birthday cakes. Chocolate is Bill's favorite. Luckily for me, it's mine, too."

"I hope it cheers him up. He looks a little down."

"You'd be down too if you had to cough up child support for two sets of kids."

"Two sets?"

"Yep. He had two with his first wife and two more with his second. It's pretty costly. He's been keeping books for some restaurant over on Colfax to help pay his support and his legal bills."

"That's too bad."

"Myself, I'm going to wait about three or four years after I'm married before I let my wife stop using birth control."

"Yeah, but doesn't that mean you'll be . . . well, kind of old before you become a daddy?"

"That's all right. I just don't ever want to be in a position where I'm desperate for money. So are you all ready to go?"

"As ready as I'll ever be, I guess."

"You'll do fine, Niecy." It was an inside joke between them that Mickey called her by a frequently used nickname for her alias, Denise. "I told Austin you'd be able to handle it, that you did a great job with me. Don't sweat it. Now, I want to know what you're going to bring me from the Ivory Coast. And Ghana. And Senegal."

They talked about what souvenirs they would get for each other from their respective destinations. Throughout their conversation, Desirée wanted to ask him something, the question that had been on her mind ever since she had been tapped for this assignment. But, as before, she found herself unable to ask. By the time they hugged each other good-bye, she left the office with her question unasked.

What did Austin Hughes look like?

The next morning Desirée pulled into McDonald's. She had a long flight in front of her, and she had forgotten to ask Eve if breakfast was being served, but even if they did she wasn't a fan of airline food. An Egg McMuffin and juice would hold her until she got to New York. Because of the time difference, by the time she landed it would be time for lunch, anyway.

An hour and a half later she settled into her seat in the coach section of the jet and fastened her seat belt. Everything was taken care of. Her apartment was sublet, her personal belongings had been boxed and put in her mother's garage and her car was parked at the airport, where her mother would retrieve it later with the help of a friend. She was on her way to New York for two weeks, to be followed by a four-week trip to West Africa—a place she'd never been to—with a man she'd never met. She sighed. It was scary, kind of like trying to feel the way to the door after the lights went out.

Two

"Ozzie, Monique's on one."

"Tell her I just left." Austin hated to put Elaine on the spot, but he didn't feel like talking to Monique. She had made him a bit uneasy ever since he had brought her with him to Phyllis's small wedding ceremony, where she'd managed to catch the bouquet. She'd turned to him with a devious smile that made her teeth resemble those of a killer shark. Lately she'd been calling frequently "just to say hello," giving him the impression that she was merely trying to stay paramount in his thoughts, even if the only way to do that was to force her way in. But he had neither the time nor the inclination to think about her. He had to get to LaGuardia and pick up Desirée Mack, the stranger who would be posing as his wife for the West African surveys. He would know very shortly whether or not the planned charade was going to work.

At the airport Austin felt foolish, holding up a hand-lettered sign with Desirée's name on it like he was a chauffeur or something, but it was a large plane and the airline representative told him the flight was nearly full. It was unreasonable to think Desirée would be the only black woman aboard. He didn't have a clear impression of what she looked like; all he knew about her was that she was, in Phil's opinion, "attractive but unconventional-looking." His first instinct was to ask if she had a ring through her nose, but he kept quiet, not wanting to break the vow he and Phil had made years ago not to exchange any type of ethnic jokes. Even Mickey said she was different, but when Austin asked what he meant, Mickey had merely shrugged and suggested that Austin see for himself. Austin wasn't impressed by all the vagueness. God only knew what would come walking off the plane.

He raised his head unconsciously when a regal-looking woman emerged from the escalator leading to the baggage claim. Instinctively he knew this was who he was waiting for.

She was strikingly dark-skinned, her skin nearly ebony against the pale blue cotton knit tunic top she wore over stonewashed jeans and tan espadrilles. Her black hair, semi-straight and quite thick, was pinned up in some kind of an impromptu twist. Her ears were decorated with wood, buttonlike earrings, and even from this distance Austin saw that the brick-red shade of her lips matched the color painted on her long nails. It was clear that Desirée Mack had style. She was perfect for surveys of African hotels; with her ethnic looks she could easily be mistaken for one of Africa's own. *He* would be the one to be labeled a foreigner.

There were many others beside him waiting to meet arriving passengers, and he held the sign high above his head when he saw her scan the crowd uncertainly. She broke out into a wide grin and walked toward him. Her teeth were strikingly white and straight, but there was a small dark spot in the center of her two front teeth—probably residue from her meal on the plane. Damn. He wasn't happy at the idea of telling her she had a piece of food stuck in her teeth. It would be embarrassing for both of them.

She came to a stop opposite him. “Hi,” she said warmly, extending her hand. “You must be Austin. I’m Desirée Mack.”

Austin lowered the sign and shook her hand. She had a firm grip . . . and lovely features. Small but expressive eyes, heavy eyebrows with a natural arch, a delicate pointed nose, what his mother would call “good bones” and skin as flawless as it was dark. And now that he was closer he could see what he initially thought was a remnant of her lunch was actually a small space between her front teeth. It really couldn’t even be called a gap; it was just wide enough to maybe squeeze the tip of a tongue into it at the very bottom.

He blinked away the inappropriate thought, unsure where it had come from. “That’s right,” he said. “It’s nice to finally meet you face-to-face, Desirée. Welcome to New York.”

“Thank you. It’s good to be here.”

Austin crumpled the paper sign and tossed it into a nearby trash receptacle. He took the flowered garment bag she held, as well as her matching overnight bag, and they fell into step with the crowd. “I can’t tell you how much I appreciate your filling in for us like this at the last minute,” he said. “I know it was a lot to ask you, to put your personal life on hold and all, especially when we couldn’t tell you exactly how long we’ll need you here.”

“It won’t be too bad.” Although Desirée would miss her mother, to whom she had always been close, there was no one else in Denver she was anxious to get back to. If anything, it would be refreshing to know she was miles away from her former fiancé, Calvin Edwards. But, of course, there was no reason to share that fact with Austin. “Besides, I’m looking forward to seeing Africa.”

“So am I.”

She looked at him with surprise. "You've never been?"

"Strange, isn't it? Since Phil and I started Wallace and Hughes I've been to Europe, the Caribbean, Asia, Canada and Mexico, but never to Africa or Brazil, the two places in the world with the most African culture. But I plan to make up for lost time."

Desirée didn't reply. She wondered what *she* would be doing while Austin was busy making up for lost time. She had a disturbing picture of being bound to the various hotel departments, doing midnight inspections of the stairwells and room service, while Austin was soaking up local culture at shoppers' markets and local bars and nightclubs. She hoped to be able to take some time to see the sights as well—the itinerary called for them to go to the Ivory Coast, Ghana, the Gambia and Senegal, for assessments of eight different hotels. If Austin Hughes decided to give her the bulk of the work while he went sightseeing, there wasn't a damn thing she could do about it. The man owned the company, or at least half of it, and as Mickey had pointed out, passing work on to subordinates was one advantage of being a partner.

Near the belt that would be delivering the luggage from Desirée's flight, Austin put down her carry-on pieces and asked for her claim tickets. She handed them to him, still stapled to the paper jacket that contained a copy of her itinerary for her ticketless travel and her boarding pass. "Two more bags with this same design," she said, pointing to her garment bag for emphasis.

Desirée studied Austin as he joined the crowd surrounding the conveyor belt, which had not yet started to move. She guessed his age at somewhere in the mid-thirties, about the same as his partner, Phil Wallace. He was about the same height as Mickey, with a clean-shaven complexion a few shades darker than Mickey's toasty brown, but Austin's frame was leaner. There were other differences, too. Mickey had a mass of black waves that Desirée suspected would get unruly and turn into a 'fro if he went too long without seeing his barber, but Austin wore his hair shaved close to his head, where it formed tiny spiral waves—and the shape of his head was suited for it, unlike many men these days who wore this type of cut or shaved their heads completely, in the process revealing pointy crowns, flat planes and other imperfections.

She was sure Austin Hughes had no problem attracting female attention, even before it was known that he was a partner in a firm with annual gross earnings in the millions. He was undeniably good-looking, but in an understated way, with deep brown eyes and what appeared to be an earnest nature.

Her personal preference had always been for men of subtle attractiveness; in her experience they were usually more humble than those whose good looks were the first thing you noticed. In other words, men like Austin Hughes. She'd spent more time than she should have wondering what the man she would be traveling with looked like. Now that she'd seen Austin, she felt a lot better about her ability to give a convincing performance in public. The two of them would probably give off decent vibes if they could get beyond the stiffness reserved for polite strangers, which of course was precisely what they were.

Desirée continued to study him as he waited at the carousel. She wondered how he had come to hook up with Phil Wallace to establish a corporation.

Austin turned, caught her eye and pointed to a bag fitting the description she had given as it rode closer to him on the carousel. She moved in to look at the I.D. tag—tapestry designs were quite popular these days—then nodded. "That's it."

Even though Desirée's bags had been loaded at the

same time, it was several more minutes before her second bag appeared. Austin carried the two larger suitcases, and she toted her garment and overnight bags.

"Why don't you wait here with the bags and I'll bring the car around," he suggested once they were outside.

"Sure."

She stood near the curbside with her bags. It was warmer here than she'd expected it to be; not bad for mid-September. The meteorologists in Denver had forecast a light snowfall for that day, the first of the season but certainly not the last.

She watched the activity around her and decided that if you'd seen one airport, you'd seen them all. It had been the same scene at DIA, with cruising taxicabs, rental car company minibuses and private vehicles taking up every foot of curbside space. People were exiting the terminal with purposeful strides, obviously knowing exactly where they were going and eager to get there.

Austin pulled up in a maroon Buick, which he had to double park alongside two cabs. He quickly hopped out and paused to unlock the trunk before effortlessly hoisting her heavy bags. She handed him the garment bag and tucked the cosmetic case into a neat corner.

"All right," Austin said with a smile as he unlocked the passenger door. "Let's hit the road. You can get a view of the skyline; it's not too cloudy today."

They talked about the company's global expansion during the ride to Westchester. True to Austin's word, she got a glimpse of the world-famous New York skyline, visible through the hazy sunshine as they crossed the Whitestone Bridge into the Bronx. She almost wished it was nighttime instead of two in the afternoon so she could see it all lit up. She knew that White Plains, where the offices of Wallace and Hughes were located, was about an hour north of the city, but she looked forward to making her first foray into the world's most exciting metropolis.

"So this is White Plains," Desirée remarked when they had gotten off the highway. "It looks like a nice city."

"It's the Westchester County seat," Austin replied. "Not too many people actually live here, but a lot of corporations are headquartered in town, and the population booms during the workweek. The rush hours are almost as bad as those in midtown."

"Do you live in this area?"

"No, I live in a small town called Eastchester, on Long Island Sound. It's about a twenty-minute commute." Austin turned down a side street of midrise apartment buildings. "This is where you'll be staying. We'll come back after we stop by the office. I need to pick up my messages, and I'd like you to meet the staff."

Desirée studied the brown brick structure. "It looks like a nice enough neighborhood," she said. "It's certainly convenient to that mall we passed."

"It's close to the office, too. You can easily walk, but there's a company car in the lot you can use."

"This isn't a company car?"

He chuckled. "No, this is *my* car."

"Oh." Desirée felt a bit flustered by her mistake. She had expected the vice president of the company to be driving a fancier vehicle than a Buick—perhaps a Mercedes, a Jag or another of those sleek foreign numbers. This car, despite being in excellent condition, was probably at least six or seven years old. She could tell because Buick, along with Cadillac and Oldsmobile, was among the last holdouts when it came to replacing the old-fashioned push-button metal door handles that protruded from the doors, with the newer types, the ones painted the same color as the rest of the vehicle, which lifted like flaps.

Apparently image was not a major concern for Austin.

Or maybe there was another reason. Maybe he was married and his wife was using the newer car. She glanced at his left hand as he drove. There was no band. That made sense; she certainly wouldn't want any husband of *hers* traveling with another woman, business or no business.

The thought of a husband automatically brought Calvin Edwards's handsome face to mind. Desirée bit down on her lip, as if the physical pain would wipe out the emotional distress that still lingered.

Austin could tell Desirée was surprised that he was driving an ordinary Buick. She was far from the first woman with that reaction. He had, after all, spent the last six years working on building the company into a recognizable name in its field. Wallace and Hughes had done well almost from day one, but Austin was by nature a conservative man. He had not been raised in wealth, and he had been quite cautious in his investments and purchases over the years. But the newly signed contract dissolved any lingering fears he had about meeting his rather hefty monthly obligations, including the mortgages on his bi-level condominium in Westchester and the nine-unit apartment building he had purchased with his friend Zachary Warner, which was fully rented and maintained by a real-estate management firm. He resolved to loosen up and enjoy himself more. This was the time for it. Everything was going beautifully. Maybe he'd buy a new car, one of those Auroras or Infinitis he admired so much, or plan to go on a safari in Kenya or Tanzania. Maybe he'd even consider acquiring another property; unlike a car or a vacation, real-estate was an investment, just about the best there was.

Most importantly, he'd cut back on the hours he put in and concentrate on finding a special someone to share his success with him. He was thirty-five years old; it was time. In the meantime there was still Monique . . .

but maybe he ought to discourage her from calling him so much.

At the office Austin turned Desirée over to Elaine Long, his administrative assistant, and disappeared into his office. Elaine introduced Desirée to Weaver Mobley, an agent who doubled as a sales associate, and part-time clerical assistant Valerie Robelli. Desirée was surprised to see that so few people worked in the New York office. The busy Boulder operation employed a full daytime clerical staff plus part-time evening help to process all the client reports. Even the office itself seemed tiny. There was a kitchenette with a tiny refrigerator and an even tinier microwave, a single unisex bathroom, a conference room and a spare office that Elaine told her was for the convenience of visiting agents. The unusual nature of the work allowed agents to live anywhere. Most were based in Colorado, but some lived in California and other states as well.

There was a warmth about Elaine that Desirée liked immediately. African-American and about forty, with her short hair worn close to her head in a glossy wrapped style, she was casually dressed in a dcnim skirt and crisply starched man-tailored pink blouse with the sleeves uncuffed and folded to just below the elbow. Elaine had the ease of someone who was quite comfortable in her job, which prompted Desirée to inquire how long she had worked for Wallace and Hughes.

"I was here three months after they opened the doors. My predecessor didn't last too long. She was qualified, but they tell me she wasn't happy with it being such a small office or the casual dress code; we only dress up if a client comes to visit. She took a job at IBM, where I understand every day is a fashion show." Elaine shrugged. "Myself, I never felt the need to be around a mob of people, nor am I thrilled about wearing heels and suits every day. You wouldn't believe how low my dry cleaning bills are since I've been here. Here, this is for you," she added, holding out a large goldenrod envelope. "It's brochures from the hotels you'll be doing, plus notes about the GM's specific areas of concern."

"That'll be a lot of help to me. Thanks, Elaine. Now I'll feel less like I'm about to jump from the frying pan into the fire, if you know what I mean."

Elaine smiled. "I know it's scary, but you'll do just fine. And Ozzie's real nice."

Desirée's brow furrowed in confusion; then she realized "Ozzie" was Austin. The nickname had a warm, fuzzy connotation that somehow didn't blend with the polite but reserved Austin Hughes she had just met. Perhaps there was a facet to his personality she had yet to see.

They were making small talk at Elaine's desk when Austin emerged from his office. "Sorry about that; I had a few calls to return. Elaine, I want to get Desirée settled in at the condo. I won't be back."

"Not ever?" Elaine asked in a playfully hopeful tone, unable to suppress a smile.

" 'Bye, silly."

" 'Bye, Elaine," Desirée said as she retrieved her purse from the back of the chair, where she'd slung it by its strap. "And thanks."

Desirée turned to him, puzzled, when he pulled over in front of a Pizza Hut restaurant. "There's a hydrant here," she said.

"I know." He reached for his wallet and pulled out a twenty. "There's nowhere to park, and I'm afraid to leave the wheel in case a cop comes by. Can you pick up the order? It's under Hughes. It should be ready; I called it in from the office. If I'm not here, I just took a quick drive around the block, which in White Plains at lunchtime can easily take ten minutes. But I'll be right back."

"No problem."

The clerk showed Desirée the pizza, which had a thin crust and was called the Edge. She shrugged. She wasn't even sure if that was what Austin had ordered, so she figured she'd give the pizza makers the benefit of the doubt.

Austin was still outside when she came out. She got in and put the box carefully on the floor between her feet. "I thought you might like something to eat," he told her.

"Thank you. That was thoughtful." Desirée had no idea the pizza was for her. It had been thoughtful of Austin to get her lunch, but it would have been more so if he had asked her what she wanted. For all he knew, she could be allergic to tomatoes or have an intolerance to cheese.

The corporate condominium was an efficiency unit, L-shaped with a sleeping alcove—with lots of windows and a spacious terrace. It was fully furnished, right down to the kitchen cabinets and drawers, filled with stoneware and utensils. The living room furnishings, covered in a nubby navy fabric, were more homey than those of a hotel suite. Desirée knew she would be comfortable here.

She went out on the terrace while Austin put her bags in the bedroom. White Plains was the perfect suburban setting, a sprawling business district with residential areas just minutes away. The downtown managed to have a cosmopolitan feel without a lot of tall buildings. Maybe it was all those sidewalk cafés. Only the courthouse and one of the hotels appeared to be higher than ten stories.

Austin joined her. "Do you like it?"

"Very nice." In spite of herself she yawned. "Sorry."

"That's all right; I figured you must be a little tired. Don't forget, you just lost two hours, and when we get to the Ivory Coast you'll lose five more."

"Seven hours, gone from my life"—she snapped her fingers—"just like that."

"But you'll get them back, eventually." Austin chuckled. "Perhaps we can have dinner tomorrow and get acquainted. We can go into New York if you'd like."

"Oh, I'd love that. I was looking forward to seeing the city up close, and I'd love to see it before we start working on properties there. Are we doing any of the luxury hotels?"

"No, not really. We'll do a basic two-day survey of a West Side hotel that's quite popular with out-of-towners who come in to shop and see the shows, followed by four days at the New York Harmon, which you might find a little overwhelming. It's got over two thousand guest rooms."

"Oh, a convention hotel."

"Yes. You'll do fine, though. Mickey said you did a great job in Arizona and up in Oregon and Washington State."

"Thanks. I was worried about being able to remember everything, but it really isn't so tough. I used to wait tables when I was in college, and I took dinner orders for up to four people without having to write it down, including special requests."

"Most of our agents started out by waiting tables while they were in school," he commented. He rushed on, suddenly feeling a tad nervous, but knowing this had to be said. "Listen, Desirée, I don't want you to get the wrong idea or think I'm coming on to you. The reason I suggested dinner is because I think we need to spend some time together before we go to Africa. It'll be to our advantage if we don't act like strangers when we're supposed to be married. I probably don't have to tell you how important this account is to Wallace and Hughes."

"I know there's a lot riding on these surveys."

"The staff at the hotels have been notified that our personnel are coming to assess their performances, and I'm sure they'll be eyeing everyone with suspicion. Asking for a couple was very astute of them. I think the staff is expecting the spy to be a solo traveler. Plus, mind-sets being what they are, I don't think a young married black couple would rate a second glance, unless we do something to tip them off. Oh, that reminds me—" He pulled a shiny object out of his pocket and reached for her left hand.

Desirée gasped as he held her hand and slipped a tricolor gold band on her finger. She hadn't seen the move coming. Although it was role-playing and virtually meaningless, the significance of the action, even as a farce, left her breathless. She braced her shoulders in an effort to keep her hand from trembling in his.

"This was Phyllis's prop. She needed to use it occasionally. Naturally, she returned it before she left. Looks like it's a perfect fit." He grasped her wrist and held up her hand for both of them to see.

"It's very nice," Desirée managed to reply. Her breathing had become uneven, and suddenly she wasn't sure if it was from the still-painful memory of her broken engagement or from Austin's firm touch.

Slowly he released her hand, his eyes on the impeccably manicured and polished nails at the ends of long, tapering fingers that were made to be adorned with rings. And her skin was soft and fragrant. Fleetingly he wondered if the rest of her body was as supple. "Yes," he agreed as he looked at her, a lazy smile forming on his lips, "very nice."

Three

"Are you all right?" Austin asked. "You look like you just saw a ghost."

"Yes, of course," she answered, too quickly.

"Have you ever been married, Desirée?"

"No. I was engaged once, though. Uh . . . what about you? Do you have a ring, too?" she asked, eager to change the subject. Casual conversation would surely make her respiration return to normal and chase away thoughts of the intimate way he'd smiled at her, as if he was privy to her most secret thoughts . . . or they were lying in bed together after making love. Austin Hughes got better-looking every time she looked at him. He had cute double lines running from the outer corners of his eyes that appeared whenever he smiled.

"Yes, but I leave it at home unless I'm masquerading as a married man."

"Do you really get that much call to do that?"

Austin shrugged. "Not too often. Some of the clients feel it helps throw the employees off guard. Where I'm concerned that's a given. I think a lot of the hotel staffs expect all the 'spies,' as they call us, to be WASPy types."

"Do you ever notice a difference in how they treat you?"

"Absolutely. Actually, my being black is like giving our clients a bonus, since they get firsthand information on how their minority guests are treated. When I'm on a job with another agent the client often gets two varying reports on the same department, especially the bar and the restaurant, and especially if it's a more exclusive hotel. But you'll find out for yourself soon enough." He winked at her.

In that moment Desirée had her answer. She might not be completely over the breakup with Calvin, but it was the feel of Austin's hand on hers that had her adrenaline pumping, not recollections of her former fiancé. There was something so sexy about a man winking, especially if that man was Austin Hughes. She inadvertently drew in her breath and hoped he hadn't noticed. The facade of being strangers was wearing off quickly.

She knew by her reaction to that gesture that four weeks of pretending to be Austin's wife was going to be quite a challenge, and she suspected it would only become more so with every moment she spent with him . . . but for reasons very different from the ones that had caused her initial apprehension.

"Here's the deal, Desirée," Austin said after the waiter set their drinks down: a tall pilsner of beer for him and a delicate stemmed wineglass for her. "These contracts mean a lot to the company. It gives us clout to have one of the world's finest international hotel chains on our client roster.

"I'm sure you've wondered about the sleeping arrangements," he continued, not waiting for her to reply. "We'll have suite accommodations at each survey. The bedroom will be your domain; I'll stay in the living area and make up the couch before the maid comes in the morning. But the important thing to remember is that every person on the staff at these hotels is going to be looking for us. Of course, they don't have the slightest idea of who they're looking for, other than that we're Americans, so that makes it all the more important that we make a convincing couple. If they suspect we're acting, we're blown. That means watching out for the little things, like me suggesting you try the veal and you saying you don't like veal. Things like that will tip off the waitperson that something's not right. In that situation, you wouldn't say you don't like veal, you'd say you didn't feel like eating veal."

Desirée smiled across the table. "I don't think we'll have any difficulties. Just remember I can't stand veal."

They shared a laugh. She certainly wasn't shy about showing her teeth, Austin thought. Not that she had anything to be ashamed of—the tiny space hardly made her look like she could be Leon Spinks's sister—but he had noticed that people with buckteeth or discolored teeth or other dental imperfections were sometimes self-conscious, covering their mouths with their hands when they laughed or smiling only with their lips. Desirée, on the other hand, radiated confidence. He liked that about her. It was more than just accepting the gap between her teeth and being comfortable with it. Here was a woman who carried herself like a queen in a world that, for the most part, dismissed that imperfection as undesirable and unattractive. He smiled at her, and as he did their eyes met and held for just a moment.

Austin cleared his throat, although there was really no need to; his voice was as strong as it always was. It was a reflex action to remind him of his place, that he was in charge, and to prevent his thoughts from going astray. He kept trying to remind himself that the vivacious woman sitting opposite him was an employee of his company and under his direct supervision. It was just so easy for his thoughts to take a personal turn where Desirée was concerned. He'd have to watch that; it could get him in trouble.

When he spoke again he was all business. "The company will reimburse you for your airport transportation. There's a cap on it, though. I forget what it is, but it's more than enough to cover the fare on a minibus and a cab to the diner where it leaves from. It's just that we don't want people chartering stretch limos and expecting us to pick up the tab."

Desirée nodded, although she was curious as to whether Austin used a limousine service. Something told her *he* wouldn't be catching a minibus at the diner to get to the airport. There was probably a special woman who would send him off with hugs and kisses.

She was curious about something else, too, but unlike her previous thought, this at least was a question appropriate for her to ask. "You and Phil Wallace founded the company. How is it he ended up president?"

Austin laughed, his laugh lines deepening. "First of all, it's traditional to have only one president of a company; it works better that way. Phil took the job because he had more money to put into the company than I did."

"That makes sense."

Austin shrugged. "Money talks; it always has. Not that I'm complaining. I've done all right for a kid from Amsterdam Avenue."

"How did you two meet?"

"At Cornell. I was there on scholarship. We used to say we would go into business together one day, but we figured it would be something like a restaurant. Phil went into restaurant management after graduation, and I worked at a series of hotels, mostly in Atlantic City, where the service often leaves a lot to be desired unless you're a high roller. One day we really got serious about starting a quality-control service for the hospitality industry. Both of us were fed up with working long hours while other folks were getting rich from our efforts."

"Most people resent that. In our case it's probably ethnic, considering our ancestors didn't accumulate anything for lifetimes of work in those cotton fields."

"Amen. Anyway, we started out doing two-day basic surveys separately. It was exhausting, not to mention a real challenge trying to be inconspicuous. But we couldn't afford employees yet, other than one secretary to answer the phone and put together proposals to clients who expressed an interest. A buddy of mine created our database system on a deferred payment plan, and our secretary did all the input, all the editing, everything. Our biggest expense was legal counsel. We did all the accounting ourselves. In addition, when we weren't traveling we were making cold calls to attract business. It was touch-and-go for a while, but then the fish started biting. We were able to use that leverage to get an SBA loan, and it's been full steam ahead ever since."

"You both worked out of New York?"

"In the beginning, yes. But then Phil got married and started grumbling about New York being too expensive to raise a family, even though he and Sandy haven't gotten around to starting one yet. They're both ski fanatics, and they considered several cities before settling on Boulder. They wanted a location that felt cosmopolitan, not isolated, yet had a lower pay scale. Most of the Boulder employees are data entry operators."

They continued talking about business throughout dinner. Both of them declined dessert. "I really enjoyed this, Austin," Desirée said as she reached in her purse for her lipstick. "It was exciting to ride down Fifth Avenue, through the theater district and then over here to . . . where are we again?"

"Columbus Avenue. That's on the West Side," he answered with a smile.

"Yes. Well, anyway, I know it was definitely the long way around, and I appreciate your taking the trouble to do it. I've always wanted to see New York."

"You can see more of it if you'd like. A friend of mine uptown is entertaining a few people at his house tonight, and I told him I'd try to stop by. We don't have to stay long, but I think you might enjoy it."

"Sure," she said eagerly.

Austin watched as she first outlined her lips, then applied a brick-colored lipstick without benefit of a mirror, all the while keeping perfectly within her lips' boundaries. "How do you do that?" he asked, leaning forward.

Desirée shrugged. "It's not that difficult. It's really just a matter of knowing where your lips are." She giggled.

"It's amazing. I've never seen anyone do that before. I have a feeling that a lot of women who try it wind up with lipstick all over their faces."

"Well, thank you for the compliment. It *was* a compliment, wasn't it?" she added, grinning broadly.

Again Austin found his eyes drawn to her smile. That space fascinated him.

Desirée noticed his change in expression. For the first time she saw the slight downward droop to the outer corners of his eyes. Bedroom eyes, her mother would call them. He had lowered his gaze, and instinctively she knew he was looking at her teeth. She wished she knew what he was thinking; his expression was unreadable. But whatever it was, she could at least tell it wasn't unpleasant. Perhaps she reminded him of someone he was fond of who also had a space between their front teeth. Or maybe he was thinking that in certain African societies having a space between one's teeth was a sign of beauty.

She was amused at her private reflections . . . and would have been shocked if she knew Austin was thinking how wonderful it would be to explore that divide with his tongue.

* * *

They took a leisurely stroll on Columbus Avenue to where the car was parked, past a horde of restaurants. On this particular September evening it was a bit too windy for al fresco dining, so the patrons seated near the windows indulged in people-watching from their seats. It was all Desirée could do not to wave at them as she and Austin passed by. She was happy tonight. Her fears no longer existed. Everything was going to be all right.

Once in the Buick, they rode uptown on Amsterdam Avenue past walkup apartment buildings mixed in with modern highrises, boutiques, cafés, bars and shops like dry cleaners and delicatessens. Desirée watched as the area changed before her eyes as they drove north. Now the streets were populated with shabbier apartment buildings, small grocery stores—bodegas, they were called—and liquor stores. Austin probably had grown up somewhere in this uptown area.

She was looking forward to a glimpse of the legendary 125th Street, home of the Apollo Theater, but they had only gotten as far as 117th when Austin turned and drove through several long crosstown blocks until they were in an area of brownstone residences, most of which bore signs of refurbishing. Desirée had heard of areas like this, where well-to-do African-Americans and even people of other races who had been priced out of the expensive properties in midtown purchased city-owned abandoned homes in Harlem and fixed them up. If it wasn't for the few buildings still dilapidated, with windows boarded up, she would have thought they were in the heart of prime residential property some fifty blocks south.

The classic architecture of the brownstones was really lovely, and it was obvious the residents who lived here were proud of the neighborhood they had created. The street, in spite of the cracked sidewalks and pothole-ridden pavement that were signs of an area neglected by the city, was immaculate. Trees had been planted at curbside, and one savvy homeowner had even installed a garage on the ground level.

"It usually isn't so difficult finding parking up here," Austin said in an annoyed tone as he slowly drove down the one-way street lined with cars. "This is ridiculous. Zack said he was only having a few people, not an army."

"Maybe someone else is entertaining tonight also. Oh, there's a space!"

Austin slowed down, then drove past. "Fire hydrant."

They found a legal spot on the next block. "Here, take an arm," Austin offered gallantly when they had gotten out of the car.

Desirée complied, thinking that Austin was definitely going above and beyond the call of duty by bringing her to his friend's home. Actually, he had gone out of his way to make her feel welcome from the moment he met her flight at the airport. She knew it was probably out of guilt because of the way she'd uprooted herself to help the company in this time of need, but anyone who saw them would think they were really involved with each other. The notion was not at all distasteful; good, eligible black men were getting to be as rare as Susan B. Anthony silver dollars these days. *But it's just business,* she reminded herself. *Anything else would be inappropriate.* Austin knew that better than anyone, she thought, remembering how he had made it a point to explain his reasons for spending time with her. Still, placing her arm in the crook of his seemed like a perfectly natural thing to do . . . though definitely not the type of behavior one indulged in with a business associate. The mixed signals were confusing. If she wasn't careful, she could lose her footing and fall flat on her behind.

"Gee, it's a lot quieter here than I expected," she remarked as they walked down the street.

"That's because it's residential. There's always activity on the main drags, especially on the weekends."

Austin guided her to a house in the center of the block. Although the view from the two large windows in what Desirée imagined was the living room was obscured by drapes, the faint strains of music drifted from the house.

"Beautiful house," Desirée observed as they climbed the stairs. "What does your friend do, rob banks?"

"Nothing quite that dangerous, though with a fair share of excitement. He's an emergency room doctor. Bought this place at a city auction about ten years ago, started renovations and moved in as soon as it had heat and plumbing. He's come a long way since those early days, when his furnishings consisted of a microwave, a refrigerator and a bed."

The door was opened by a heavyset, suit-clad man with a drink in one hand and a handkerchief in the other. "Welcome," he said, extending his hand. "I'm Larry Vickers."

Austin shook his hand and gave their names.

"Zack's in the living room," Larry told them. "I volunteered for door duty for a while; it's cooler."

They wiped their feet carefully on the mat, not wanting to leave marks on the gleaming hardwood floors that were only partially covered by scattered area rugs. An elegant staircase with an oriental runner was on their right, and an arched doorway on their left led to the living room.

The room was large, accommodating the twenty or so guests comfortably. Some were standing and talking, some sitting and others dancing. A clean-shaven man approached them immediately. "Ozzie, glad you could make it."

The two men shook hands, and Austin introduced Desirée to Zachary Warner. "Well, hello there, Desirée," Zachary greeted, taking her hand.

"Hello." She was immediately struck by how good-looking Zack Warner was. Flawless deep honey-brown skin was the backdrop for perfect features, the crux of which were electric blue eyes that were somewhat out of sync with his coloring. The lighting in the room was dim, but nonetheless she blinked at the sight of those eyes. His looks were too outstanding for her taste, but definitely worth appreciating. She found herself wishing she had an unattached friend to introduce him to.

"Desi's here from Colorado. She's going to be my travel partner, now that Phyllis has left," Austin explained.

"I see," Zack replied. "Well, welcome to New York." He still held her hand, but he let it fall just as the moment was about to become uncomfortable.

"Thank you. You have a lovely home."

"Thanks. Of course, Ozzie modeled his after it, but you know what they say—imitation is the sincerest form of flattery."

Desirée merely nodded. She hadn't been to Austin's home, although Zack presumed she had. Besides, her ears were still ringing with the sound of the intimate way in which Austin had shortened her name. "Desi," he called her. No one else had ever called her that, not even Calvin. She liked it.

"Here, let me give you the grand tour," Zack said, taking her arm. Desirée welcomed the opportunity to see the rest of the house. She didn't notice Zack turn and cock his head toward the back of the house, silently conveying a message to Austin.

"Were you coming with us, Austin?" she asked over her shoulder.

Austin's reply was lost as he was practically covered by a squealing female who, judging from the way she flung her body against his, was delighted to see him. "Ozzie! How long have you been here?"

"We just walked in."

The woman released her hold on his neck and turned. She looked surprised, but not hostile, to see Desirée, who had stopped with Zack to watch the interaction.

Zack, ever the gracious host, performed the introductions. "Monique Oliver, Desirée Mack."

Monique released her death grip on Austin's neck, and the two women exchanged casual hellos. Desirée turned expectantly to Zack, who guided her out of the room, his hand on her shoulder.

Four

Monique watched them leave. "So that's your new agent?" she asked Austin.

"Yes. She's from Colorado."

"You didn't mention it was a *she.*"

"Does it matter, Monique?"

She shrugged. "Not if it doesn't matter to *you.*"

Austin didn't like the turn the conversation was taking. He had been dating Monique for a year, but he had known nearly from the start that there would never be anything substantial to their relationship. Any passion he felt for her was confined to the bedroom. Although their friendship was far from dull—they genuinely liked each other and had personality traits in common, with ambition and organizational skills heading the list—it had failed to ignite with the fiery flame that was the difference between easygoing camaraderie and an ardent love affair. If anything, their alliance had made him realize just how nice it would be to have a woman in his life with whom friendship would develop into something deeper.

He had never made Monique any promises, nor had he ever made any demands on her. Now it bothered him that she expected him to inform her about any female he had contact with, Wallace and Hughes's newest quality-control agent in particular.

Monique slipped her arm through his, "Anyway, I'm looking forward to next weekend."

"Huh?"

"Next weekend. The New York Harmon. You invited me, remember?"

"Oh, yes. I'm sorry, Monique; I really didn't forget. I guess I've got the African surveys on my mind. We leave the week after next, you know."

"I'm so envious, Ozzie. Wouldn't I love it if I could go with you." Monique's brow wrinkled. "Wait a minute. Is that girl going with you?"

Once more he found himself unruffled by Monique's demeanor. "If you mean Desirée, yes; she's coming. She's Phyllis's replacement."

"Well, Phyllis was different. I *knew* Phyllis." Monique pouted. Austin felt her arm grow stiff in his, and after a moment she unlinked them with more movement than was necessary. He knew she was trying to make a point, but it made no difference to him; it wasn't as if he was trying to hold on to her. "Excuse me a minute, Ozzie," she said in a voice deliberately cold and distant.

He resisted the urge to say "Gladly" and simply murmured an acknowledgment.

Zack appeared as Monique was making a quick exit toward the kitchen, in the rear of the house. His eyes went from Monique's rapidly retreating form to Austin. "What's goin' on, man?" he asked.

Austin shrugged. "I don't know what her problem is."

"I do."

"And?"

"She's jealous, Ozzie. She sees you come in with a real fox whom she knows you've been out with all evening. Monique wants to be the only one on your arm. And let me tell you, that Desirée is one *beautiful* black woman."

"Zack, she works for me."

"Since when does that make a woman off limits? Hell, men have been marrying their secretaries for years, as well as their kids' nannies."

Austin chuckled. "You're way off base, chum. There are certainly no marriage plans. Desi works for me, nothing more."

"Desi, huh? Sounds to me like you've gotten cozy with her already."

"What're you getting at, Zack?"

"I can tell by the way you shortened her name. I've never heard you call Monique 'Monie' or 'Eekie,' that's for sure."

Austin realized he had changed the way he thought of Desirée and was a little embarrassed. "Oh, that. It just slipped out."

"I don't know if you realize it, but that's the second time you called her that in five minutes."

He hadn't realized. This time he didn't answer; instead, his eyes scanned the room. "Where is Desirée, anyway?" This time he was careful to use her full name.

"Well, don't look now, but she's talking with an admirer in the hall. He cornered her before we could get up the stairs. We'll have to do the tour later."

Austin knew he was being baited, but he still felt Zack's comments were off the mark. Desirée was an attractive woman, no doubt about that. But New York was full of beautiful black women, Monique included, who didn't work for him. As far as he was concerned, that changed everything. He had always frowned on mixing his personal and business lives. Phil Wallace, whose wife Sandy had originally been hired as a Wallace and Hughes agent, teased him about it all the time. For Austin it was a matter of principle. He had always felt that his race prompted greater scrutiny of his professional behavior, even though that wasn't really fair, and he wanted his reputation to be impeccable. While he was friendly with the female agents he traveled with, there was never any tiptoeing in and out of each other's hotel rooms late at night. And there was practically no socializing with co-workers beyond an occasional impersonal lunch, unless it was with Phil or Mickey, both of whom were among his closest friends.

The only reason Desirée was with him at the party was because he felt he owed it to her to show her a good time. Surely it had been a sacrifice for her to drop her life and come running to New York for two months. The least he could do was make sure she was enjoying herself. And as for shortening her name, after all, they were going to be traveling together, for all outward appearances as man and wife. Why shouldn't they be a little chummy? A good rapport between them would only help get the job done more effectively.

Austin recognized some friends of his and Zack's. As he circulated through the crowd, he found his gaze periodically going to both doorways, the one leading to the hall and the other that led to the dining room.

He had taken a seat near a couple he knew and was conversing with them when Desirée returned. But she was not alone; the man's classically handsome features were vaguely familiar to Austin, but he couldn't remember where he might have seen him before.

Even in the midst of conversation, Austin again found his gaze wandering over to where Desirée stood. She was wearing a pale yellow sweater with a billowing brown paisley print skirt that grazed her slim ankles, and narrow tan skimmers on her feet. The earth colors were quite flattering to her rich complexion. Tonight her thick hair was braided in four neat cornrows from the hairline to the crown, where they joined to form a bun. Twisted gold loops dangled from her ears. Funny . . . her ebony skin tone, textured hair and the space between her teeth were not the standards of beauty he had grown up with, yet he couldn't seem to take his eyes off her. The very personification of a Nubian queen, she was by far the most exotic woman present.

Amy Ferguson tapped Austin's knee. "If you ask me, he looks as good in person as he does on TV," she whispered.

"Who is he, anyway?"

"Schuyler Audsley, from Channel Two News."

Austin nodded. He generally watched a different network, but if there was a big news story breaking, he often put his remote control to use and flipped channels. Now he remembered seeing the man who was deep in conversation with Desirée, reporting various news stories. He had Schuyler Audsley pegged. He was a smooth type with deep pockets, just the sort who could really impress a woman who, despite a moderate degree of sophistication, had only been in New York two days. He felt responsible for Desirée and didn't want her to be taken in by manufactured charm.

Austin's view was suddenly obstructed by Monique, who emerged from the dining room hand-in-hand with a male guest, with whom she began to dance just four or five feet in front of Austin. It was a slow jam, and he knew Monique was trying to make him jealous, but all she had accomplished was to annoy him because she was blocking his view of Desirée. It was a fairly large room, and it was just like Monique to stand right in his path, as if he really cared that she was dancing with some other man.

He excused himself and went to the dining room, where the rectangular cloth-covered table held liquor, mixers, ice, food and utensils. He mixed a vodka and orange juice, then took a sip to test the mix.

"Hi, Ozzie. Zack told me you were here."

"Syd!" Austin put the glass down to embrace the woman who stood smiling at him. "It's been too long. How've you been?"

"Just fine. I hear you're going to Africa."

"Yeah, Wallace and Hughes has gone international. We've got contracts for South America and Asia as well."

"Oh, that's wonderful! Which countries are you going to?"

"Hi!"

Austin recognized Desirée's voice, so vibrant it packed an entire personality into a single syllable. He immediately noticed she was alone, out of the clutches of her new acquaintance. "Desi," he replied, "I want you to meet someone." He reached for her hand and gently pulled her in his direction. When she was standing slightly in front of him, he dropped her hand and ran his palm up the length of her arm until it rested on her shoulder. "Syd, this is Desirée Mack. She's going to be coming with me on the African surveys. Desirée, this is Sydney Chambers. She lives downstairs."

"Downstairs?"

"On the ground floor, behind the burglar bars." Sydney chuckled. "But believe me, I was lucky to get it. There's a terrible shortage of rental units in the city, what with everything going co-op and condo. It helps to have a cousin who has a brownstone. And who co-owns an apartment building in Westchester if I want to live up there, which I don't," she added.

"Oh, you're Zack's cousin?"

"All my life."

Desirée took a closer look. Although Sydney's eyes were brown, she had the same complexion and features as Zack. Desirée liked her immediately. She chatted with Sydney and Austin about the upcoming trip for a few minutes, until Skye Audsley located her and asked her to dance.

* * *

"I'm ready whenever you are," Austin said in a low voice.

Desirée glanced at her watch. To her surprise it was after one A.M. "Stopping by" at Zack's had turned into a stay of almost three hours.

"Sure," she said quickly. "Just give me a few minutes." She had spoken to just about everyone in attendance at one time or another, but there were two people she wanted to say special good-byes to.

Desirée found Skye talking football with a few other men in the kitchen. He saw her approach and moved away from the others, putting his arm around her shoulders. "I'll bet you're coming to tell me you're leaving."

"Yes."

"Just my luck," Skye said with a display of mock disappointment. "The most fascinating woman I've met in ages is about to take off for Africa for a month. I hope you'll give me your number, Desirée; I'd really like to see you again."

"Sure, I'd like that." She reached into her purse for a pen, then began to laugh. "I just realized I don't know what it is. Not by heart, anyway." She'd called her mother after she arrived and given her the phone number to the condo but had not yet memorized it.

"In that case," Skye said as he reached for the pen she held, "I'll give you *my* number. When did you say you were leaving?"

She told him. "I'll be on assignment most of that time, though. But I will have a few hours Tuesday afternoon," she added, "and I'll be in the city, too." She knew from talking with him that he lived on West End Avenue.

"Why don't we have lunch?" Skye suggested. "I wouldn't want you to forget me while you're away."

Fat chance. Aloud she said, "Sounds good. I'll be in touch in the next few days."

"I look forward to it." Skye bent and kissed her cheek. The touch of his warm lips against her cool skin elicited a smile, but the truth was, Desirée's arm had been tingling all evening from the friction Austin had created when he ran his hand up her arm just before he introduced her to Sydney. She'd first experienced that bolt when he fitted the wedding ring on her finger. There was something about his touch that was pure magic.

Next she sought out Syd, who was talking with Zack and a few others. "Oh, are you leaving?" she asked when Desirée tapped her shoulder.

"Yeah, it's about that time. I wanted you to know that I really enjoyed meeting you."

"Me, too. Let me give you my number. I'm sure it can be a little scary, being in a new city where you don't know anybody, even if you're traveling most of the time. Everybody needs a friend."

"That's real sweet of you, Syd."

"I'll go write it down for you. Be right back."

Zack embraced Desirée chastely, as if they had been friends for years. "Don't believe everything they say about New York, Desirée. There are plenty of nice people here."

"Yes," she agreed, "and I talked to a lot of them here tonight." In a lower voice, she added, "I've heard that the upper class in Harlem tend to be bourgeoisie, but there wasn't a snob anywhere around."

Zack squeezed her arm. "You were expecting everyone to be talking about income taxes, investments and *La Boheme?*"

"Let's just say I *didn't* expect to find a tray of pig's feet in the kitchen. And to see it vanish inside of five minutes," she added with a laugh.

He joined in the mirth. "Sure made everybody forget

about the chicken and ham in a hurry. It's funny how things we turned our noses up at as kids are coming back as delicacies. I can't even afford to eat catfish anymore; the fillet is up to something like six bucks a pound."

"All set, Desirée?" Austin asked, suddenly appearing at her side.

"Yes, I was just saying my good-byes." He had come from the rear of the house, where she suspected he had been talking with Monique. Why did that possibility invoke such a feeling of disappointment?

Syd showed up and handed Desirée a folded piece of paper. "Give me a call any time."

"I will. Thanks, Syd."

"All right, guys," Zack said as he walked them to the door. "You be careful in Africa, Desirée. Stay out of trouble. And keep this guy out of trouble, too." Zack cocked his head toward Austin and winked.

They had just stepped out into the night air when Austin yawned, his entire body stretching. "Excuse me," he said sheepishly.

"It's all right. I'm sure you had a long day."

"Actually, I left work at two. It's those two drinks I had. Don't tell anybody, but alcohol tends to make me a little sleepy."

"Why not let me drive? You'll have to tell me which way to go, of course."

"No, I'll be all right. I just needed some fresh air after all that cigarette smoke in the house. A few minutes of this and I'll perk right up."

"Well, if you're sure . . . but if you're not a drinker, what do you do when you're surveying a hotel bar? You can only knock over so many glasses."

"I find the closest potted plant and dump it. I've left a trail of intoxicated plants on three continents."

* * *

The late hour and the fact that they were both a little tired precluded conversation on the way home. They had crossed the Harlem River when Austin commented, "I hope the party wasn't too long for you. The time went by rather quickly, at least for me."

"Not at all!" Desirée exclaimed. "I had a great time, so much that I didn't realize how long we stayed. I met some very nice people, too. You have nice friends."

"Well . . . I can't say they're *all* my friends, although Zack and I know a lot of the same people. Some of them I'd never seen before. Like that guy you were talking to, even though he looked familiar to me." Austin was surprised at how easily the lie formed on his lips. It must be his line of work; sometimes he felt like "professional liar" was the most accurate job description for what he did.

"His name's Skye Audsley. He's a TV news reporter. I forget which network."

"Oh, yeah; now I remember." Austin stole a glance at Desirée. He had hoped to be able to determine how excited she was at the prospect of dating a television personality, but her expression was impassive. He wished he knew of a way to tell her to be wary without her resenting it, but he couldn't find the right words. Wisely, he kept quiet. After all, it really wasn't any of his business. Desirée was a grown woman. It was *his* problem if he felt responsible for her. Or was his apprehension due to something other than a feeling of responsibility?

Parking was at a premium in White Plains. Austin pulled over by the cars that lined the street in front of the condominium and turned on the flashers to indicate he'd only be double-parked for a minute. They alighted at the same time.

Both elevators were waiting in the lobby. It was a

quick ride to the eighth floor. At her door she said, "I enjoyed tonight, Austin. Thank you."

"I'm glad you had a good time."

Desirée unlocked the door. "I don't think we'll have any problem fooling anyone with our little charade. We get along well enough to give the appearance that we've known each other for years." She flipped on the foyer light, stepped inside and turned to him. "Thanks again, Austin. I'll see you Sunday afternoon."

"Good night, Desirée." Spontaneously, Austin bent and kissed her soft cheek.

She saw the action coming and thrust her chin upward so he wouldn't have to bend so far. She smiled, thinking how fortunate she was to be paired with such nice men for her assignments—first Mickey, now Austin.

Her body tensed slightly when Austin's fingertips grazed her chin. A gentle but firm pressure turned her upturned face toward his, as his warm, moist lips moved along a diagonal trail to her mouth.

She gasped. This was the last thing she had expected from Austin Hughes, her *boss*. . . .

At that instant Austin's tongue slid into her open mouth and began an erotic exploration, alternately with squeezing the tip of his tongue through the modest space between her front teeth. His fingers still held her chin, and a fingertip moved to stroke the corner of her lips. With his other hand he cupped her shoulder in an attempt to bring her closer. Desirée spread her palms on his chest, not to stop him, but in an effort to prevent the kiss from getting too intimate. She knew the action was pointless. She was being thoroughly kissed by an expert, and there was no denying that this was very, very personal.

Her tongue intertwined with his. Inside his mouth she could taste a hint of vodka. Perhaps *that* was why her mouth was burning.

Instinctively she knew it was about to end. Austin's

hand slowly fell away from her chin and their lips gently broke apart.

She stared at him expectantly, not knowing what to say.

"That probably shouldn't have happened," he said, his voice low with embarrassment. "But I think it had to, and I can't say I'm sorry it did. Good night, Desirée."

The elevator that had brought them upstairs was still there, and in an instant he was gone, leaving her gazing out on an empty hall.

Five

"All right, here we go," Austin said as they rose to enter the general manager's office for the traditional exit interview. "I think it would be best if I handle him. Just smile and look pretty."

Desirée was stunned at the blatant sexism of his comment. "What? This isn't my first GM meeting, Austin."

"I know, but it's your first with me." He put his finger to his lips as he held open the door of the hotel's business offices. "Shh."

She walked through the door, her face a stony mask.

"Well, that's over," Austin remarked as they left. "You did fine."

"There wasn't much for me to do except sit and smile like a Kewpie doll. You suggested I let you do the talking, remember?" Desirée tried to keep the bite out of her tone, but she felt his request had been unfair and unwarranted. She was a professional, and in her years as a meeting planner she had worked with many sales directors, a position generally one step removed from general manager. Did Austin think she was going to put her foot in her mouth? Mickey had always encouraged her participation in these interviews.

She knew everyone had different management styles, but one thing was certain: She had no intention of continuing to be the invisible woman. Austin would have to change his way of thinking real soon. In the meantime it wasn't worth getting worked up over. In a casual tone she said, "The whole experience was a real confidence booster. It showed just how much they need our help. I can't believe how many things are wrong with the place."

"I guess a multimillion-dollar renovation doesn't go as far as it used to."

"There's an old saying, 'You can't make a silk purse out of a sow's ear.' "

Austin chuckled. "I know it well. It was a favorite expression of my grandmother's."

She looked up at the behemoth of a hotel behind them. Nearly a thousand rooms, all designed to cater to budget travelers. Still, at rack rates of upward of $150, it wasn't exactly cheap, and on top of that the service had been horrendous. Like all Wallace and Hughes agents traveling within the United States, Desirée performed her surveys under an assumed name, presently "Denise Miller," and the front desk clerk had called her "Denise" instead of "Ms. Miller" when she checked in. That was bad enough, but instead of merely handing her the key card with the room number discreetly written on the paper jacket, he told her what her room number was, speaking so loudly that she insisted he change it—and this time not broadcast it to everyone within earshot. It had gone downhill from there, and she was glad it was over.

Austin handed his parking ticket to the valet, then glanced at his watch. "We've got a couple of hours to kill before we check in at the Harmon. How about lunch?"

"Actually, I made plans for this afternoon. Can I meet you at the hotel?"

Austin looked dubious. "Will you be able to find it?"

"Avenue of the Americas—I mean, Sixth Avenue at Fifty-third Street, right?"

"Right . . . but do you know where Sixth Avenue is?"

"Well, the logical place is between Fifth and Seventh," she snapped, annoyed. First he told her to keep quiet at the meeting, then he thought she wouldn't be able to find a building so large it took up an entire city block. Did he think she didn't have a brain in her head? "Don't worry, Austin, I'll take a taxi. Oh . . . would you mind terribly carrying my luggage in the car? It's not much, but it's kind of awkward to carry around with me."

"But you can't check in to the hotel without luggage."

"Oh, that's right. This is getting difficult. We're not supposed to have a connection, so I can't ask you to come down and get my bags out of your car. Do you have any suggestions?" Except for occasions where married couples were requested, the agents usually worked separately on property, which made it more difficult for the hotel staff to identify them. Anonymity was relatively easy to attain in the larger New York hotels with thousands of guest rooms.

"Here's what we'll do. Ride over there with me now, and you can bring your luggage in and ask if you can leave it until you're ready to check in. I'm sure they'll do it for you. You can even make a front desk survey out of it. It'll be one less thing for you to do later."

Desirée beamed. "That's fine."

The valet delivered the car and put their bags in the trunk. "I wanted to tell you how nice you look," Austin said as he opened the passenger door for her. She was quite stylish in a tailored tan suit, white silk jacquard blouse and low-heeled tan pumps.

She stiffened and quickly averted her eyes. "Thank you."

Austin regretted the words the moment they were out. Desirée had seemed edgy ever since he picked her up on Sunday afternoon, and he knew why. It was that kiss he had so brashly helped himself to on Friday night. He knew it had been a mistake—and he had never before taken such liberties with women agents—but he hadn't been able to help himself. As he bent to kiss her cheek something had cried out to him to taste her lips. Now she was unable to relax around him, to the point where a simple compliment had her suspicious about his motives. He had hoped to talk to her about it over lunch, but apparently she had other plans, probably with that dude from the news, the one who looked like the groom on top of a wedding cake.

When he got behind the wheel he noticed her fingertips were tapping nervously on her lap. He considered talking to her about it now, but there really wasn't time. Even in busy midday traffic, the New York Harmon was less than ten minutes away from their present location.

Still, he'd have to bring it out in the open before they left for Africa. With all this tension between them they wouldn't fool anyone into believing they were married. Well, maybe they could, but he didn't want the hotel staff to be buzzing about the American couple who obviously weren't getting along. They were supposed to be inconspicuous.

He just wished he knew what to say.

The moment Desirée got into the backseat of the taxi she let out her breath in relief. It had been a difficult forty-eight hours.

She had been shocked by Austin's actions in her doorway on Friday night. He had seemed so amiable and they'd had so much fun, she certainly saw no harm in a friendly peck on the cheek. How was she to know that same friendly peck would turn into something that would shake her to the root of her soul, a kiss she had been unable to get out of her mind and had relived every night before falling asleep since it happened four nights ago?

It was marvelous, but also frightening. Was he going to expect this from her when they traveled together?

Maybe she was reading too much into it. It might be nothing more than the alcohol he'd consumed at Zack's party gone to his head. He had certainly been a perfect gentleman through the survey they'd just completed. He had seemed rather anxious for her to join him for lunch. Perhaps he wanted to clear the air, which had grown undeniably thick between them. Or maybe he was just worried she'd slap him with a sexual harassment suit.

At any rate, she was glad to be away from him and having lunch with Skye Audsley. Now, *there* was a man who knew how to keep a peck a peck, she thought, remembering his good-bye kiss at Zack's party. She sighed again. She supposed she was willing to give Austin the benefit of the doubt. If this type of behavior wasn't limited to a one-time indiscretion, she'd know soon enough. No harm had been done, really . . . if she overlooked the sleep she'd lost while she repeatedly relived the feel of his lips on hers . . . and the fact that she'd kissed him back with equal fervor, leaving no doubt of the dormant feelings he'd awakened in her. It had been too long since she'd been thoroughly kissed.

No sooner had she had that thought than the taxi pulled over in front of the restaurant where she had arranged to meet Skye. She fleetingly wondered if there was some symbolism there. There was no denying this was what she needed—the company of an exceedingly handsome man who seemed charmed by her. It was definitely a change of pace. Skye Audsley was one of the best-looking men she'd ever met, and she was curious to see where their acquaintance would lead, in spite of her lifelong habit of steering clear of men with looks of his caliber.

She knew where her caution originated. In second grade she'd had a terrible crush on the best-looking boy in her class. When she approached him and admitted her feelings he had laughed at her and called her a spook. She'd cried all the way home.

She lowered her eyes to try to erase the unpleasant memory of childhood cruelty. When she raised them she glanced at the meter and did a quick mental calculation for a tip as she reached into her wallet.

Someone rapped on the window. "I'll get it," Skye said. He handed the driver a bill, then opened the door for her.

"Thank you," she said as she gracefully got out of the cab. "I didn't even see you."

Skye held out his hand to assist her. "It's easy to get lost in a crowd in New York. You look lovely, Desirée."

She didn't bother to try to hide her smile. "Thank you. You look pretty good yourself." Skye looked ready to go before the cameras, in a black suit, white shirt and geometric tie in black, white and red.

"It's not every day I meet a beautiful woman for lunch."

She smiled again. *Good Lord, one lunch with this man and I'll end up with permanent laugh lines from all the smiling he'll have me doing.*

"They're holding a table for us. I don't know if you're familiar with Indonesian cuisine, but they serve Burmese and Thai as well."

"I'm crazy about Thai."

After a relaxing lunch during which they talked about their respective hometowns—Skye was from Buffalo—as well as their careers, they took a leisurely stroll across Eighty-ninth Street to Lexington Avenue and then proceeded south. Desirée was surprised how quickly they traveled on the short north–south street blocks, especially after the minihikes required to get from Second to Third avenues and again between Third and Lexington. Before she knew it they were down in the mid-Seventies.

"Time for me to get back to the newsroom," Skye said after a quick glance at his watch. "What time do you need to be at the Harmon?"

"Not until four at the earliest."

"You've got some time, then. It's not quite three."

"If you're getting a cab, drop me at Fifty-ninth Street. I can shop at Bloomingdale's for a bit, then walk over to the hotel. Let's see. Fifty-third . . . that's six blocks down and . . . I always get confused with this part. After Lexington is Madison—"

"Park."

"That's right. Park Avenue, then Madison, Fifth and then Avenue of the Americas—I mean, Sixth. Four blocks, the long ones. I guess I'll try my skill at hailing a cab."

"Didn't you get the first one?"

"No, the doorman took care of it." She smiled at the memory. Austin had offered to see her to her destination, but she'd politely declined. With whom and where she was dining was none of his business.

"You won't have any problem. Here, try your luck now."

Desirée moved to the curb and raised her right hand, her index finger extended. In a matter of minutes a cruising cab stopped. She lowered her body and gracefully got into the cab hips first, then slid over to give him room.

"Hey, not so far away," Skye complained good-naturedly. "Don't you know it's tradition to sit close together in the back of a taxi? Don't you watch old movies on the late show?"

She moved toward the center until her thighs were parallel with his.

"That's better," he said as he put an arm around her shoulder.

* * *

In the lush atrium of the IBM Building, Austin was talking to Phil Wallace from a pay phone, courtesy of his corporate telephone calling card. "The GM was hoping for a better performance from his staff this time out. He's looking forward to getting the completed reports."

"Well, at least the crummy job they did will guarantee he'll sign for more coverage next year," Phil replied. "How's Desirée doing?"

"I listened to the tapes she made, and she did fine. Of course, the Harmon will be more challenging for her. But I think she's up to it. This job built up her confidence."

"You two getting along all right?"

"Maybe a little too good."

"All right, I'll ask—though I have a feeling I'd rather not know. What do you mean?"

"We had dinner Friday night and stopped at a get-together Zack was having on the way back. Everything was fine until I kissed her good night."

"You kissed her? On the cheek, right?"

"Well, it started out like that, but then my hormones started in on me and I took a detour."

"You . . . what the hell were you thinking, Ozzie? This could be big trouble, with a capital *T*."

"I know that. I plan to do what I can to smooth things over as soon as I can get a few minutes alone with her." Austin felt it ungentlemanly to state that in the heat of the moment Desirée had kissed him back.

"Didn't you two ride down together?"

"Yes, and she chattered the whole way about a lot of general interest stuff. It was like she was afraid to stop talking."

Phil's groan came in loud and clear. "Oh, fine. Listen, Ozzie, you'd better make sure you get her to relax before you set foot in the Ivory Coast. This could blow the whole deal. You two are supposed to be bonded and relaxed, not distant and tense. And she can always decide she'd rather quit than go to Africa with you. I don't even want to think about what a mess that would be, now that Eve's issued all the tickets."

"Don't worry, Phil; I'll take care of it. Our cover won't be blown." Austin was regretting having said anything to his partner, who tended to get panicky where business matters were concerned.

"I'm counting on you. We've got enough trouble as it is. The GM at that spa up in Idaho called yesterday afternoon. It seems his final package was full of errors. He noticed them just by glancing through it; the answers didn't correspond to the comments. Like there was a 'no' for the question 'The guest was approached by a waiter/waitress in less than two minutes,' but the comment was 'almost immediate.' "

"Well, how'd that happen?"

"I don't know, but I'm going to make it my business to find out. In the meantime I assured him that we would get a revised report, including the stats, overnighted to him."

"Who did the data entry?"

"Karen Bowman. I can't even question her; she's taken a few days off. But what really bothers me is that the report was packed without being proofread."

"What did Diane say?" Diane Brown oversaw the preparation of all client reports, including editing, proofreading and packing.

"She says it was. She keeps a notebook, and her initials were by the hotel name."

"Hmm. That could be. Maybe the agent checked the wrong box. We'll have to put the typists and proofreaders on alert to watch out for comments that don't correspond to the answers. Who was the agent?"

"Chuck Lowe."

Austin fell silent. A beefy former policeman, Chuck

specialized in bar surveys. With his help, hotel management had successfully caught dozens of employees who were stealing in the usually laid-back atmosphere of bars and poolside cabanas. Lately there had been signs that in the process Chuck might have started drinking too much himself. Could his alcohol intake be responsible for him making errors?

"I know what you're thinking, chum. I'm on it."

"I hope this doesn't blow the account."

"The GM wasn't happy, but I think I showed enough genuine remorse to mollify him. Hmph. The things I do to make this company succeed."

"You mean the things you do to get that fat bonus at the end of the year."

"Yeah, well, what can I say? Later, man. Keep me posted."

The check-in process completed, Desirée walked toward the bank of elevators. The level of service here was miles above that of the previous client. The employees at the Harmon showed as much polite deference as the others had been rude.

The sheer size of the hotel was staggering. Designed to accommodate large groups and conventions, it had over 2000 guest rooms. Austin told her that the popular Ebony Fashion Fair was held here when they came to New York.

The front desk clerk had remarked during check-in that the hotel was nearly full, prompting her curiosity about how the housekeeping staff kept up with all the work. The hotel appeared to be exceedingly well maintained, with its beautifully landscaped driveway that was like an oasis in the heart of midtown Manhattan, and elegant lobby. Her room, furnished in pleasant but rather basic hotel style, was spotless. No dust on the windowsill or the drapes, no grime on the sink or tub and no spiderwebs under the bed. One of Wallace and Hughes's main rules was that there was always room for improvement, but her inspection of the accommodations had found nothing that needed fixing so far. If anything was amiss, it wasn't readily apparent.

She studied the room, trying to identify anything where maintenance had been glossed over. Surely the staff routinely cut a few corners here and there, especially at times like this, when they were near capacity. Her eyes settled on the huge king-sized bed that dominated the room. Thoughtfully, she reached into the desk drawer, took out a pencil and carefully marked the inside of each pillowcase with an X. She marked the top and bottom sheets in similar fashion, in an area where it wasn't readily visible. If the marks were still there after housekeeping was through with her room tomorrow, she would have one shortcut identified. While the Harmon wasn't considered the cream of the crop—its size and definite hotel-like atmosphere set it apart from the more exclusive, elegantly furnished hotels on the Upper East Side—it was still one of New York's more expensive lodging houses. Certainly the guests who were shelling out in excess of two hundred dollars a night to stay here deserved to have fresh linens every day unless they requested otherwise, which she knew energy-conscious guests sometimes did.

There were plenty of outlets to survey in a hotel of this size. Desirée had more than enough to keep herself busy. She ordered her dinner through room service and made a report of it, then settled in in front of the television.

In the morning the routine started over again, with breakfast in the coffee shop. Desirée's contact with Austin had been minimal. He was staying in an upgraded room on a different floor, as was usual for the senior agent. But she knew they would have to get together eventually.

The knock on the door came at four that afternoon. "Yes?" Desirée asked cautiously through the closed door.

"It's Austin."

She opened the door. "Hi. Come in."

Austin sat at one of the chairs by the window. "How's it going?"

"Pretty well. I did the business center a little while ago. Typed out a letter to my mother." She laughed.

"I've been practicing my French, getting ready for Africa. I'll be going down tomorrow to see the multilingual staff. I don't know nearly as much as you do, but I'll ask a simple question, like what time it is. If they can understand me, I guess I've done all right."

Desirée was uncomfortable when he mentioned her French. She had listed that language on her résumé, reasoning that she was entitled to do so because she had studied it in high school. She'd never expected people would assume she was fluent, nor did she feel it would come up, since at the time she applied the only foreign cities Wallace and Hughes serviced were London, Tokyo, Hong Kong and Bangkok. Paris and French-speaking African countries were not on the roster. She was afraid to tell Austin her knowledge of the language wasn't as good as he and everyone else thought.

"So how's your room?" he asked.

"Oh, it's all right. I've got a nice view, at least." She suddenly became aware of the room's oversized bed and quickly went to the desk, turning the straight-backed chair so she faced Austin. At that moment the phone at her elbow began to ring. "Excuse me." She reached for the receiver and stated a soft greeting, breaking out into a smile when she recognized Skye's voice.

Austin stiffened. He could tell she was talking to a man by the smile and the slight softening of her voice, and he had a good idea who the man was. Not that he was jealous . . .

Wait a minute. Who are you trying to fool? He'd meant it when he told himself he didn't care what Monique did, but that was Monique. With Desirée it was different, and he knew it.

"Tomorrow? That sounds wonderful. But . . . can I call you back a little later? All right."

"Sorry," she said when she hung up.

"No problem. I just wanted to suggest that we check out the restaurant together tonight."

"That'll work. It's tomorrow night that's not good for me."

He nodded, knowing she referred to her phone call. "Uh . . . you do know that the company frowns on socializing while on a survey?"

A tightness immediately formed in Desirée's jaw, and she straightened her spine. "Wait a second, Austin. Even jurors are entitled to have something of a social life, although what I had in mind was more like drinks, not a conjugal visit. I'm doing my job, and you said yourself I'm doing it well. I want it understood that Wallace and Hughes is not going to have me on call twenty-four hours a day. They don't pay me enough for that. If that's the type of career I want, I'll run for president." In her vehemence she had leaned forward as she spoke, and now she sat back in her chair and folded her arms in defiance.

Austin tried to appease her. "Desirée . . . I was just making a statement. No one is denying you the right to a social life. But you have to be careful that your cover isn't blown. Regardless of how many thousands of guests are staying here presently, we always have to use our aliases when we're around people. We can't have someone come in asking for Desirée Mack's room if you're registered as Denise Miller. All the employees know it's been about six months since the last survey, and they're looking for us. One word from the front desk and it's all over." It was in each client's contract that if management learned that agents had been identified, the survey was automatically voided, with Wallace and Hughes having to pick up all expenses. That could be quite costly, especially if travel was involved. This had yet to happen and probably never would—Austin felt that if they ever had been recognized, the employees simply kept their mouths shut and just concentrated on doing a good job in order to get a good appraisal.

She was unyielding, keeping her arms folded. "He knows I'm registered as Denise Miller. He won't give it away."

Austin sighed. "Listen, Desirée, there's been bad blood between us since the weekend. It's my fault, I know. It was inappropriate for me to kiss you. I'm sorry it caused so many problems between us. I assure you it won't happen again, but please let's put it behind us. We're going to be working together closely for the next several weeks on a new account. I don't need the added stress, and neither do you."

She sighed. "Yes, I agree." Suddenly it was all too much. This room was too small for the two of them, that king-sized bed and the still-vivid memory of last week's kiss. Her hands fell to rest in her lap. "It's all right, Austin," she said in a softer tone.

"Is it really?" he asked, rising.

At first she didn't trust herself to speak as he moved closer to where she sat. "Of course," she said after a few moments of silence. He stood before her, gazing at her intently. "It was only a kiss, Austin," she added, trying to downplay the stirring of emotion she had felt while in his arms. "It's just that I . . . I was afraid you might start making demands of me. You know . . . things I had to do if I wanted to keep my job."

Austin winced at the thought. "I'm not that kind of

man, Desi," he said softly, unaware that he'd shortened her name again. "I've never had to resort to pressure to get a woman's company. And I'll promise you this right here, right now: I won't kiss you again unless I have your permission."

The tissue partially extending from a decorative box on the desk swayed with the breeze he created as he swept past her. "I'll be by to get you at seven-thirty for dinner," he said in a tight voice as he left.

Desirée sat still for several minutes before rising to lock the door. What a mess this had become. She and Austin had gone from two people with a growing fondness for one another to two people who vacillated between unnatural stiffness and being at each other's throats; all because of a kiss so impassioned she found herself thinking about it a dozen times a day.

She knew her statement about him using his position to extract sexual favors from her had pained him, but she also felt he deserved honesty. She didn't believe in her heart that Austin Hughes was the type of man to practice sexual harassment, but on the other hand she had to be realistic. The kiss they shared was enough to make her uneasy about what the future held, and it had. At least after talking to him she felt fairly confident that it had been a one-time incident; Austin's hurt had been authentic. It was unfortunate that her relief had to come at the expense of his feelings, but she had to make him understand her fears.

Six

Austin knocked on her door at precisely seven twenty-eight, looking dashing in a camel-colored blazer, striped shirt and brown slacks. The only thing that spoiled his appearance was his dour expression. One look at him and Desirée knew if she didn't ease the tension right now, their dinner would seem eternal.

She held the door open in invitation. "Come in for a minute, will you?"

When he turned to face her, she closed the door, leaning against it with a sigh. "Austin, I can't bear to spend an evening with you if you're going to be so hostile toward me. I've always believed in being open about my feelings, and I felt you deserved to know exactly what was on my mind. I really didn't believe you would put pressure on me, but it was still a possibility I had to consider. Can you blame me? I mean, we gave off enough sparks in that hallway to light up the Las Vegas Strip. Can you honestly say I was foolish to be concerned?" Realizing too late that she had given more information than she should have, she bit her lower lip in nervous anticipation of his response.

Austin raised an eyebrow. He hadn't expected Desirée to be so brutally honest about what she'd felt when he kissed her. It was yet another appealing facet of her personality. "No," he answered, "I guess I can't. And even though I had a feeling I knew why you were so edgy, it still stung when you put it into words."

"I don't want there to be anymore hard feelings between us." She searched his face anxiously.

"None; I promise." He took her arm. "Let's go eat; I'm starved."

Dinner in the hotel's restaurant was a pleasant affair, now that they had dispensed with the touchy subject of sexual harassment. The food was mediocre, but the service was excellent.

They concluded by discussing in soft voices the proper way to report on food presentation. Austin stressed that because taste was a personal matter, all comments on reports had to be restricted to the way the meals were presented and whether or not they had been prepared to specifications. "A steak shouldn't be pink inside if you wanted it well done, and you shouldn't have to ask again for sour cream for your potato if you requested it with your order."

"I agree. They did get my steak right, but that potato felt hard, like it had been in the microwave too long."

"That's not surprising. My shrimp scampi tasted bland."

"Even if my dinner was delicious, I can't finish it all anyway. I'm still full from lunch." Desirée reached for her purse as she prepared to dispose of her uneaten food. This way no one would be suspicious about her sudden lack of appetite; it was highly irregular to order a twenty-five-dollar meal and leave most of it sitting on the plate.

She usually kept her purse in her lap and discarded the contents of her plate a forkful at a time, but this was one of those times when the table at which she was seated was isolated enough so she could simply rest her purse on an extra chair—there were four seats at the table—and just pour the food off, then discreetly replace her plate on the table.

As she opened her purse wide, she couldn't help feeling a little sorry for Austin and the other male agents who had to eat most of their restaurant orders, since they didn't walk around with handbags. Austin and Mickey probably had developed vigorous workout routines just to keep all those meals from showing. The somewhat pudgy Phil Wallace, on the other hand, probably didn't bother.

Austin gasped when she replaced her plate—the entire operation had only taken about three seconds. "Desirée, the bone!" he hissed.

But their waiter was already upon them to remove their plates. "May I take—" he began before breaking off, wide-eyed. In that instant Desirée realized her gaffe. While some residue of potatoes and vegetables remained on her plate, she had unwittingly deposited the entire T-bone, including the inedible bone itself, into the personal trash bag in her purse. No wonder the waiter was thrown.

He quickly regained his composure and again offered to take her plate. "Would you folks like to look at our dessert menu?" he inquired as he gathered both of their plates.

"Not unless you've got a Snickers bar on it," Austin replied.

"No, sir; I'm sorry."

He chuckled. "That's all right. I'd have to wait at least a half-hour to digest my dinner before I could eat anything else, anyway. You can just bring me the check."

When the waiter was out of earshot they dissolved into muffled laughter. "Desirée, how could you be so careless?" Austin hissed.

His tone was an odd mix of mirth and concern, but not anger. They both saw the humor in the situation. "I don't know what I was thinking," Desirée replied. "Oh, what he must think of me!"

"He probably thinks you're bringing the bone home to your dog."

"A treat for Rover. Now I know how people feel when they go to those all-you-can-eat buffets and get caught stashing food in their purses to bring home for later."

Austin turned serious. "You realize if this happens in Africa we're dead meat. If we're traveling in a foreign country we obviously won't have a dog with us."

"I promise, I'll never do it again."

Back at her room door, Desirée had a strange sense of déjà vu, recalling what had occurred after she let herself into the apartment last Friday night. But this time Austin simply wished her good night, adding, "I'm glad everything's okay with us."

"Me, too. I'll see you tomorrow, huh?"

"Sure."

After they parted she relaxed in her room. The evening had gone quite well, in spite of her unfortunate comment about the sparks between them. At least Austin hadn't seemed upset by it. She was glad he chose not to respond; that was definitely not the direction any conversation between them should be taking.

She felt so much better now that the tension had dissolved. Still, she wished there was something she could do to apologize for practically labeling him a blackmailer.

Suddenly his comment to the waitress came back to her, and she had an idea. Desirée reached for the phone. "Hello, Concierge, is there anywhere around here that I can get a Snickers bar?"

* * *

Desirée nervously stood outside Austin's room on the hotel's Tower Level. In her hand she held a Snickers candy bar. She didn't understand why she was having second thoughts about her gesture of goodwill.

This is silly; there's nothing to be nervous about. Quickly, she knocked on the door before she changed her mind . . . and before someone noticed her standing here and reported the presence of a loiterer to the hotel's security office.

The door was promptly opened, but not by Austin. Monique Oliver's hand rested on the doorknob, her dark brown hair grazing the shoulders of her cream-colored nylon robe. From the way it fit loosely over a matching nightgown, Desirée could tell it had been thrown on, probably when Monique heard the knock.

She quickly masked her surprise, hoping the other woman hadn't noticed. "Oh . . . hello."

"Hello. I remember you; you work for Ozzie." Monique's triumphant smile told Desirée she had failed to control her facial expression hastily enough.

"Yes, that's right." Desirée held out the Snickers bar. "Would you give this to Austin?"

"Yes, I'll give it to him when he comes out of the shower. I don't know where he'll put it all, though. We just ordered room service. In fact, I thought you were them."

"I appreciate it. Thanks." Desirée had barely turned away when the door closed. Maybe she was imagining it, but it sounded more like a slam.

She muttered a curse under her breath. No wonder she had last-minute reservations about bringing Austin that candy. A sixth sense was trying to warn her of Monique's presence.

The irony of Austin's comment about not entertaining while on a survey wasn't lost on her. Skye was only coming to take her to dinner—and that was where it would end—but it was obvious what activity Austin would be indulging in with Monique once he emerged from his shower. Who did he think he was, anyhow? First he told her to speak only when spoken to at the GM meeting, then he suggested it wasn't proper for her to spend an hour or two with one of the few people she knew in New York after her work had been completed for the day. He certainly wasn't letting this survey interfere with *his* personal life. It was like that old expression, a favorite of mothers everywhere, "Don't do as I *do,* do as I *tell* you to do." Well, she had news for Austin Hughes: She was twenty-nine years old, too old to be treated like a child.

Then she realized confronting him would only bring back the bad feelings they had just eradicated. It was a relief to be done with all the tension of the past few days, and the last thing they needed just before their trip was to renew it. She decided it would be best simply not to mention the incident. Besides, once Monique told him that she had left the candy bar for him, it would all be in the open anyway, and Austin would realize he had been caught not following his own advice.

Austin picked up the Snickers bar from the desk. "Where'd this come from?"

"Oh, that." Monique reached for the brush on the nightstand and began to vigorously brush her thick locks. "Your assistant dropped it off."

He broke into a smile. "That was nice of her. I was too full in the restaurant to eat dessert." Then he frowned. "Where was I when she came by?"

"In the shower."

"Damn. I wish I'd been able to answer the door. I didn't want her to know you were here."

"What!"

"Just this afternoon we had words about entertaining while on a survey. This makes me look like a hypocrite."

"Don't be silly, Ozzie. The rules don't apply to you. You're a partner. She's only a junior agent."

He shrugged. "Still . . . so when were you going to tell me she came by?"

"Well, pardon me if your assistant and her little gesture weren't paramount on my mind," Monique replied frostily. Then her voice took on a softer, more intimate quality. "I was more concerned with showing you how much I missed you . . . and having you show me how much you missed me." She put the brush down and deliberately let the sheet fall, exposing her naked torso. "Come on, lover, I'm not done with you yet."

Desirée opened a large goldenrod envelope and let all the forms she'd completed and the tapes on which she had recorded her observations spill out on the bed, then began the process of organizing them into large plastic bags with zipperlike closures. There had to be a form completed for each department within the hotel she had assessed, as well as a taped overview of all contacts, whether they were direct or indirect. By organizing them this way she'd make sure nothing was missing.

She had the television on while she worked, but nonetheless, the harsh ringing of the telephone startled her. Her room was equipped with two phones, one by the bed and the other on the desk. She climbed over the papers on the large bed to get to the other side quickly. "Hello?"

"Thanks for the candy," Austin said.

"You're welcome. I thought you'd appreciate it."

"I did, in all the ways you meant it."

Desirée knew he was saying he recognized it as a peace offering.

"I'm sorry I was indisposed when you stopped by. Uh, Desirée . . . I have to tell you I feel a little foolish about what I said this afternoon."

The corners of her mouth tilted upward and her eyes shone with mischief. "You mean you didn't expect me to find out you were, uh, *entertaining* while on a survey, which of course is a direct violation of company policy?"

"Uh . . ."

"Well, you *did* say you didn't have to resort to pressure to get a woman's company."

"You're not making this any easier."

She giggled. "Can you blame me? But it's all right. I know the rules only apply to peons like me and not to founding partners. Besides, I think I made my position on the matter clear."

"Yes, you certainly did," he agreed, remembering her fiery declaration of where she drew the line. "I'll see you tomorrow, eh?"

"Good night."

Austin replaced the receiver and sank back into the multiple pillows on the bed. Eyes closed, he took a bite of the candy bar she had brought him. Snickers was his favorite candy. That had certainly been a nice thing for Desirée to do.

He was deep in thought when Monique emerged from the bathroom, where she had gone in a huff after he declined another lovemaking session. He had begun to feel that perhaps the flame had gone out between them, at least for him. She, on the other hand, was apparently thinking they were headed in the direction of commitment. Where she had gotten that idea he didn't know. He'd never done anything to encourage her; in fact, he'd even suggested that he didn't want to monopolize her time, a hint she had evidently chosen to ignore. It was probably time to break it off before things got out of hand.

"You're acting very strangely, Austin," Monique commented as she caught her hair in a coated rubber band at the nape of her neck. "I think it has something to do with that woman."

"Don't be ridiculous, Monique. I'm just feeling a bit on edge. We've got a big problem in the Denver office that might have cost us a client. I already apologized to you for being distracted." *What more do you want?* he added with silent annoyance, knowing this was not the time or place to end their relationship. There was still time before he left for Africa.

"You're sure it has nothing to do with her?"

It grated on his last nerve to hear Monique repeatedly refer to Desirée as *she* and *her,* but never by name. "Look, Desirée is new in town, she doesn't know anyone, and she's doing the company a tremendous favor. I thought the least I could do was take her to dinner. And I was glad we stopped by Zack's; she made a few friends there."

"Yeah. Skye Audsley certainly seemed interested. I guess it's something all men go through from time to time, to see how sweet the juice really is."

Austin had had enough. "Listen, Monique, I don't know why you're so down on Desirée. From what I've seen, she's never given you any reason to dislike her. She's a very nice person, and I don't ever want to hear you refer to her in a negative way again."

Monique stared at him angrily, her expression transforming into a sly, knowing smile Austin didn't like. "Uh-*huh,*" was all she said.

The elevator came to a halt and opened.

Desirée's heartbeat accelerated as she reached for the plastic key card to her room. She wondered how long it would be before she could unlock a door without thinking of that kiss with Austin.

"Nice," Skye commented as he walked into the room.

"Not too bad. Of course, when I'm picking up the tab myself my budget runs more to HoJo's."

Skye turned to her and pulled her into his arms in a fluid movement. "I've enjoyed the time we spent together, Desirée," he said. "I'm going to miss you. I hope you don't forget me while you're away."

She noticed his eyes had narrowed and his voice had grown uncharacteristically husky. It was a good thing he didn't talk like that normally. He wouldn't have gotten far in the field of broadcasting sounding like a male version of Tallulah Bankhead.

Good grief, girl, snap out of it! She was thinking about everything except the matter at hand because she didn't *want* to think about the matter at hand. Aloud she said, "I won't forget. It'll give me something to look forward to when I get back."

He kissed her then. Desirée stood still, waiting for a sensation that never came. There was no rush of oxygen to her brain, no feeling of floating . . . just a fairly pleasant tingle that couldn't begin to compare with what she'd felt when Austin kissed her. She'd been afraid of that, and now that her fears had materialized she trembled slightly in Skye's arms.

"Of course," he whispered when their lips separated, "we can always make a fabulous memory for you to take with you . . . to keep you cool on those hot African nights." He cocked his head toward the bed.

She smiled and shook her head. "No . . . I don't think so."

"Oh, well," he said matter-of-factly as he released her, his entire attitude changed within the space of a few seconds. "Can't blame a guy for trying."

"I'm not upset, Skye." Actually, she felt like laughing.

She knew he'd felt the vibrations of her body and probably thought it was in reaction to his kiss. *If only he knew.* His swift change in demeanor was frightening. Delivering the news of the day was probably a close relation to acting. She would never be able to tell if he was being sincere or merely giving a performance.

"Good. I'll talk to you when you get back. You take care of yourself over there."

"I will."

Desirée closed the door behind him. She felt strangely relieved to know the moment she had half anticipated and half dreaded was over. She wondered if Skye had actually thought he might be successful in getting her into bed. He wasn't only drop-dead gorgeous, but a high wage-earner who could easily have any woman he wanted. It surprised her that he would be interested in a quality-control agent from Denver, especially one who looked like she did.

She had no illusions about her looks in a world where it was okay to be black, but not *too* black. She knew people often laughed and made snide comments behind her back—or her face—about the darkness of her skin. First there was the second-grade heartbreak of her first crush. Then later on, she had gotten in several fights because of it, especially during Idi Amin's reign of terror in Uganda. Fellow students used to ask her in deadpan fashion if the notoriously cruel dictator with the blue-black skin was her father. Finally, there was the astonishing conversation she had overheard between Calvin and his parents when they didn't realize she was within earshot, which led to her walking out of his apartment, but not before she told them what she thought of them and their attitude.

But through it all she wore her skin well and made no apologies. As a child her mother always told her that she was just as pretty as any other girl and a lot prettier than many. They were special people, she had said, descended from the Fulani of West Africa.

It had all been fabricated, of course. Helen Mack had as little knowledge of her lineage as any other African-American family unless they were related to Alex Haley, but one day during a trip to the library Desirée saw why her mother had chosen that particular ethnic group with which to claim kinship. The Fulani were something of an exotic people, with narrow noses and unusually shaped eyes that set them apart from other Africans, even if none of the people in the library book pictures were as dark as she.

There was a definite trend among prominent African-American men in their choices of wives and girlfriends, with most of the ones she saw choosing was what Oprah Winfrey described as "cupcakes," attractive women who just happened to have light skin and long hair. As for the rest, well, most of them were with white women. Sure, she had tons of hair, but she usually wore it sedately pinned up, not cascading loose. No, she simply didn't fit the mold. Why had she caught Skye's eye?

She knew better than to think he would be pining for her while she was away. A month was a long time, and she was realistic enough to face the very real possibility that he would be seeing someone else by the time she got back. That was okay by her, but it really hadn't occurred to her before now that it would be difficult to maintain any romantic attachments with all the travel she would be doing. What would happen if she met someone she really wanted to spend time with?

At that moment she realized the only person she'd be spending time with for the next few weeks would be Austin.

* * *

"Austin, what's a throg?"

"What?"

"I saw a sign for the Throg's Neck Bridge. What's a throg?"

"I don't know. I guess I never really thought about it. Maybe it's a cousin to the troglodyte."

"A what?"

He shrugged. "Nothing." Austin realized that Desirée was too young to remember the popular R&B novelty song from the Seventies. He'd only been a kid himself when it was out, but it had been a favorite of his older sister. He knew from their conversations that Desirée was an only child.

"I'm just glad traffic wasn't bad," she commented. Everything had gone smoothly. Austin parked in a lot near the airport, from which they were shuttled to the terminal. They checked in without incident and now were just waiting to board their plane.

"It's one of the advantages of taking a nighttime flight. Unfortunately, most of our flights are scheduled during the day, and the traffic can be miserable, but at least by the time we reach our destination we can check in right away."

He reached for her left hand and turned it over. "Where's your ring?"

Having her hand swallowed by his larger one so suddenly startled her, and she gulped. It was like she'd swallowed a golf ball; it was several moments before she could speak. Why did Austin's touch always affect her this way? "In my change purse. Don't worry; I'll put it on before we get to the hotel." She noticed he was already wearing his. "I can't believe we're finally going. I can't tell you how excited I am." It was the truth; she *was* excited—both about the trip and by Austin's hand, which still covered hers.

He increased the pressure on it slightly in response.

"You're not alone. I've been looking forward to this for weeks, ever since the deals were finalized." He frowned. "Damn. I just realized I forgot to call Phil. I was in and out of the office today, but there were a lot of last-minute things I needed to do. He left messages for me both at work and at home, which means it might be urgent."

Desirée looked at her watch. "We won't be boarding for another twenty minutes or so, and in Denver it's only eight-thirty. Do you have his home number with you?"

"Yeah. I guess I'll try to reach him now."

While he was gone Desirée fidgeted with excitement in her seat. They were finally on their way. She hadn't expected him to offer her a ride to the airport, figuring Monique would bring him. Perhaps Austin's girlfriend was sulking about his going away for so long in general, and the fact that she was going with him in particular.

She flipped through one of the magazines she'd bought at the newsstand. It contained a retrospective of fashion models and included her two favorites, Lauren Hutton, who like herself had a space between her front teeth and who, at least later in her career, had insisted on proudly smiling without the device that had concealed it; and Alek Wek from the Sudan, who cut a striking figure on runways and magazine covers with her ebony beauty.

Even the article wasn't enough to contain her excitement. She checked her watch for the fifth time in ten minutes. She hoped she would be able to sleep on the plane.

The plane wasn't full, and because there was no one assigned to the middle seat in their row Desirée and Austin were able to get a little more room in the otherwise narrow seats by lifting the armrests and stretching out.

Desirée surprised them both by falling asleep half an

hour into the flight, but Austin had too much on his mind to rest. Phil had just given him some disturbing news. Karen Bowman denied having done the input for the botched Idaho spa job. Karen, a divorceé who changed boyfriends like most people changed linens, had been one of their first employees in the Denver office. She did an excellent job, despite the demands of single parenting two young children and a social life that kept her up until all hours and was the source of much office gossip. Phil said he believed her, but if Karen was telling the truth, it meant the work was deliberately being sabotaged, a disturbing thought. By whom and for what reason was yet to be determined.

Austin immediately suggested revamping the system to include personal security codes that only he and Phil could access to find out who had input what. Phil had laughed and said he was having a computer consultant come to the office the next day for just that purpose. He warned it was going to be expensive—the consultant's fee was fifty dollars an hour, an added expenditure that would ultimately come out of their own pockets.

Austin found himself visualizing all the employees in the Denver office, trying to figure out who would have a reason to do them in. He came up with nothing.

His eyes drifted over to the sleeping Desirée. In repose she looked lovely. She simply had closed her eyes. There was no snoring, gaping or drooling.

He took advantage of her sleeping stance to stare at her unabashedly, and she unwittingly cooperated by shifting in her seat so that she faced him. Her dark skin looked like smooth chocolate against the vivid royal blue blouse she wore and, he thought with a lick of his lips, it was probably as sweet. It was probably no coincidence that she always wore highly flattering rich colors or pastels and avoided less complementary hues like red, navy and black.

His gaze went to her mouth. Her lips had parted slightly when she changed positions but then closed. Either way they looked luscious and kissable.

There in the darkened plane, Austin allowed himself to admit he was attracted to Desirée Mack. It had been there from the very beginning, the day she walked off the plane at LaGuardia, but he'd stubbornly refused to acknowledge he could be interested in a subordinate, even when Monique expressed her suspicions. He'd even tried to convince himself that kissing her had been no more than a momentary urge he'd acted on recklessly. Even when Skye Audsley entered the picture, he'd only been partially honest with himself, but now it was time for the truth to set him free. He hated the thought of her in some other man's arms . . . because he wanted her in his own.

He was at a loss. Throughout his career he had always made it a point not to get involved with anyone connected with work. It hadn't been a problem, because never before had he felt drawn to any of his associates or employees. He thought of Desirée instantly, especially at night when he was at home alone, wondering why he had spent six figures on a house that felt cavernous to him. It was crying out to be filled by the puttering about of a wife and the antics of children. But he had been too busy building his company to search for Ms. Right. Just imagining Desirée relaxing with him on the sofa or helping him prepare a meal in the kitchen was enough to bring a smile to his lips. He wanted to know all about her, what she felt passionate about, what was important to her.

He also knew he was in an awkward position; he was unable to do anything to pursue Desirée without having her think it was a condition of her job. And then there was the promise he had made to her last week. "I won't kiss you again unless I have your permission," he had said.

The only way to get anywhere with Desirée would be to somehow make her *want* him to kiss her.

Seven

The Air Afrique flight was uneventful. It made one stop in Dakar, Senegal, which would be the city from which they would depart Africa to return to the States when the surveys were complete. Although Desirée was excited at knowing she was actually in Africa, she also knew they were far from their final destination in the Ivory Coast. The distance between Dakar and Abidjan was roughly the same as between Washington, D.C., and St. Louis. She found herself feeling glad they weren't flying all the way to the East Coast, which would probably take another seven hours or so. Africa was a tremendous continent; only Asia was more expansive.

At last they landed in Abidjan, claimed their luggage and went through customs. Desirée felt uncomfortable as the male officer inspecting her baggage lingered over her lingerie. She lowered her eyes while he was examining the folds of her favorite lace-trimmed nightgown.

"Is this necessary?" Austin demanded as the officer stared at Desirée with heavy-lidded deliberation while his hands were all over her nightgown. "It didn't take you this long to go through *my* belongings."

"Just doing my job, monsieur," the officer replied in a monotone. He continued with his maddeningly slow search, probably just to remind Austin who was in charge. But Desirée refused to give in to him again. The next time he looked for her reaction she fixed an icy stare on him, and he responded by promptly zipping her bags closed and announcing he was through.

"Thanks for sticking up for me," she said to Austin when they had regained possession of their luggage.

"The S.O.B. was out of line. I ought to report it."

"No, Austin, that's not necessary. I'll just wash out my underwear before I put it on." In a reflex action she squeezed his arm affectionately.

There was another delay while they changed some of their dollars into local currency, but finally they were on their way.

In the taxi Desirée fingered the wedding band every few minutes, unaccustomed to having it on her finger.

"Looks like any moderately large American city, from the skyline," she commented as they approached the city center.

"For a while Abidjan was the leading city in West Africa," the cabbie, who had told them in French-accented English that he hailed from neighboring Togo, "but about a dozen years ago it fell apart after the drought and coffee and cocoa prices went down."

"You wouldn't know it to look at it, at least from this point. It certainly looks prosp—" Austin cut himself off when he suddenly realized they were now traveling through an impoverished area. Shacks sat closely together, wash hanging everywhere, barefoot children whose feet and legs were caked with street dirt and people moving about oblivious to the contrasting patterns between their shirts and their slacks or skirts.

The driver laughed. "This is Treichville."

"Trashville?" Desirée repeated haltingly, unconsciously altering the pronunciation slightly in her effort.

Again the driver laughed. "Yeah, that's it!"

* * *

A ride over the Charles de Gaulle Bridge spanning the lagoon that surrounded the city put them in the business district, leaving the slums of Treichville behind.

They would be conducting surveys of two competing hotels in Abidjan. The site of their first assignment was centrally located and quite attractive.

Although the local time was not quite one o'clock, an early check-in had been arranged for them, a service many hotels provided for foreign guests whose flights arrived in the morning. Austin handled the check-in with the front desk clerk. All of their reservations during this trip had been made under the name of Mr. and Mrs. Austin Hughes; aliases could not be used in foreign countries requiring passports. Of course, both Desirée's passport and her airline tickets bore her true surname, but Austin had gotten the typesetter at a local print shop the company patronized to create an authentic-looking marriage certificate in case the legality of their relationship was questioned, in which case Desirée would tell them she merely hadn't gotten a passport that reflected her married name.

The bellman literally dropped their bags and left the suite, offering no information about the hotel.

"Well, he was helpful," Desirée remarked. Then she proceeded to look inside the closets and behind the shower curtain.

"What are you doing?" Austin asked.

"Making sure no one's hiding in here. I always do that when I check in, no matter how nice the hotel is. The only reason I left the door shut is because you're here. Otherwise I usually prop it open with one of my bags so someone will hear me if I scream."

Austin shrugged. He supposed travelers couldn't be too careful these days, particularly women. He popped a tape into his microcassette recorder. "I'm going to dictate the check-in, including the hospitality of our bellhop."

"Go ahead. I'll do the room inspection. Can you go in the other room so our recorders don't pick up each other's voices?"

"Sure."

After he went into the bedroom Desirée studied the room. It was cozily furnished and had a marvelous view of the lagoon, as had been promised when the booking was made. Then she reached for her own recorder and identified herself by agent number, giving the date and name and location of the property being surveyed. "This is a survey of the room condition after check-in. At twelve-twenty-five P.M. Greenwich Mean Time, the agents entered the accommodations . . ."

She moved about as she dictated, pausing as she searched for dust and thin spots in the carpeting. In the powder room she noted that there was no grime in the bathtub and that the top sheet of the toilet tissue was folded to a point for easy grasping. When Austin emerged from the bedroom she went in to complete the overview. The Bible was in place in the drawer of the nightstand, there were hangers in the closet and the blow dryer worked, but there was a lipstick stain on the carpet and the mattress had not been turned in six months, according to the rotation label.

After they had completed their paperwork, Austin suggested lunch. Desirée, famished after the too-small portions of breakfast served on the plane, agreed.

Over a casual meal of fried chicken and French fries in one of the hotel's restaurants, the conversation was lively as Desirée tried to polish Austin's extremely vague French, which was even more shaky than her own. She felt a lot better. She might not be fluent, but Austin didn't know enough to be able to tell. Besides, most of the staff seemed to speak English anyway. She was so caught up in the fun, she forgot that Austin was supposed to be her husband until her memory was jarred by the way the staff was smiling at them.

"They probably think we're newlyweds," Austin whispered.

Desirée's thoughts immediately went to the king-sized bed in their suite, and her face grew warm. She quickly reached in her purse for her lipstick, which she applied with a sure hand without benefit of a mirror. Austin's obvious fascination with her feat made them both burst into laughter, and again she felt at ease.

As they were leaving the restaurant, Austin suggested they check out the pool and surrounding cabana area and snack bar. Desirée went to change while Austin dictated his report of the restaurant while it was still fresh in his mind. Although she felt safe with him so close by, she locked the door behind her. It would be embarrassing for them both if he walked in while she was changing.

Curiously, she wondered what Austin would think if he saw her naked. In Denver she regularly went rollerblading and bike riding to keep in shape, as well as doing occasional aerobics with the ladies on TV. Although her rear end was a bit more prominent than she would have preferred, it was firm, and her waist was well defined. There was nothing really wrong with the way she was built; it was her coloring that she was concerned about. Would he be turned off by her great expanse of ebony skin? And why on earth was she even *thinking* about how Austin would react to her body in the first place? She needed to get a grip. This was business, all business and nothing but business.

She had changed into her print maillot and was tying the matching sarong around her waist when Austin knocked. "Desirée . . . I'll meet you down there, okay?"

"All right." She started to tell him she was almost

ready but thought better of it. It was just like a man to not want to wait two minutes.

Besides, with Austin gone she saw no need to rush. She rubbed sunscreen into the skin of her face, shoulders, arms, legs, feet and as best she could on her back. She knew it would be courting trouble to ask Austin to do it; she could barely handle his grazing her hand, which was considerably less sensitive than her back.

Her relaxed hair was still in the old-fashioned style she had worn on the plane, with two braids caught high and wound around each other across the top of her head. It looked pretty good, considering she had slept during the long trip, but a few stray hairs—probably straggler split ends—were threatening to come loose from her hairline. She brushed them into place and applied fresh lipstick, then studied herself from all sides in the large rectangular mirror that hung over the dresser. Impulsively, she turned all the way around and lifted the sarong. The suit covered her bottom nicely. Desirée knew that a swimsuit was the skimpiest attire she would ever wear in public and, always conscious of her generously proportioned behind, she wanted to make sure she would not be an unpleasant sight.

She needn't have worried. It was apparent from the affable looks she received that she was anything but offensive. A suit-clad man in the elevator asked her a question in rapid French, to which she replied with her standard, *"Je parle très mal le français."* Undaunted, the man asked her in accented but comprehensible English if she was from Ghana.

Desirée smiled. She had caught the words "Cotê d'Ivoire" in his original question. No doubt he was asking something like what part of the country she was from. Her lack of fluency in French had answered *that,* so he had merely gone to the nearest English-speaking country in this heavily French-settled region of Africa.

The ironic truth was that her complexion actually was darker than that of many of the Africans she had seen so far. "I'm American," she replied.

"Ah. Well, welcome to Cotê d'Ivoire."

"Thank you."

She had been carrying her sunglasses, a contemporary version of the cat eye style that had been so popular in the Fifties, and she slipped them on as she went through the doors that led to the pool area. It was cool this afternoon—the African sun felt just comfortably warm—but it was certainly bright.

Austin was relaxing on a lounge chair, reading a newspaper. He happened to turn a page as she was approaching, and when he caught sight of her, he lowered the paper to his lap.

His eyes were hidden by horn-rimmed sunglasses with dark green lenses, but the way his head was turned in her direction left little doubt about the focus of his gaze. Desirée was dismayed by the instantaneous rapid rise and fall of her chest. There was no way she could hide it from him; the snug-fitting swimsuit made it impossible to conceal. Austin would think it was nerves, but Desirée knew better. Her body was reacting to having struck a chord in a man she had found undeniably appealing from the very start.

So what if he was her boss? she thought. He was also a man, and it was clear he found her desirable.

She suddenly realized she was using Austin's status as her employer as an excuse for not getting involved. Even after half a year, the wounds from her broken engagement were still raw. But when Austin had raised her chin and kissed her senseless, nothing else had mattered. She had been desperately wrong to think that Skye Audsley could make her forget. It was Austin's touch that she craved. She wanted—no, she *owed* it to herself—to see what lay beyond that spark.

But it was futile. She had alienated him permanently when she shared her fears with him. She would never forget what he'd said about not kissing her unless he had her permission. It was just a nice way of saying, "When donkeys fly."

Perhaps it was just as well. Even though he was her boss, being paired with him was only temporary, and she would most likely work under Mickey or another one of the senior agents when this was over. She would be returning to Colorado and Austin to New York, and they would hardly ever see each other again. Despite Eve Brown's obvious elation over her new East Coast love, Desirée felt two thousand miles was too far a distance to allow for maintaining a relationship. The most she saw resulting from acting on her impulse was a brief dalliance that would be over with the last survey, and while she was sure it would be memorable, she felt she deserved better. She wanted the comfort of a good man who would still be around the next month, and the next year.

She thought she had found him in Calvin Edwards, but she had been wrong, and it still hurt. She wondered if the pain and apprehension that had plagued her since then would ever go away. Thank God her mother had taught her the art of self-love early in life, or she might have ended up with zero self-esteem. Helen Mack was a wise woman. It was almost as if she knew the heartache that awaited her only child.

Desirée tried to put it in the back of her mind. The prospective in-laws who hadn't accepted her lived in Missoula, Montana, halfway on the other side of the world. She shouldn't be wasting her thoughts on them.

"Hi," she said to Austin as she sat in the neighboring lounger. "Catching up on local news?"

"I'm trying to, but it's not easy. It's printed in French. Hey, you got here awfully quick. I just stopped in the lobby to get a paper, and I haven't been here two minutes." He opened his mouth to tell her that she looked fabulous, then changed his mind. He had to make sure she was relaxed, and complimenting her appearance would only make her tighten up quicker than heat-straightened hair at a crowded party.

He stared at her thigh, partially visible through the wrap opening of her sarong. It was smooth-looking, like a strip of dark chocolate; and the jungle print of her ensemble, consisting of elephants, lions, leopards and trees in earth tones on an off-white background, was about the most attractive wrapping he could imagine.

Safely concealed by the lenses of his sunglasses, his gaze traveled upward. The stretch fabric of her one-piece suit hugged her bustline. Austin had never seen her wear anything quite so form-fitting. Her chest seemed to be heaving slightly. Given their history, she was probably a bit jittery about wearing a swimsuit in front of him, but her nervousness was only accenting her nicely rounded form. There was a lot of woman in that suit, he thought with admiration. Beneath his trunks, he felt himself stiffen.

"C'mon, let's go swimming," he said. The water was probably freezing, but the equivalent of a cold shower was just what he needed to calm him down. In another minute he'd be salivating. He stood and held out his hand to her in invitation.

Desirée looked up at him, puzzled by his sudden eagerness to swim. She shrugged before removing her sunglasses, swinging her legs to one side of the lounger and accepting his hand as she got to her feet.

The moment their hands touched, a current of electricity bolted through them. Desirée gasped and quickly pulled her hand back. For a moment they simply stared at each other. She was the first to avert her eyes.

Austin was the first to speak. "Are you coming?"

Her head jerked up at the phrasing, but there was only earnestness in his expression, not the sly look of someone who had knowingly used a double entendre.

"Yes." She got to her feet and untied her sarong.

Austin was wearing an unbuttoned, short-sleeved tan shirt over black trunks. He pulled off the shirt and tossed it on the lounger, placing his sunglasses on top of it. Desirée watched as he confidently walked to the lip of the pool and dove in. She cringed as he hit the water, having always been more of a gradual, work-your-way-in type of swimmer, before walking around to the pool's shallow end.

She had made it as far as the next-to-the-bottom step when she saw a dark form gliding in her direction under the water. Austin emerged just two feet in front of her. "What's taking you so long? The water's great!"

"You must be a member of the Polar Bear Club. This is probably only mildly warmer than the Arctic." She advanced to the bottom step and grimaced as the cool water rippled around her hips and abdomen, as well as the exposed skin of her lower back. The shock of the contact caused her nipples to harden. Her body was certainly betraying her today. She needed to conceal her reaction, and quickly.

There was only one way. "Okay, here goes," she said. She pinched her nostrils shut and bent her knees so she was wet up to her shoulders, then she leaned backward until she was in a floating position, buoyed by the gentle rippling of the water.

The water felt less frigid to her skin once her entire body was wet. She quickly became acclimated. With her eyes shut and her arms outstretched, she felt weightless as she floated. Her system was still operating on Eastern Time, and it was about the time she would be taking it easy before preparing to go to sleep for the night, even if here in Abidjan it was only three-thirty in the afternoon. She was glad Austin was doing most of the day's reports; she was too groggy to be accurate.

Desirée yawned. It was not an attractive thing to do, she knew, but in her fatigue she didn't bother to attempt to stifle it. The water always made her tired, and at the rate she was going she wouldn't make it to dinner. She would suggest to Austin that they survey room service around dinnertime this evening. She would eat a light meal and then get into that king-sized bed, alone.

And no doubt have the same sweet dream of kissing Austin that she'd had every night for a week.

Eight

Desirée didn't know how long she had been floating, nor did she care. She was comfortable drifting aimlessly with the flow of the water.

She was thinking that it was probably time to go upstairs and truly get comfortable when something lightly brushed against the sensitive soles of her feet. She let out a squeal and splashed wildly with her arms as her feet thrashed out for the pool floor. She soon learned she had drifted into the deeper water when her feet failed to touch the bottom. Sputtering from the water she had taken in, she caught her breath and swam the few strokes to the pool's edge. "What was that?" she breathlessly asked Austin, who was leaning against the edge only a few feet away.

"Me."

His face wore a broad grin, and she scowled at him. "I hope you're proud of yourself for scaring me half to death, not to mention almost drowning me."

"I'm sorry, Desi. It's just that you looked like you were about to drift off to sleep, and I didn't want you to drown. Actually, for you to react so suddenly you must have been closer to nodding off than you thought, which can be very dangerous."

"I wasn't nodding off," she protested. "I knew I was in the water; it covered the sides of my face. The only reason I jumped up was because it tickled. As a matter of fact, I was just about to call it a day. But if you thought I was about to fall asleep, a simple 'Wake up, Desirée' would do, don't you think?"

"All right. No more pranks." He closed the distance between them. "I think we've had enough watersports for today. Let's go back to the suite."

For the first time she became aware of his bare chest. She hadn't had time to notice the well-developed biceps of his arms and pectorals of his chest, the latter visible through a sparse coating of coarse hair, before he dived into the pool. Austin had a lean build, and fully dressed there had been no hint of the marvelous physique before her now.

She knew she was staring, but she couldn't help it. The mere thought of being cradled against his firm body made her breathless. Finally, knowing she had stood mesmerized for far too long, she blinked and raised her eyes to meet his. The intense gaze she encountered embarrassed her. It was obvious he knew precisely what she had been thinking.

"Desi," he began, leaning toward her, his voice low and sensual.

"You're right," she interrupted in a voice ringing with forced cheerfulness, "we need to be getting back." She turned away, swam a few strokes to the metal ladder and climbed out.

"I'll get you a towel," he offered.

She was planning on using the one already on his chair but knew he wanted to include an interaction with the cabana clerk in his report. "Thanks," she said, not turning to look at him. If she had, she would have found him staring intently at the expanse of exposed back in her deep-cut maillot, as well as her round, ample hips.

Austin watched the sway of her hips from side to side in the natural flow of her walk. *What a woman.* He had no idea she had such a nice behind; she was partial to those long, hip-hiding tunics. The best part was that she didn't appear to know how good she looked. Her erect carriage had more to do with confidence than arrogance. He was disappointed when she replaced her sarong after wiping the excess water from her body with his towel.

As soon as he returned to their suite, Austin retrieved his handheld recorder from the closet and began to recount the service he had received from the cabana personnel. Desirée noticed his eyes were on his newspaper as he recorded. She wondered why. Note-taking in public was strictly against company policy; the agents were required to remember all the details of their encounters until they could put them on tape in the privacy of their own rooms.

She shrugged and went into the bedroom, where she gathered a fresh change of clothes plus a few essential toiletries and took them in the bathroom. Because Austin's clothing was in the bedroom as well, she left the door open in case he wanted to get some dry clothes, locking the bathroom door before she began to undress and unbraid her hair.

As she vigorously scrubbed her scalp, she found herself singing the chorus of the Rodgers and Hammerstein classic from *South Pacific,* "I'm Gonna Wash That Man Right Out of My Hair."

That's what you *think.* Great day in the morning, Austin looked good in those trunks. Permission to kiss her, indeed—the smoldering look he had given her in the pool made her want to throw her arms around his neck and offer him her mouth . . . as well as anything else he might be interested in. It amazed her that she had been able to go on as if nothing out of the ordinary had happened. The static that blazed between them when he took her hand said it all.

She wrapped a towel around her head and dried off, then she slipped into what she referred to as her trusty, a tan nylon sleeveless shirt dress with white polka dots. While clearly loungewear, its just-above-the-knee length, button-down shirtfront, stiff white collar and abundance of extra fabric—the A-line cut was so full, even a very expectant mother could fit into it—made it entirely suitable to wear in front of a man with whom she was not intimately involved. It was certainly not even remotely similar to that sexy outfit Monique was wearing in Austin's room at the Harmon.

She was replacing the shampoo in favor of lotion when she heard Austin's voice. "Did you leave me any hot water?"

He was standing in the doorway, arms folded in mock accusation. Desirée giggled. "Well, if I didn't, the GM will certainly be interested to hear about it. Quality hotels like this one aren't supposed to run out." She glanced at him again; he was still wearing his swim trunks and open shirt, the towel he'd used to dry off now draped around his neck. "I thought you would want to put on something dry before now."

"Nah, I figured I'd just wait until after I showered." The playful stern look returned. "I just didn't think you'd take this long." As he walked past her to the bathroom he muttered in an audible tone, "You never hogged the bathroom like this before we were married."

"Sorry, dear," she replied, sounding like a perfect TV wife.

Desirée was in the living room, slowly working through her hair with a setting lotion, parting it neatly and styling it in thick Jamaican-style braids, when Austin emerged, clad in khaki slacks and a shirt. "Wow, you've got a lot of hair," he declared as he took in the strands that cascaded to the middle of her back. "No wonder you were so long in the bathroom."

She sighed. "My hair takes forever. It's my mother's influence. I kept her awfully busy keeping it neat when I was small. She always said there was no such thing as not being able to grow hair, that it's the condition of the ends that determines whether it stays or breaks off. I know she's right—I've had friends who were always complaining about how their hair wouldn't grow, but whenever they relaxed it or colored it, it was never long before they needed to touch up their new growth. But taking care of it is a real time-consuming process."

"Why don't you just cut it?"

"I think about it all the time. But it's been this length ever since I was about ten. I've never worn it any other way. You see, it wasn't very 'in' to be my complexion when I was a kid; not that it's exactly a desired look now. The other kids used to tease me because I was so dark. It was important to Mom for me to have long hair as sort of compensation. I might have been teased about my complexion, but a lot of the girls were envious of my hair.

"Anyway," she continued, "I saw a lot of women with their hair braided during the ride from the airport; apparently it's a popular look over here. This way I'll fit right in with the locals." She recounted the incident in the elevator with the French businessman.

"Sounds to me like he was flirting."

"No, just making conversation." Desirée knew it was an innocent conversation, but the truth was, she usually received more attention from Caucasian men than she did from African-Americans. She remembered Whoopi Goldberg saying the same thing when an interviewer asked her why she never dated black men.

Austin sat beside her on the sofa and fingered the lustrous strands. It looked abrasive but was soft to the touch. "You look like you're in for the evening."

"Are you kidding? I'm exhausted, and doing this hair has worn me out."

"I was hoping you'd want to hit a hot spot tonight."

"Tomorrow, maybe. I need some time to get my system acclimated to the time difference. But I won't be upset if you go without me." She meant it; she really was tired.

"No, we've got plenty of other nights. Why don't I order room service for dinner? We need to get a report on them during peak hours anyway." He reached for his tape recorder and the newspaper. "Guess I don't need this anymore."

"I noticed you were writing on it and looking at it when you made your report."

"I'm going to give you a tip: You can make notes if you make them inside a crossword puzzle."

"So that's what you were doing with the paper. It's not like you can read it, much less do a crossword."

"Yes, but nobody knows that but me."

"Why don't you do this one?" Austin suggested with a wave of his hand when someone knocked on the door. "It'll give the girls a break from the sound of my voice."

Desirée opened the door. "Good evening, Madame Hughes," greeted the white-coated young waiter as he pushed the rolling cart into the room.

"Good evening," she managed to respond. Austin's taking care of all their needs this afternoon had given her zero contact with the staff. It sounded so strange to be addressed as "Madame Hughes."

The waiter removed the lids from the plates, confirming what had been ordered, then replacing them. He slid two chairs over to the tray. "Can I get you anything else?" he asked, addressing both Austin and Desirée, who looked at each other. Desirée shook her head.

"I think that will do it," Austin said. He reached into his back pocket and pulled a few Ivorian notes out of his wallet. "Here you are, uh, Isaac," he said, reading the waiter's name tag. "Thank you."

"Thank *you,* sir. I hope you both enjoy your meal, as well as your stay at our hotel."

"By the way, Isaac," Austin said, "is there a nightspot near here that you would recommend for American tourists?"

"Well, Monsieur Hughes, the lounge right downstairs is very nice. They always have live entertainment, usually either piano and vocalist or kora music."

"Kora music?" Austin repeated.

"I believe you Americans call it a harp."

"I see. I guess that means they don't have dancing."

"No, monsieur, they do not. But there are places in Treichville that are, uh, quite lively. That's where most of the clubs are. Some of them are more reputable than others, of course. Treichville can be a very dangerous part of town, for residents as well as tourists. Please be careful if you go there."

Desirée smiled. Isaac had done the right thing by recommending the hotel lounge first. The GM would be glad to know he wasn't endorsing other nightspots to hotel guests unless pressed.

"Thanks for the information, Isaac." Austin saw the waiter out.

Austin uncovered the plates and took Polaroid shots of them while Desirée recorded her report, at one point getting down on her knees to check the condition of the cart. She suspected her performance was being quietly monitored and wanted to cover everything.

When they were done they pulled up chairs on either side of the cloth-covered cart and ate companionably. *Just like two old married people,* Desirée thought. She was enjoying this easy camaraderie with Austin, even if it did start her imagination running wild. How would it feel to really be married to him, where they would both retire to the bedroom at the day's end instead of him bedding down on the sofa?

The sleeping arrangements worked with no complications. Each night Desirée and Austin bid each other good night before she retreated to the bedroom, at which time he opened up the sofa and made his bed with the spare blanket from the closet shelf and a pillow Desirée gave him from the bed. When morning came, they rose early, and by the time they left their suite to get breakfast there was no sign that anyone had slept on the couch. For extra protection against accidental entry by the maid or other hotel personnel, Austin even adopted Desirée's hotel safety ploy of inserting a door stop into the door, a surprisingly effective deterrent for what was essentially a wedge of rubber.

Friday was check-out day. Austin felt uncomfortably warm in a long-sleeved tailored shirt and tie. "I'm glad we're meeting with the GM early," he called out as he fastened his tie clip. "This way we'll be able to come back and change clothes. It's too damn hot to be wearing a jacket and tie."

"Are we going straight to the next hotel?" Desirée called from the living room.

"No. I think it's best we leave our luggage here for a few hours. We can go to the market, then get our bags when we're done."

"I can't wait. This place is lovely, but I feel like I've been cooped up long enough."

"Have you forgotten last night already?"

"No, of course not." Not hardly, she added silently. Their survey complete save for one or two departments and reports to write, including the extensive summary, she and Austin had slipped out to dine at a maquis, the Ivory Coast's major contribution to African cuisine. Braised food was the specialty at these rustic restaurants, most of which were open only for dinner. They had sat across from each other on wooden benches perched beneath a straw roof, the open-air surroundings affording them a picture-perfect view of the lagoon, and celebrated the success of Wallace and Hughes's first African survey over a meal of savory fish, chicken, rice and wine. They had not exchanged a single cross word the entire evening, and it had been all business, but in spite of herself Desirée found her mind wandering again. The romantic environment was intoxicating. It was a perfect evening for a couple in love . . . or falling in love. Ah, to be one of those lucky people, she had thought as she looked at the other couples present with naked envy.

Afterward they had walked back to the hotel along the wide Boulevard de Gaulle. They were not alone; the soccer game at the stadium nearby had just let out. About halfway there, Austin reached for her hand and held it until they arrived back at the hotel. She waited for him to comment about it simply being a natural gesture for a young married couple that the hotel personnel would expect, but he did not address it and neither did she. She was glad he'd left appearances out of it; it was beginning to grate on her nerves that his every action toward her was part of playing a role.

"It was a wonderful experience, every bit of it," she said now. "Of course I haven't forgotten," she added as she moved to the doorway of the bedroom. "I guess I'm just anxious to cut loose a little. I feel like a child who's been on her best behavior all week."

"You could have cut loose down at the lounge," Austin said as he slipped into his suit jacket.

"Sure, to harp music," she replied with a laugh. She closed the distance between them and reflexively adjusted his shirt collar, which wasn't lying properly because his tie was twisted beneath it. "I want to dance, Austin, not just sit and listen politely like I'm at a concert. I know *you're* a mature man, but I'm still in my twenties, you know," she added with a smile.

"I'm thirty-five, which is hardly ancient," he responded dryly. "But if it's dancing you want, it's dancing you shall have. Tonight we'll go to one of the real hotspots. I'll get Isaac or someone else at the hotel to recommend one."

They spent most of the day at the big market in Treichville. The selection was staggering, and the variance in pricing for similar merchandise was quite wide. Desirée lost all track of time as she bargained for fabric, beads, masks and other wood carvings. She helped Austin pick out gifts for his parents and for Elaine, his secretary.

The impatient rumbling of her stomach at one-thirty convinced her that it was time to break from shopping and get something to eat. She followed her nose to a street vendor who was selling rice and some kind of sauce, but Austin appeared before she could order. "Getting sick is not an option while we're here, Desi. That means you'll have to watch what you eat. Restaurant food is best, and good restaurants, not street stalls or luncheonettes."

"This woman's kitchen is probably a lot cleaner than those of most restaurants," Desirée grumbled as she allowed herself to be led away. She hated it when Austin was bossy; it made her feel like she was five years old instead of almost thirty.

"Maybe so, but we can't afford to take a chance. It's just like not drinking water or soda unless it's bottled or canned."

She glared at him and complained, "You're acting more like my father than my boss."

"Just watching out for you."

Desirée was miffed by his words. He might as well have said straight out that he was protecting the company's investment, she thought with irritation. He didn't have to be so blunt about it. There was nothing wrong with a little pretense of him caring what happened to *her* just because . . . well, just because.

After lunch at a nearby Ethiopian restaurant, where flattened bread took the place of eating utensils, they returned to the market. Austin helped Desirée carry their purchases to a taxi. They rode to the hotel, where their survey was completed, retrieved their luggage from the front desk and continued on to the hotel where they would spend the night between surveys, in the Marcory section of Abidjan near Treichville.

"Are you sure this place is all right?" Desirée asked, eyeing the blue stucco low-rise situated on a side street so narrow it was little more than an alley.

"Sure. Someone at the hotel recommended it. The InterContinental it ain't, but remember, we're paying for this one ourselves."

"But the company reimburses you, doesn't it?"

"Sure. The problem is that the level of accommodations here in Abidjan jumps from inexpensive places like this to the luxury places; and believe me, a corporate refund won't be enough to cover any of those. Needing a room between jobs is actually rare. Usually we go out of one hotel and into the next if it's in the same city, but since so many surveys are being done at one stretch, we got a day off between these two. Enjoy it; there will be times when we'll go straight from one site to another."

"Hmph," Desirée muttered as she helped get the luggage out of the taxi's trunk. "To me, inexpensive means someplace like a Motel Six, and this place looks *nothing* like a Motel Six. It looks more like one of those no-name places you see on the old state roads motorists used before the interstates were built. Most of the ones still standing rent rooms by the hour." She turned at the sound of an approaching vehicle.

A limousine came to a halt in front of the hotel. A dark-skinned, suit-clad man arose from the backseat; then he turned and extended his hand to assist his female companion. She watched them disappear inside while Austin paid the driver.

"Did you see that?" she asked, jabbing him in the ribs.

"Yes. Probably a big shot in the government."

"Coming to a hotel at four in the afternoon without luggage."

Austin shrugged. "I guess the woman isn't his wife. Oh, that reminds me: You can take off your ring. We're not married here, remember?"

Desirée had to tug a bit to get the wedding band off her finger; it seemed to want to stay just where it was. She must be putting on weight already, no doubt from all the meals she was ordering each day. She slipped the ring into her change purse and zipped it securely shut.

The hotel lobby was nicely decorated, with the walls painted a cheery mint green, rattan-framed chairs with colorful vinyl cushions and ceiling fans. Desirée immediately felt more comfortable. Besides, she thought wryly as the dignitary and his companion swept past her, the hotel couldn't have been too bad a choice if government officials used it for their trysts. That meant they were clean as well as discreet.

She turned her attention to the conversation Austin was having with the clerk. "A room, sir?"

"Actually, two rooms. For the night."

"Ah, for the *night!*" the clerk replied, obviously taken by surprise. "Of course, monsieur. Would you like adjoining rooms?"

Austin didn't even look her way. "Yes, that would be fine."

Desirée immediately folded her arms and glared at him. There he went again, with that damned take-charge attitude of his. Who said *she* wanted adjoining rooms?

She was still in that defiant position when he turned and handed her a piece of paper and a pen. "You have to fill—" he broke off when he noticed her stony stance. "What's wrong?"

She let her arms drop. The man was hopeless; he hadn't a clue. Aloud she said, "Nothing's wrong. Here, let me fill this out."

"Not too bad, eh?" Austin asked.

"No, actually, it isn't." Desirée's eyes did a rapid inspection of the modest room. There were a few burn marks on the cheap blond wood bureau and nightstand, but other than that it looked all right. She pulled back the floral print bedspread and fingered the sheets. They were crisp—just-changed crisp. Crease marks were visible on the sheets, as well as the pillow cases. Then again, if what she'd just witnessed was typical of what went on here, laundry was probably the hotel's biggest expenditure. It wasn't all that surprising how good they were at it. "Just think," she said, "I'll be able to write my mother and tell her I stayed in a real life Ivorian brothel." As they carried their belongings to the elevator they had seen another empty-handed couple enter and request a room.

Austin chuckled. "Did you catch the clerk's amazement when I told him we'd be staying the night? I do want you to know, Desirée, this little detail was something the man at the hotel failed to mention about this place. If he had, we wouldn't be here now. But it should be all right for one night. There's a bar downstairs, and they serve hamburgers, fish sandwiches and fries."

Desirée looked at the wood door with its flimsy lock, "supplemented" by an equally feeble hook-and-eye. She would definitely be using her door stop. "You know, I was a little upset when you took adjoining rooms without consulting me, but now I'm kind of glad you did. It'll be comforting to know you're right in the next room."

"I thought you'd feel better if I was. It didn't occur to me to ask if it was okay with you. I guess I should have; sorry." He nodded toward the door that connected their rooms. "We can leave that open if you'd like."

"All right." It was more than what they'd done in the elegant setting of the client site they had just left, where she had not only closed the connecting door at night but locked it as well.

They had dinner in the lounge, where the lighting was low enough to suggest it was a place for discretion. It was clear that this was a place to go on those occasions when it was better not to run into large numbers of people. Austin got the name of a local club from the bartender, who said he would be going there himself when his shift ended. "Just watch your back," he cautioned. "Sometimes tourists are targets for thieves."

In the solitude of her room in the time between dinner and going out for the evening, Desirée took time to write her mother a letter. She mentioned how nice Austin had been to her and how well their ruse of being husband and wife was going. She paused, inadvertently chewing the top of her pen—an unpleasant habit her mother's many reprimands over the years had failed to break her of—and wondered if she should mention anything else, like that controlling manner of his that got on her nerves but was strangely comforting at the same time, or even give a physical description.

She threw her pen down in sudden exasperation. If she was going to do all that, she might as well say what a good kisser he was. *That* would certainly pique her mother's interest. Desirée reached for the pen and abruptly signed off. She wouldn't devote any more space to Austin than she needed to.

Nine

Desirée looked around happily. It was only nine-thirty, but the joint was jumping. Most of the people appeared to be locals. It was easy to spot the tourists; their wide-eyed expressions said it all. Here was a side to the Ivory Coast that wasn't seen in the sophisticated hotel lounges mostly frequented by French expatriates, who engaged in witty conversations around immaculate piano bars. This was the type of place where patrons reflexively brushed off chair seats before sitting down. The vinyl upholstery of the bar stools had been liberally taped down where needed with pale yellow masking tape that seemed to glow in the dim lighting.

Makossa music blared from the speakers, and there was a crowd on the typically undersized dance floor. Regardless, Desirée and Austin worked their way into the flock of bouncing bodies. Dancing nearby was a man they both recognized as the bartender from the hotel where they were staying. The music was too loud for verbal communication, so they used the universal language of smiles and waves to greet him.

The music was intoxicating, a panorama of what African culture had contributed to the world of song. The Camerounian makossa beat blended into the more laid-back style of the British singer Princess, and from there it was onto South Africa and the sound of Hugh Masekela, and then across the Atlantic to Jamaica for the legendary Bob Marley. There was something sensual about the varying beats that made Desirée's muscles loosen, along with her inhibitions. Eventually she found herself merely rotating her shoulders and hips in fluid movements, occasionally lifting her arms for emphasis.

Austin eyed her with interest. In a tank top and matching miniskirt with an Aztec-inspired navy design on a tan background, and her hair textured with waves from being braided while still wet, she certainly looked like a local woman enjoying an evening out. It was almost as if she had been put under a spell, what with those swaying movements and her facial expression—she alternated between closing her eyes as she sashayed her feet and looking at him directly with sensually parted lips and a gaze that had become uncharacteristically heavy-lidded.

Austin imitated her smooth maneuvers with a little hip motion of his own. At one point when her hands were raised he raised his own and pressed his palms against hers. Their arms spread, he moved in close, the front of their bodies coming within inches of each other with their slow rotations. They weren't shaking or rattling, but they were definitely rolling. His gaze locked with hers, but Desirée threw him off guard by pulling her arms away and turning so her back was to him. Austin responded by closing the little distance between them and lowering his hands to her hips, gently rubbing his palms on the sides of her waist and feeling her pelvis revolve against the length of his fingers.

Desirée didn't miss a step. If anything, she became even more bold, leaning her upper body backward a bit, confident that he stood close enough behind her to prevent her from losing her balance. He loved the way she threw her head back; it reminded him of that night back in White Plains when he kissed her. A hungry shudder ran through him at the thought of that kiss, combined with the mental picture of her beneath him in bed, wiggling her hips forward to meet his.

The music of Senegalese recording artist Youssou N'Dour was being featured when a weak-kneed Austin led an exhausted Desirée by the elbow to a vacant table in the corner, from which the view of the dancers was partially blocked by the huge speakers of the sound system. Austin signaled a waitress and ordered drinks, Ivorian beer for himself and white wine for Desirée. "That was the best workout I've had in months," he said after the waitress left, dabbing his forehead with a paper napkin.

"See, a little dancing is good for you," Desirée replied. She tried to make light of it; now that their dance was over, she felt embarrassed by her lack of constraint. She could only imagine what Austin was thinking. What had gotten into her she didn't know; perhaps it was the ghost of her African ancestors—the female ones—urging her on. "The music is wonderful. I would have kicked off my shoes if there hadn't been so many people on the floor, but I know how to make room." She thrust her bent arms to the side, pretending to elbow nearby dancers. "A little rest and some wine and I'll be ready to do it again."

"Well, it might take me a little longer to recover. Remember, I'm older than you are."

They shared a laugh, and then Desirée caught Austin's eye as a brown-skinned woman with her hair styled in Senegalese twists joined them, uninvited.

"I hope it's all right if I sit here," she said belatedly. "This seems to be the only table available." She smiled, revealing even white teeth. "You American?" she asked, directing the question to Austin.

"Yes. New York."

"And what do you think of Abidjan?"

"It's a beautiful city, with the lagoon and all. It came

as something of a surprise; I really wasn't expecting to see any thirty-story buildings."

At first Desirée assumed the questions were directed to Austin because he, unlike herself, did not look like an Ivorian, but she grew increasingly annoyed as the small talk continued in this pattern. Damn it, she was dark but she was hardly invisible, and she resented being ignored. But at least Austin was making eye contact with her as he responded to the woman's questions, attempting to draw her into the conversation.

The waitress appeared and languidly set their drinks in front of them. "That'll be thirty-five hundred francs," she announced.

"I sure am thirsty," the woman declared, and at the moment Desirée realized why she had been giving Austin all her attentions. Desirée looked at him now, curious to see how he would react. He was busy counting out francs, muttering under his breath about the high cost of alcohol in Abidjan.

"Anything else?" the waitress inquired as she accepted the money.

"Nothing for us, thank you," Austin replied.

"You?" the waitress asked the woman, who in turn met Austin's eyes with her smoky stare. Desirée watched as Austin returned the stare, his eyes suddenly gone cold. The waitress shrugged and moved on, and the woman followed suit, her loquaciousness a thing of the past as she gathered her shoulder bag and left without a word.

"Brazen little hussy, wasn't she?" Desirée remarked with a smile.

"I don't like being hustled," Austin answered. "I suspected that was what she was up to from the start, with all the flirting she was doing."

Desirée felt herself beginning to soften toward the woman. Everybody deserved to have a little fun. She didn't agree with the woman's blatant tactics, but she was obviously thirsty and probably didn't have much money. "Oh, well," she said. "No harm done, not really. It's not like you and I—"

"We just danced together, Desirée, and now we're sitting together. If that's not enough, we're wearing wedding rings." Before they left the hotel Desirée had commented that she planned to wear her ring as a safeguard against unwanted male company, and Austin had gone along by wearing his, too—not that its presence had been a deterrent to the now-departed interloper. "Maybe you and I *aren't,* but nobody knows that but us."

She was surprised by his vehemence. Did his anger stem from the woman's attempts to play him . . . or because their relationship wasn't as intimate as it looked to the outside world? "Anyway, it's over," she said. "It was only a drink. Not really worth getting upset about."

"It's more than just a drink, it's the principle. I've heard of places where women are paid by owners to get customers to buy them drinks. Half the time they don't even drink them. Why do you think the first words out of her mouth were, 'Are you American?' "

Desirée looked around. "Well, don't look now, but she's got herself another live one. At least this one's unattached." She turned around to find Austin looking at her strangely. She realized all the anger had gone out of him.

"Do you consider yourself attached to me, Desi?"

It was a loaded question, one she'd unwittingly asked for and that was asked of her in a low, seductive tone, but she decided to make light of it. Everything was going so well between them. They were at ease with each other and she wanted that to continue.

She held up her left hand and pointed to her gold-encased ring finger. "How can I not feel that way, wearing this all the time? I feel like I've been branded 'til death do us part."

They smiled at each other comfortably—oh, how she loved those laugh lines of his—but their attentions were quickly diverted by the sound of raised voices coming from the dance floor. The voices were French, but the emotions transcended language barriers. It was clear that two men were exchanging angry words. Desirée craned her neck to see around the speakers. The crowd around the men was moving back as the music simultaneously came to a halt. A burly man she surmised was the club's bouncer was approaching as fast as his considerable bulk would allow. One of the men shoved the other just before the bouncer got to them, sending the man sprawling into the crowd. He quickly got to his feet.

The bouncer moved between the two men, facing the one who had done the pushing. By his gestures Desirée could see he was trying to reason with him, but the man wasn't having any. He pointed at the man and then at a woman who stood nearby, speaking in rapid French. Then the other man said something to him, something that obviously didn't sit well. Although the bouncer was considerably heavier than both men, the man to whom the uncomplimentary comment had been directed managed to push him aside. As the bouncer lost his balance and fell to the floor, the man who had pushed him lunged at the other man. The crowd squealed as they rushed to get out of the way of the men, who had become a mass of rapidly flailing arms and legs as they rolled about on the dance floor.

The bouncer got to his feet and struggled to separate them, assisted by one of the bartenders. The man whose wife had apparently been unfaithful to him shook off those who were trying to restrain him and backed up a few feet, simultaneously reaching inside his jacket. The next thing Desirée knew, the sound of gunfire roared through the club. Her own scream was lost in the other cries that immediately rang out. She felt an arm clutch her waist, and the next thing she knew she was being pulled to the floor. Austin lay sprawled atop her, providing a haven for her between his body and the wall at her side. "Don't make any noise," he commanded in a whisper. "The police should be here soon."

He could tell from the cries of pain that several people had been hit. The gunman was apparently holding the onlookers at bay. From the way they periodically cowered, Austin surmised the man was waving the gun and threatening to shoot. His grip tightened around Desirée's shoulder as the gunman's shouts became louder. He was moving closer to the main entrance, probably with the intention of preventing anyone from leaving or entering.

Austin knew the dim lighting in the club paired with the dark colors of his clothing were advantages. People at nearby tables had also scrambled to get under them when the shooting started. He wished he and Desirée had been sitting closer to the emergency exit in the rear so they could slip out.

He could feel her fear, her hand clutching his arm and her rapid staccato breaths on his neck. "Shh . . ." he soothed. "It's got to be almost over. Don't worry, sweetheart. I won't let anything happen to you."

It had been quite some time since he'd been this close to her. For what had to be the hundredth time he relived the one time he'd kissed her. Right now he felt he'd give anything to feel her pliant lips yielding to his once more. The only thing that stopped him was the need to keep his eye out for any sudden moves by the obviously unstable gunman. But having her this close was stirring up feelings Austin couldn't ignore. He allowed himself a moment of respite and cupped the far side of her face, rubbing his cheek against hers. In spite of the danger they were in, he felt the beginnings of an erection forming. It would be impossible for Desirée not to be aware of his desire for her, not with his body nearly flush atop hers. All the more reason for him to tell her—provided they got out of here—that he was crazy about her.

Lying beneath him, Desirée's hand clutched his upper arm with one hand and his back with the other, afraid to let him go. She closed her eyes and felt her body relax. Her face was in the blissful position of being stroked by the pads of Austin's fingers on one side and rubbed by his cheek on the other. He felt a little scratchy, but nonetheless divine. This was crazy, she thought as her tension was replaced by other urges—they could be shot dead at any moment, and here she was feeling sensual. And so was he; she could feel his arousal pressing into her hip.

She closed her eyes and prayed she wouldn't die before she had a chance to make love to him.

Austin didn't know how the Ivorian police would handle what was essentially a hostage situation. The wrong approach could do a lot of damage if the gunman became nervous. Unfortunately, now that he had changed position, Austin and Desirée were not nearly as safe as they had been just minutes ago should there be any further gunfire. He considered moving a few feet to behind the speakers, but even they were positioned in a manner that would afford little protection, and he could hardly start rearranging furniture at a time like this.

A voice amplified by a megaphone spoke to the gunman. Austin listened carefully, but he couldn't understand what sounded like a command. He looked at Desirée and gestured to her to translate. She shook her head, and he figured she was too frightened to be able to understand.

After thirty seconds with no response, the order was repeated, louder this time. "What'd he say?" Austin hissed.

"I don't know."

He frowned, then tentatively raised his head for a better view, and Desirée propped herself up on her elbows and craned her neck so she, too, could see.

The gunman walked over to the still form of his wife. He knelt and embraced her, his body shaking with silent sobs. Then he gently put her down and raised the gun to his head.

"No," Austin said aloud. In his concern he forgot himself and sat up, moving from under the table.

Desirée moved behind him. "Oh, my God," she said, her voice breaking. When the shot sounded she buried her face in his neck to muffle her scream.

"The bouncer was shot, the wife, the wife's boyfriend and a bystander," Austin related. "Fortunately, they're all expected to recover, even the boyfriend, who got it in the belly."

"But the wife . . . she was so limp, I thought she was dead."

"It's a cinch her husband thought the same thing. She must have just lost consciousness from shock."

"And she was definitely stepping out on her husband with the other man?"

"Hey, they did have guilty written all over their faces."

"Yes, I suppose they did." Desirée shook her head. "It was just awful. I keep seeing that man shoot himself—"

"Maybe I should get you something to help you sleep."

"No, I'll be fine." She looked at him, apprehension in her eyes. "Just don't go too far away."

He squeezed her hand. "I won't; I promise."

They were sitting in the bar of their hotel. The quiet atmosphere was just what they needed after the violent episode in Treichville. The bartender who recommended the nightclub to them had also returned to this subdued environment and had filled Austin in on what he'd learned about the condition of the victims.

Desirée took a final sip of her wine to the closing strains of Jonathan Butler's soothing guitar. The jukebox was silent, as if signifying the end of the evening. "I guess I'm ready to go up," she said.

Austin held her hand from the time he paid the bill until they got to her room. His authoritative presence soothed her nerves, but when she unlocked her door with him standing close behind her, her hand shook a little.

Once they were inside, Austin made sure the door was locked behind her. "Did you want to leave the door open?" he asked, pointing with his chin to the door that connected their rooms.

"Yes. I'd feel a lot better."

He quickly moved to take her in his arms, catching her off guard. "Desi . . . if it wasn't so late, I'd arrange for us to stay someplace nicer. I know you'd be more comfortable elsewhere." His hands rested broadly on her back.

Desirée relaxed against him; he felt so strong, so safe. "It's all right," she said softly. "Who could have known the one night we were at that club would be the night that man would choose to confront his wife and her lover?"

"Claude at the bar was saying that they've closed a lot of the clubs in Treichville because of trouble breaking out. Looks like that one will be closing its doors as well." Austin chuckled. "Then he told me about another place over there. It's not one of those snooty jetset places; they really party, but the management keeps a tight rein on their clientele. I just wish he'd mentioned it earlier; that's where we would have gone." He stepped back a little so he could see her face. "Are you sure you're all right?"

"Yes. I just had a few bad moments when I wasn't sure if we were going to get out of there alive."

"I was concerned about that myself. But I knew I had to get out of there so I could do this one more time."

Desirée saw his head start on its slow descent. She raised hers to meet him halfway, her lips parted. His mouth met hers in a feather-soft persuasion, not once, but three agonizing times before he finally pressed his lips to hers, worked his tongue inside her mouth and kissed her in earnest. Desirée stood on tiptoe and encircled his neck with her arms.

The fireworks she had felt before were very much in evidence now. Her heartbeat was skyrocketing, her flesh tingling, but the kiss was surprisingly gentle. Austin was doing his best to put her at ease. What a wonderful man he was, she thought. Considerate, thoughtful, good-looking . . . and a fabulous kisser.

She cocked her head to one side as his lips left hers to nuzzle her neck. Her grip around his neck tightened, and she made no attempt to conceal her contented sigh as he gently puckered the delicate skin of her throat.

Austin returned to claim her mouth once more, playing with the space between her teeth and teasing her sensitive palate with the tip of his tongue.

"I know I was supposed to ask for permission," Austin said matter-of-factly after the kiss ended, "but I just couldn't help myself. I hope you didn't mind." Once more he nuzzled her cheek. "I don't know what's happening between us, Desi, but I know I was crazy at the mere thought of anything happening to you. And it wasn't because I was thinking of the company's liability."

"Oh, Ozzie," she said, so relieved that his thoughts of her weren't limited to what she meant to Wallace and Hughes that she didn't realize until after the fact that she'd used his nickname. When she'd first heard it, she'd thought it didn't suit him, but this was the warm, fuzzy facet to his personality she had wondered about. She looked up at him and smiled. "I'm glad we're both all right."

He released her then. "Why don't you try to relax?" he suggested. "I'll check on you in a few minutes."

She nodded. "I'm going to close the door while I change."

In his room Austin took out his phone card and placed a call to Phil. The seven-hour time difference between Greenwich Mean Time and Rocky Mountain Time meant it was still early in Denver. He wanted to get the latest on the situation in the office.

Phil was at home. The security system in the computer network would be installed the following week, he said, and in the meantime he and his secretary were taking it upon themselves to personally check every report that went out of the office, which they would continue to do until the saboteur had been identified and dealt with. "I'm concerned, though," he added. "It's going to be a bit much for Maddie to handle on her own after I leave." He was scheduled to take off for Paris in a few days as part of the Accolade Hotel's surveys.

"You can always ship them to Elaine."

"Yeah, but that would mean she'd have to get someone to help her, and the other two in the office would learn about our problem. The fewer people who know about this, the better."

"Come on, Phil, you don't think anyone in New York has anything to do with this, do you? Everything's happening out there."

"I know I'm being overly cautious, but I feel better this way. I'm reluctant to even call in outside forces, but Maddie's going to need a temp to help her. Everything has to be checked, no matter how small the client is."

"I agree."

"So how's it going in Abidjan?"

"It's rough over here, man." Austin briefly covered the events at the nightclub.

"Damn. With all that going on, you might as well have stayed in New York. But it could have been worse, like a fire. I'm just glad that nut didn't take anybody else out with him."

"Yeah."

"Desirée all right?"

"She's wonderful."

"Wonderful? Wait a minute," Phil said. "Don't tell me you two have started something over there!"

"What if we have? If I recall, that's how you met Sandy." Phil's wife was no longer a full-time agent, but she still occasionally accompanied her husband on assignment and would be going to Europe with him.

"Yeah, but you've always been so adamant about not mixing business with pleasure. I never had a problem with it."

"Listen, Jack, this call is expensive. We can talk about my principles when we're both in the same country."

"A word of caution, my friend. You haven't confided in Desirée about this problem we're having, have you?"

"No. It has nothing to do with her, and it's not like she can do anything to help."

"Good. Like I said, the fewer people who know about this, the better. As it is, there's no way I could keep it from Diane, since I'll have to instruct her that all client packages are to be brought to Maddie before they're wrapped."

"That means Rita and Jennifer know, too," Austin said, referring to Diane's assistants. "This little circle of those in the know is getting bigger and bigger."

"I've had a meeting with the three of them and told them I expect this to be kept on the Q.T. If they feel their jobs are at risk if they blab, they're more likely to keep quiet. I didn't give them any explanations for why we're doing it, either."

"I'm sure they'll be able to figure it out, Phil."

"I can't help that. Even after I find the sonovabitch who's behind this, I don't want it to become public knowledge. It might give someone else ideas about trying something, knowing what not to do to keep from getting caught. In the meantime everyone is a suspect, so watch the pillow talk, okay?"

Austin felt his temper flare. "Now, wait a minute, Phil. Are you suggesting that Desirée might be involved in this?"

"All I'm saying is that no one is to be trusted beyond you, me, Maddie and Elaine. Gotta go, man. Keep in touch." Phil broke the connection.

Austin stared at the phone in anger. He felt like breaking his partner's neck for even suggesting such a thing. Phil knew him well enough to know he was angry; that was why he had hung up so abruptly.

Desirée changed into a dusky rose nightgown before emerging from the bathroom, feeling that slipping into something pretty would help her nerves. Through the adjoining door she could hear Austin talking on the telephone, and she jealously wondered if it was Monique. She hadn't given too much thought to the woman Austin was involved with, but now she had to. Perhaps she has misinterpreted his earlier concern for her safety. How could he possibly be so callous as to call another woman after he'd kissed her so passionately and possessively? How serious was it between them? She was going to have to find out, and quickly.

She slipped between the cool sheets and pulled the covers up to her collarbone. She was already dozing when she felt a presence in the room and sat up with a start.

"It's all right; it's only me," Austin said. He had been standing at the side of the bed, watching her sleep, and the sudden movement when Desirée sat up caused the covers to fall forward, exposing her upper body. He stared openly at her figure. The lace-trimmed, shimmery material held up by spaghetti straps hugged her breasts snugly. Although the thin nylon that made up the majority of the gown prevented it from being sheer, he could just imagine her nipples, looking like two dark chocolate drops on top of the beautifully shaped mounds of her breasts. He felt heady as he remembered how they had felt against his chest as they lay on the floor of the nightclub, like two small, firm pillows that welcomed his weight.

Desirée knew he was staring. Her first inclination was to grab the sheet and cover herself, but then she decided she would not hide from him. Defiantly she straightened her posture.

At last Austin tore his eyes away from her. "I'm sorry. I didn't mean to startle you. I just came in to make sure you were all right."

"I'm fine. I guess my sixth sense told me someone else was here." He looked embarrassed, she thought. She wondered what his thoughts had been as he stared at her sleeping form.

"If you're sure you're all right, I'll say good night and leave the door open."

"Thanks. Good night, Austin."

Desirée rocked her head from side to side in her sleep. She and Austin were in the club, watching in stunned disbelief as the man with the gun raised it to his head and pulled the trigger. She hid her face into the haven of Austin's neck to keep from seeing the destruction of a human life, but not before a fine red mist surrounded the man like an aura of death. . . .

She tossed wildly in her sleep, trying to rid herself of the horrible memory but too deep in repose to realize all she had to do to be rid of it was open her eyes. A cry of terror escaped from her throat as the scene played in her dream over and over again.

Slowly she became aware of large hands shaking her shoulders. "Desirée . . . Desirée. Wake up. I know what you're dreaming about, but it's all over and you're all right."

She opened her eyes. She shook her head, not knowing the identity of the person who was kneeling beside her on the bed. She squinted, trying to make him out in the dark. "Austin?" she whispered.

"It's me, sweetheart. You were crying out in your sleep."

"Oh . . . I couldn't get it out of my mind. It was so awful!" She shut her eyes and pressed her palms against her temples in an effort to block the images out.

He instantly pulled her into his arms. "I knew I should have brought you a stronger drink to help you sleep. This was a hell of a traumatic experience." He began to rock her gently. "Come on, go back to sleep. I'll stay with you all night if you want."

Desirée didn't answer; she was afraid to. Now that her eyes had adjusted to the darkness she realized he was shirtless, wearing only a pair of blue cotton drawstring pants. Austin Hughes could make her forget everything except his overwhelming sex appeal. Paired with his considerate nature, he was irresistible . . . and suddenly she knew she had fallen captive to his charm and was in love with him. Right now that was all that mattered. She'd worry about Monique tomorrow.

She settled against the cocoon of his chest, confident

that she would have no further nightmares. Soon she was asleep.

As the sound of Desirée's even breathing alternated with the whir of the ceiling fan, Austin began to feel drowsy himself. He allowed himself to slide down into a reclining position next to her, and she made a murmuring sound and snuggled up against him with her back and hips. He lay on his side and wrapped his arm around her slim waist, planting the lightest of kisses on her bare shoulder and inhaling her fragrant lemon-scented skin. He had never felt such tenderness toward Monique, and he was glad he'd suggested that farewell dinner with her before he came to Africa—not farewell as in bon voyage, but to their long-running liaison. Desirée had awakened emotions in him that had been secondary to his work for years. It warmed his heart to know that she felt so comfortable with him that she could go right to sleep once he was at her side. Much as he longed to make love to her, that knowledge would have to hold him for now.

In that intimate posture they slept, each dreaming of only happy thoughts.

Ten

"Ah, yes, Mr. and Mrs. Hughes," the Ghanian front desk clerk said. "I'm afraid we had to alter your booking."

Austin frowned. "Alter it how?" he asked.

"Well, sir, President Rawlings has some important visitors who are staying in our hotel and needed suite accommodations. Mr. Thomas Stuart, our general manager, arranged for the transfer of your reservation. He is refunding your credit card in full and asks that you stay here as our guests."

"We only have a single room instead of a suite?" Desirée asked, her voice higher pitched than normal in her concern, which bordered on panic.

"We regret it could not be helped," the clerk replied. "Mr. Stuart left word that he would be available to speak with you personally about the situation if you so desire."

"It's fine. We understand completely, and I'm sure our accommodations will be comfortable," Austin replied graciously.

"But, Austin—" Desirée began.

"It's all right, Desi," he broke in, a discreet warning contained within the simple statement.

"It's one of our finest rooms," the clerk was saying. "A little larger than the standard rooms, with a comfortable sitting area. And," he added with no change in his expression, "it has the king-sized bed you *had* requested."

Desirée realized it would not do to object to the change in accommodation. To a real married couple it would not make a difference; actually most people would be overjoyed at the prospect of staying at such a fine hotel for nothing. But she and Austin *weren't* a real married couple. Austin Hughes the hotel guest would be issued a credit card refund, but Austin Hughes the quality-control agent always received a credit from the general manager after a survey was complete; it was part of the process.

She was enjoying working with him since that awful night in the Ivory Coast. Her fears had diminished with the light of day, but it had felt very strange to awaken and find herself wrapped in Austin's embrace, close enough to ruffle his chest hair with her breathing. For a few uneasy moments she could not remember what had transpired between them, but then it all came back. He was in her bed because she needed the comfort of his presence to sleep, a comfort he willingly provided without taking advantage of her fear.

Their remaining time in the country was punctuated with an indefinable but special air. They took a tour of the city before checking in at the second Abidjan hotel. It went well, and immediately after presenting their preliminary findings they left for the airport for the flight to Ghana, stopping at the Federal Express office to send off the completed tapes, Polaroids and written forms and reports for both Ivorian appraisals. In all that time neither of them had mentioned the night they "slept together"; but this! How were they going to get through spending three nights in the same room, in the same bed?

A bellman showed them to their room, which was, as the desk clerk promised, quite lovely. A plump love seat and two wing chairs were arranged in a conversational corner, some feet away from the king-sized bed that was covered with a spread in a pattern of dark red flowers.

Desirée stared at the love seat. She had brightened when the clerk mentioned a sitting area in the room, thinking the easiest way out of their dilemma would be for Austin to sleep on the couch. What she hadn't counted on was the couch being a love seat. No one could sleep on that unless it was in a sitting position, which would be miserably uncomfortable.

She turned to look at Austin, who had retrieved his handheld recorder and was busy making a report of the check-in process. Apparently the stark reality of their predicament had not yet registered to him. Not wanting him to be aware of her anxiety, Desirée instead turned and looked out the window.

The view from the windows overlooked the capital city of Accra, which seemed to be a hodgepodge of the ancient and the modern. While not exactly impoverished-looking, the low-rise buildings and abundance of trees was more in keeping with Desirée's mind-set of what a major African city would look like, much more so than the tall glass and stone towers of Abidjan. And, she thought wryly, Accra was probably a lot safer. . . .

It was taking Austin forever to dictate his report, she thought impatiently as she walked around the room, automatically brushing her fingers on the furniture and checking for dust. This occupied her only for about thirty seconds, and afterward she sat down in one of the chairs, the cushions of which embraced her like an old friend. With nothing else to do, she listened as Austin recounted the desk clerk's smooth handling of the news that their reservation had been downgraded. Whoever transcribed this report was certainly in for a surprise, she thought; in her experience one check-in report could barely be differentiated from another, whether it be it in Hartford or Hong Kong.

Finally he put the tape recorder down. She waited expectantly for him to comment about the unsuitability of the love seat for a bed, but instead he merely sat on it and said, "Nice place, eh?"

Desirée raised her chin. She didn't know if he was deliberately ignoring the subject of sleeping arrangements or not, but she could be just as cool as he. "Yes, it's lovely," she agreed. "At least it has a coffeemaker."

"Just remember, I take mine hot, black and sweet."

"I'll try not to forget that," she replied dryly, refusing to as much as blink at the double entendre. So much for impersonal small talk. Since Austin's comment had turned the tide of the conversation, she might as well address the topic that was uppermost in her mind. "Did they ever change your booking when you were traveling with Phyllis?" Desirée asked.

"Phyllis and I did a fair amount of surveys together, but it was only maybe four or five times that a client asked us to pose as husband and wife, and when we did we always had a suite. But then, you have to consider that in larger American cities there's usually no shortage of upper-echelon hotels. In African cities there's usually just one, maybe two at the most, places per city that would be suitable for VIPs. People probably get bumped over here all the time." Austin chuckled. "It's just as well it never happened. Phyllis's boyfriend Eddie—now he's her husband—wouldn't have been too happy about it."

"And neither would Monique, I'm sure." The words were out before she could stop them.

"She would have gotten over it," he said dryly. "And as for Phyllis, that was a completely different situation. She and I had worked together often enough to know each other reasonably well by the time we were asked to pose as husband and wife. I don't mind telling you, I was more than a little uneasy about you and I being able to pull it off, since we'd never met."

"I had doubts myself."

"But," Austin continued, "I was never interested in sharing a bed with Phyllis, any more than she was interested in sharing a bed with me."

While Desirée hadn't taken offense at his comment about how he liked his coffee, when paired with the unspoken implication of his last statement it became too much. "What's going on with you, Austin?" she demanded as she got to her feet. "Are you deliberately trying to make me uncomfortable with all these snide comments?" The stress of having been forced to stay in a room with only one bed was bad enough without him insinuating that neither of them was interested in using it to merely sleep in. Maybe that was how *he* felt, but how dare he speak for her? She'd about had it with his controlling attitude.

Instead of standing and facing her, Austin settled back into the cushy love seat and spoke with a calm Desirée found maddening. "No, Desi; I'm not. On the contrary, I want you to be completely at ease with me, as you were at that hotel in Abidjan."

"Well, innuendo is *not* the way to put me at ease," she snapped.

Now Austin stood. His words were soft and soothing as he faced her. "It wasn't meant as innuendo; it was meant to tell you I'm very much attracted to you. But you should know by now that you don't have to fear for your safety with me. Or maybe you don't know, Desi. I saw that panicked look in your eyes when you saw the room had just a love seat and not a full-size couch. I've never seen a raccoon the moment it gets trapped, but I suspect the look in its eyes would be the same."

"So I find it unnerving. Can you blame me? What are we supposed to do, Austin?"

"Well, of course the ideal solution would be to request a cot, but as you know we can't do that."

"So what *do* we do?"

"We sleep in the bed together. It's big enough for you to sleep on one side and me on the other. I'll even sleep with my head in the opposite direction to make the most of the distance. We can straighten it out before the maid comes."

"And I guess Monique will get over *that,* too?"

He met her gaze. "Monique is not an issue. She and I aren't seeing each other any more."

She couldn't suppress her surprise. "You aren't! Wasn't that rather sudden?"

"No, not really. We both felt it coming. There are always signs when a relationship has run its course or gone as far as it's going to. We were together mostly out of convenience more than anything else." He wanted to ask if she really thought he would have kissed and held her the way he had if he was still involved with Monique but decided against it. Desirée was a woman who believed in being brutally honest, and he would only get his feelings hurt if she said yes.

For three interminable nights they, as Austin suggested, slept in the bed on opposite ends and with opposite heads. Desirée grudgingly admitted that Austin was right: The bed was so big she barely knew he was in it with her. She barely knew he was there, yet she *knew* he was there.

Desirée lay on her right side, her right hand resting on her left shoulder, remembering how glorious it was when it was Austin's warm, large hand on her bare skin when he stayed with her in the Abidjan hotel the night of the shootings. She *had* trusted him completely that night in the intimate confines of the much smaller bed, and that was when she thought Monique was still a part of his life. Now that she knew otherwise, thinking about him wasn't enough. She longed for him to touch her, to taste her, to fill her. She knew all it would take was a word from her to make her dream come true, but she was too practical to walk down what she viewed as a sure road to heartbreak. When the surveys were over she would be heading back to Denver. She wanted a lasting love affair, not a two-week fling. The next time she gave her heart, body and soul to a man she was determined to have a happy ending. Making love to Austin now would only make it more difficult when the inevitable separation came.

On the other side of the bed, Austin, too, kept thinking of that night in Abidjan when they had bonded like never before. He was haunted by the memory of the feel of the feminine softness of her body as he lay atop her while the gunfire rang out at the club, shielding her from harm, of how in her fear she'd clutched his forearm, and his response of whispered words of comfort. And later at the hotel, when he lay beside her in bed, his arm finding a home in the niche between her waist and the swell of her round hips, laying together on their sides like nesting spoons. The fresh, fragrant scent of the soap she used mixed with that of her own natural warmth emanated from her pores to entice his sense of smell. How he would love to be that close to her again, instead of on opposite ends of the bed, so far away that they were practically clinging to their respective edges to keep from falling out; and to get another glimpse of her in a feminine nightgown, not a sleep shirt like the one she had on now, an oversized number modeled on the style of a football jersey and with about as much sex appeal, even if she still managed to look cute. Of course, he thought with a smile, Desirée could wear a horse's feed bag and still look good.

It was an uneasy three nights, but somehow they got through it. The hardest part was sharing a single bathroom, which made for a strange kind of nonintimate intimacy. This was most apparent their last morning there, while they were dressing for their meeting with Thomas Stuart, the hotel's GM. At one point they found themselves sharing the mirror, Desirée pinning her hair in a French roll and Austin tying his tie.

Desirée took a hand mirror and turned around to inspect the back of her head. She wanted her roll to be smooth, with no bumps or gaps, and because of her abundance of hair getting it just right could be difficult. "Not bad," she said aloud. Then she turned around again, put down the mirror and picked up her lipstick.

"I thought you didn't need to see what you were doing to put on lipstick," Austin remarked.

She smiled a Mona Lisa smile. "Is that a hint for me to get out of the bathroom?"

"Not really. I kind of like having you here next to me. It's the closest we've been in days."

She knew he was make a veiled reference to their sleeping arrangements. "I know it's been difficult, Austin, and I really do appreciate . . ." she trailed off, not sure of what words to use.

"You appreciate me being on my best behavior," he said flatly as he secured his tie to his shirt with a gold stickpin. "And you're damned right; it wasn't easy. The way I see it, Desi, you're denying us something we both want." With that he left the room.

She whirled around and followed him with quick, short steps. "I really do appreciate your not applying any pressure on me," she snapped sarcastically.

"Oh, yeah; I forgot. You'll say I demanded you sleep with me as a condition of your job. Damn it, Desi, when are you going to get it that this isn't about an employer and employee? This is about two people, a man and a woman, who are drawn to each other the way a magnet draws paper clips." His tone became more gentle, almost cajoling. "It's about you and me, baby. Work has nothing to do with it. And don't tell me you don't feel it; I know better. I can sense it every time I'm close to you. You probably don't realize it, but it's in plain view, in your eyes, even in your breathing."

She turned away, knowing she couldn't convincingly argue and afraid it showed on her face. In a tone that was all business she said, "I think we should get going. We don't want to be late." And so help her, if he told her to keep quiet during the interview, she was going to tell him something most unladylike. She was sick and tired of Austin Hughes dictating what she was feeling and what she should and shouldn't say.

Austin sighed. The way he saw it, he was merely sharing his honest feelings with her, as she had with him on several occasions, and it bothered him that she was avoiding the issue. She obviously wasn't in the mood for honesty, but, considering they were due in the GM's office in ten minutes, this was not the best time to discuss it anyway.

At the meeting Desirée was pleased to let Austin do most of the talking for once. Her mind was elsewhere. Austin was right about how she felt, but how did she know his desire for her wasn't simply because he and Monique had broken up and he was feeling the need to be intimate with a woman? She wasn't interested in providing sex for convenience's sake.

She was thankful they were done at this site. One more night of sharing a bed with him under these conditions would be too much for her.

Thomas Stuart looked confused. "Mr. Hughes . . . Ms. Mack . . . you are not married?"

"No, sir, but we feel confident that your entire staff thinks we are," Austin replied.

"Well, this puts a different face on things. The change in plans must have created difficulty for you."

Desirée loved the way Mr. Stuart spoke; to her there was nothing more pleasant to the ears than British English. "Unfortunately, all our upgraded rooms come with king beds. I asked Robert on the desk to downgrade your room. Again, once I realized he put you in the next best thing to a suite, there wasn't much I could do about it without arousing curiosity."

"That's quite all right, sir; we managed just fine," Austin replied briskly. Desirée gave a weak smile. She shifted in discomfort as the general manager looked first at Austin, then at her. Was she imagining the slight smile on his lips? Had he presumed they were having an affair?

"I see," Mr. Stuart said. When he spoke again it was to inquire about how the hotel had rated. This was the main concern of all the GMs; after all the forms had been input, a complete set of statistics would be distributed to all the hotels within one group, to senior management as well as each GM. Naturally all the managers were anxious for their properties to be at, or at least near, the top. Mr. Stuart appeared visibly relieved to learn that his hotel was one of the best-run Austin and Desirée had seen. His expression did not change when Austin cautioned that the survey as a whole was not over; they still had a number of sister properties to assess.

At the close of the meeting Austin and Desirée shook hands with Mr. Stuart, who was the first African general manager they had encountered. Desirée could have listened to him talk all afternoon. The front desk clerk and other hotel employees spoke in the same crisp, clear tones. "Will you be leaving the country right away?" he asked.

"Not until tomorrow," Austin replied. "We just did two straight jobs and have a day off coming."

"To do some sightseeing and shopping," Desirée added, finally having found her voice. "And, of course, eating."

"Ah, well, I recommend the Flip Bar rooftop restaurant on Liberia Road. Or Kinbu Gardens, which is on the ground but is open air. It's a wonderful feeling to sip a cold beer on a hot day like today while the trees shield you from the sun."

"Sounds good. Can you recommend a midrange hotel for us?" Austin asked.

"The Ringway is supposed to be quite nice. And it's right down the street from the Apollo, if you're interested in seeing what our people do on a Saturday night. Accra is a very lively city."

Austin and Desirée exchanged glances. "I don't think we're ready for lively nightlife," he said. "We witnessed a shooting at a club in Abidjan. A domestic dispute that ended in suicide."

The GM shook his head. "That doesn't surprise me, not in Abidjan. They need to shut down that red-light district; they're always having some kind of trouble over there. But if you want someplace quiet, there's a lovely guest house out by the botanical gardens. It used to be Kwame Nkrumah's weekend retreat when he was president. It's rather far, but the bus from the taxi park will take you right there, and once you're there you really won't have to leave for anything. There's a restaurant right on the property."

"Oh, that sounds wonderful," Desirée said.

"Here, let me call them and make sure they have accommodations available tonight. If they do I'll ask them to hold them for you until this evening. You'll have to do all your shopping and sightseeing this afternoon while you're in the city; if you're flying out tomorrow you probably won't get another chance."

"We really appreciate this, Mr. Stuart," Austin said as the GM picked up the telephone on his desk.

"No problem. The way I see it, you two have given me a gift with the news of how well my hotel is run, in spite of my having to inconvenience you. It's only right that I return the favor and give you a gift as well. Why don't you two change into whatever you plan to wear this afternoon and stop in on your way out? By then I'll have an answer for you."

As she and Austin left the office Desirée wondered why Mr. Stuart had referred to his securing of hotel reservations for them as a "gift." The way he spoke, anyone would think he was picking up the tab!

"Austin, you look positively regal."

"Maybe, but I feel a little silly. I can't picture myself going out on the street in this getup." He was draped in colorful kente cloth, which the market vendor had wrapped around him toga-style.

Austin turned to the vendor. "All right, how much?"

"Sixty."

"Sixty cedi?"

"No, sixty American dollars."

Austin shook his head. "Sixty dollars for an outfit that makes me feel foolish? No, I can't see it."

"That's because it is genuine kente cloth, hand woven," the vendor replied.

In the end Austin settled on a ready-made shirt and slacks in a red-and-black cotton print made from lower-priced adinkra cloth—"It won't make me feel as conspicuous," he said—while Desirée purchased more material, including high-priced kente cloth in a rayon blend. "What are you going to do, open a sewing shop?"

Austin asked her. "Between this and what you got in Abidjan, you'll certainly have enough to do that."

"This is a once-in-a-lifetime event for me, and I'm going to make the most of it. I'll be sewing up a storm when I get home."

By "home," Austin knew she meant Denver. His body tensed. He hated the idea of her leaving New York. He was going to have to see if he could extend her stay there. If he couldn't tell her more clients wanted surveys performed by a couple, he would have to think of something else.

Actually, after six years, Austin had grown weary of the constant traveling and intended to move Weaver Mobley, who mainly was involved in sales, into agenting on a full-time basis. Then he could take on the securing of new clients full-time. Weaver seemed to have lost his knack lately; he hadn't closed a sale in some time. It had been Austin who landed the Accolade account. He planned to perform only an occasional survey, while he attempted to attain the same success in his personal life as he had in business. But he'd gladly put those plans on hold if Desirée remained in New York. After all, when it came to what was missing from his personal life, she could definitely be part of the solution.

Eleven

After shopping they had a lunch of jollof rice and palaver sauce. A Ghanian specialty similar to paella, it did not contain the staple of many an African's diet, the yam. A visit to the W.E.B. DuBois Memorial Center, located in the house where the American Pan-Africanist spent the last five years of his long life, completed their activity in the city center. Upon returning to the hotel, Mr. Stuart informed them that their booking had been confirmed, and they both found themselves looking forward to relaxing for the rest of the day. The strain of three nearly back-to-back full surveys was beginning to wear on them.

Their bags had been held at the front desk. "This suitcase is getting harder and harder to close," Desirée commented before they left their room, as she struggled to get the two sides to meet.

"Here, I'll do it," Austin replied. "I guess you don't want to ship these back."

"I wouldn't even consider it. If my purchases get lost, I'll have nothing to show for this whole trip."

"I still can't believe all that material you bought. And that hideous wood carving."

"It's a fertility doll. After all, I want to have loads of children when my time comes. All I have to do is carry it in my purse and it's guaranteed."

Austin laughed aloud at her seriousness. Then he

found himself wondering what a child he and Desirée created would look like. He chuckled at the irony of the thought, chalking it up to being more lonely than he realized. Desirée was avoiding intimacy with him like it was the plague, and here he was daydreaming about making babies with her. It was ridiculous.

The bus driver informed them that their destination was some thirty-five kilometers away, which Austin calculated was a shade over twenty miles. "It shouldn't take too long," he said.

It took forty-five minutes, during which time Desirée began to feel the effects of several hours of walking around in eighty-five-degree heat. Shooing away the numerous mosquitoes buzzing around hadn't helped, either. There was little relief to be had in the confines of the minibus, which was not air-conditioned. She leaned her head toward the window, shifting repeatedly in her attempts to obtain a position of comfort.

Desirée felt his arm before she heard his voice. It moved across the back of her neck, and his hand settled on her shoulder, pulling her to him. "Here, Desi," he said, his voice barely above a whisper. "Lean on me."

She didn't argue. He felt so perfect, strong yet soft at the same time. In minutes she was asleep, her head cradled against his chest.

It seemed she had barely closed her eyes when Austin was nudging her awake. "Look, Desi. God, it's beautiful."

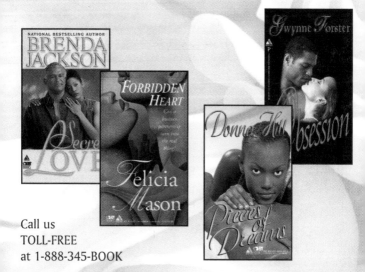

Desirée grudgingly opened her eyes and turned her head to face the window. The sight she beheld was enough to make her forget her annoyance at having been awakened from a sound sleep. The botanical gardens were a virtual shangri-la of flora—delicate, bell-shaped jacaranda, orange-red tulips, daffodil-like yellow olean-

Accepting the four introductory books for FREE (plus $1.50 to offset the cost of shipping & handling) places you under no obligation to buy anything. You may keep the books and return the shipping statement marked "cancelled". If you do not cancel, about a month later we will send 4 additional Arabesque novels, and you will be billed the preferred subscriber's price of just $4.00 per title. That's $16.00 for all 4 books for a savings of 33% off the cover price (Plus $1.50 for shipping and handling). You may cancel at any time, but if you choose to continue, every month we'll send you 4 more books, which you may either purchase at the preferred discount price. . . or return to us and cancel your subscription.

THE ARABESQUE ROMANCE CLUB: HERE'S HOW IT WORKS

PLACE
STAMP
HERE

ARABESQUE ROMANCE BOOK CLUB
P.O. Box 5214
Clifton NJ 07015-5214

der and pink temple flowers bloomed among the tall silk-cotton trees and bougainvillea shrubs. Even from this vantage point Desirée could see several brick-lined paths that led through the setting. "Oh." The syllable escaped from her lips in an extended breath. "It's like a fairy-land."

The bus stopped on the curved driveway in front of a large, graceful Colonial-style mansion. As Desirée disembarked from the bus she immediately noticed how being just slightly north of Accra affected the temperature. In the city the heat had been stifling, but here it was heavenly, with an aromatic breeze that held the natural sweet scent of the surrounding flora.

The inside of the house looked as if a family—undoubtedly a well-to-do bunch—lived there. Desirée glimpsed a Chesterfield sofa, area rugs over the tan carpet and cherrywood accent tables in the living room on the left. A man appeared from the other side of the stairs at the sound of the heavy oak door closing behind them. "Good afternoon," he greeted. "You must be Mr. and Mrs. Hughes."

"I'm Austin Hughes," Austin said as Desirée glanced at the gold band she still wore. Obviously Mr. Stuart hadn't clarified that she and Austin weren't married. That seemed strange, she thought. It wasn't as if they would be sharing a room.

"Mr. Stuart called me about you. I have your room all ready."

Room? Desirée whirled to look at Austin, who in turn gave her a slight nod, as if silently telling her not to panic. "You have a lovely property here. Tell me, do you have many rooms?" he asked the clerk.

"Only six. You two were very fortunate. We were sold out but had a last-minute cancellation."

Desirée could stand it no longer. "Austin, may I speak with you alone for a moment?" she asked sweetly.

Austin flashed the man a confident smile. "Excuse us." Then he deftly took Desirée's arm and walked her into the living room.

They spoke in low voices, Austin going first. "You don't have to tell me," he said. "I'll make it easy on you. You'd rather go back to Accra than stay here and have to share a room with me."

She hesitated; he looked so hurt. "Actually, I'd like to," she answered. "Sharing a room is only going to lead to more arguing for us. But now that I've thought about it, I guess we shouldn't offend Mr. Stuart, when he was nice enough to make the arrangements. I mean, he *is* a client. But why did he have us put in one room?"

"Because that's all they had available. Didn't you hear him?"

"No wonder the man thinks we're married."

"Lucky for us he does, or we probably *would* be waiting for the bus back to Accra. People here aren't necessarily as open-minded as they are in the States."

Desirée wasn't sure where her next words came from; she supposed it was from her heart. "Oh, Austin, I'm so tired of fighting with you."

"Then we won't," he replied matter-of-factly. "Come on. It'll be okay." He took her hand.

Their conference over, they followed the man to his small office in the foyer, located in what Desirée suspected had once been a large closet.

She fingered her wedding band while Austin registered them, looking up to see the man smiling at her. "Newlyweds?" he inquired.

"Actually, we've been married over a year now," Austin lied as Desirée scrambled for a response. "I'm an importer, traveling on business. Mr. Stuart was kind enough to recommend this as a nice, out-of-the-way place after the hustle and bustle of the city."

"I'm sure you will be very comfortable here. By the

way, the dinner buffet is served between six-thirty and eight. Jackets are required for gentlemen." The man handed Austin a key, the old-fashioned kind that had become obsolete in most hotels but were probably still in use in bed-and-breakfasts. "Room Six. It's at the very end of the hall on the right. I'll have the luggage sent up shortly."

Austin thanked him. He gallantly offered Desirée his arm, and together they climbed the graceful curved staircase. "How'd you like to come home to this every night?" he asked.

"A little too grand for my taste. Just give me the proverbial house in the country."

Again he fleetingly wondered what she would think of his condo. Would it meet her qualifications for a house in the country? He thought of how she had straightened his shirt collar in their suite in Abidjan, the most domestic behavior she had ever exhibited toward him. What a difference from a similar incident with Monique, who had merely said, "Your collar is crooked," and let him fumble with it himself.

It was a long walk to the end of the hall, and when they finally reached Room Six Austin unlocked the door and they entered a virtual paradise in yellow and white.

The first thing Desirée noticed was a tremendous bed draped in white mosquito netting. It was an exotic touch, complemented by the light brown rattan furnishings, pastel print cushions and ceiling fans. There was even a small Juliet-type balcony. Her breath caught in her throat. This was a room made for romance, and she was here with a man who seemed to be perfect for her—and they would sleep in it on opposite sides of the bed, more willing to fall out than risk touching each other accidentally. A pall began to descend over her previously lighthearted mood.

Austin didn't notice the subtle change in her; instead

he made a joke. "Where's my tape recorder? I need to make a check-in report and do a room inspection."

In spite of her apprehension, Desirée chuckled. Her weeks as a quality-control agent had sharpened her senses as to how she was treated in a hospitality situation. She doubted she'd ever again be able to walk into a restaurant and not be conscious of how long she waited for someone to seat her, how long it was before her order was taken and the meal delivered. It felt inconceivably good not to have to be concerned about it for a change.

"Hey, look at this!" he called from the bathroom.

She followed him inside, where he stood looking at a rustic shower that had been made from a bucket.

"Check this out," he said.

"You've got to be kidding. There must be a real one here someplace."

"This is real, all right. There's a hose."

"A hose!" she exclaimed. "A hose?" she repeated dubiously.

"I think it's neat. But we'd better hurry if we don't want to miss dinner. It's already a quarter past six."

She waved a hand. "You go first. I know how anxious you are to try the amenities, be they ever so primitive."

"I can't do anything until our bags get here," he pointed out. At that precise moment there was a knock on the door, and they burst into laughter when they realized the bags had arrived.

Austin emerged from the bathroom looking quite tropical in a peach-colored short-sleeved shirt and tan slacks. He slipped into a beige textured sports coat as Desirée looked on. He certainly was handsome, she thought with admiration.

She decided not to take the time to shower; she could do that after dinner. Instead she freshened up and pulled on a print sleeveless sheath in varying shades of pink, dusty rose, lilac and chartreuse. The bun her hair had been styled in that morning was still intact. A few strokes of lipstick in a deep raspberry and some rouge for her cheeks—she could be generous with the bright red color because of the richness of her complexion—was all the makeup she needed.

"Wow," Austin exclaimed when she emerged. "That was much quicker than I expected."

"Stop thinking in stereotypes," she said sweetly. "All women don't take hours to get dressed."

"You know, you look different somehow; I can't put my finger on what it is."

"It's the lipstick. Different shade."

"No, it's something else. I had the feeling earlier, before you had the lipstick on. It's been gnawing at me ever since. Ah!" he exclaimed. "It's your hair."

She patted the strands on the side of her head. "Oh, yes. The salon was on the list of outlets they wanted surveyed, so I had a wash and set. It always comes out better when the pros do it."

"It looks real nice." Her hair had a shine to it that hadn't been there before. He found himself wondering what it would look like if it was loose, fanned out against the whiteness of an encased pillow.

Dinner was served at an oblong cloth-covered table for twelve with high-backed chairs in the large dining room. Desirée was surprised to see that all of the other chairs were taken; she'd expected the guests would come down at different times over the serving period.

She and Austin introduced themselves to the friendly guests, most of whom were European. From the conversation Desirée surmised that the average stay in this part of Ghana was two nights. She flashed a genuinely felt smile when someone asked her if she lived in Ghana, by now having grown accustomed to others' perceptions of her. "I'm American," she replied, "but who knows? Perhaps my roots are here in the Gold Coast."

A red-jacketed, black-bowtied waiter came from the kitchen and offered them the contents of a tray. Desirée helped herself to hot, steaming rice and then a mixture of stir-fried beef and vegetables in gravy. A bowl of salad and plate of rolls were already on the table.

The conversation was lively, the mood unhurried. Still, as the last ones to arrive, Desirée and Austin were still having their dessert when the last remaining guests departed. "Mr. Hughes, Mrs. Hughes. Since you're only going to be here one night, you must be sure to take a walk through the gardens. They're especially lovely at night," the woman suggested as they exchanged good nights.

"Thank you; we'll do that," Austin replied. "We can talk about them at breakfast tomorrow morning."

"Oh, didn't you know? Your first morning they bring breakfast to your room as part of their service."

"How considerate!" Desirée exclaimed.

"They want to preserve their reputation as a romantic hideaway," the man remarked.

"Well, 'Mrs. Hughes,' are you game for taking a stroll through the gardens?" Austin asked after the couple had left.

Desirée shrugged. "Sounds like something we shouldn't miss," she replied. She and Austin were younger than the other guests by at least a decade, and all through dinner she had noticed smiles that spoke volumes, no doubt sparked by memories of their own younger days, when their marriages were still new. If only they knew, she thought wistfully, as the now-familiar feeling of frustration over the confusion of their role-playing descended over her.

"Let's go," she said, pushing her unfinished apple pie à la mode back slightly and placing her napkin on the table. "It feels strange with just the two of us at this humongous table." Best to take a look around and get it over with, so they could return to their room and another night of sleeping at opposite ends of the bed. It was going to be a long night, she thought unhappily, but she saw nothing she could do about it. If she didn't give in to her desires she would be unhappy, and if she did she would only be giving herself a temporary happiness, which in the long run was worse than unhappiness.

They walked to the front door and together stepped out into the night.

Twelve

The gardens were well lit, but it was still too dark to see the true glory of the brilliant blooms of colorful vegetation before them. Austin reached for Desirée's hand as they made their way down the path, which was furnished with an occasional lacquered wooden bench.

By unspoken agreement they continued walking, going down one path and up another. "This garden is a lot larger than I expected," Desirée remarked. "I suppose we ought to pay close attention to which way we're going so that we don't get lost."

"The main path is easy to find. It's wider than the others, for one, plus you can see the house from it. We'll be all right."

They continued to walk in companionable silence, Austin searching for the words to tell her about his growing feelings for her, when he felt her shiver. "You're cold," he said.

"Maybe just a little."

He stopped walking and dropped her hand. In an instant he had removed his sports coat and was wrapping it around her shoulders. "Better?"

"Much, thanks." She turned to smile at him, but the smile faded when she saw the expression of naked yearning in his eyes, visible even in the dusky night.

The next thing she knew she was in his arms, his strong hand grasping the back of her neck as he kissed her hungrily, his lips making demands she wasn't sure she could meet. With his other hand he cupped her rear and pressed it against him, leaving no question of what he craved. Desirée's tongue mingled with his, leaving a moist trail on his lips. Her arms went around his back, her eager hands exploring the rippling muscles she could feel through his shirt.

The murmuring sounds of their ardor, actually quite faint, filled their ears, and when Austin broke the kiss Desirée made no attempt to control her breathlessness. She looked up at him, her eyes reflecting confusion.

Austin's hands moved to rest lightly on her shoulders. "Desi—believe me, I'm not in the habit of being so demonstrative in public places . . . even if there's no one around to see. I guess I got carried away."

"It's all right," she said softly. "It looks like I got carried right away with you."

His arm still around her, they headed back toward the house. When they arrived he held the front door open for her but did not follow her inside. "You go on up," he said, handing her the key. "I need a few minutes."

She could tell he was troubled by what had just happened between them. Wisely, she nodded her agreement to him, knowing this was not the time to intrude on his thoughts.

Once upstairs, Desirée immediately prepared to take a shower. She rummaged through her tightly packed suitcase for something to wear to bed. In her attempt to pack light, she had brought only three sleepwear items, but the blue-and-white jersey-style sleep shirt needed to be washed after wearing it the past three nights in Accra, when she and Austin had shared a bed. Well, she and Austin were *still* sharing a bed, but she wasn't going to wear a garment that had lost its freshness, no matter how appropriate it was. Still, she was reluctant to put on one of her gowns; they were too inviting. In the end she settled for her trusty, the polka-dotted housedress that could easily double as sleepwear. The thing didn't even wrinkle.

She brushed her teeth at the sink and then stepped into the shower. Between the closed bathroom door and the shower spray, she did not hear the insistent knocking at the door.

It was steamy in the bathroom. Desirée cautiously opened the door to see if Austin was back, then remembered he had given her the key, which meant he had no way to get in. She opened the door to let some cool air in, then toweled herself dry.

The mist on the mirror was already clearing. She began removing the pins that held her bun in place. When she was done she realized she had left her brush in her tote bag. She wrapped the towel around her and secured it between her breasts, then plodded barefoot over to the dresser, where she'd left the bag.

She had barely reached inside when she heard a key in the lock. Her hand flew to her chest, the only movement she had time to make before the door opened and Austin walked in.

"Hey, I was knock—" He broke off when he saw her attire.

"I . . . I was in the shower."

"I guess that's why you didn't hear me." He couldn't take his eyes off her. She was a stunning sight to behold, with her slightly tousled hair tumbling past her shoulders and a skimpy white towel a sharp contrast to her berry black skin. She'd never looked sexier. "I went downstairs and got an extra key from the desk," he explained.

Wordlessly they stared at each other, Desirée instinctively tightening the towel around her, aware that its small size barely covered her.

"You certainly know how to tempt a man," he said, licking his lips.

"I just ran out for a minute to get my brush." She blinked at the glint of desire in his eyes. "Austin—don't look at me like that. You're making me nervous."

"You *should* be nervous." He moved toward her, closing the distance between them in a few quick steps. "I want to make love to you, Desi. Right here, right now. If you don't want me to, say it now, and I'll sleep downstairs. I can't spend another night this close to you and not touch you the way I want to. I've wanted you since Abidjan, probably even before that. I've been carrying it bottled up inside me, and tonight—well, it's like the cork has popped and it's all come out. That's why I kind of lost it in the garden."

She could only return his hungry stare, which was all the encouragement Austin needed. He pulled her into his arms and proceeded to ravage her mouth. Desirée moaned under the pressure of his insistent lips and tongue. She dropped the brush and wrapped her arms around his neck, her hands clutching the base of his scalp as she pressed her body into his.

She felt Austin's determined hands squeezing her backside through the towel, then roaming down to her thighs and up over her waist and to her breasts. Still kissing her like a man starved, he began to move toward the bed until he fell backward on it through the opening in the mosquito netting, bringing her with him.

When the kiss ended Desirée, on top of him, moved to sit up. In their frenzied groping the towel had come loose, and now it fell. She made no move to cover herself; instead, her eyes went to Austin, anxious to see his reaction.

Austin's approval was evident in his hungry stare. She

was perfectly formed, her small breasts round, her stomach flat, her pubic hair neatly trimmed. He reached out and almost reverently touched a breast, his palm barely touching a sable-colored nipple, which quickly grew stiff in response. He leaned in to taste it.

Desirée arched her back, her head leaning back and her eyes closed. When it stopped she raised her head and opened her eyes.

Austin was looking at her with unabashed admiration. "You're perfect," he said.

"I am?"

"Like Venus herself."

She shrugged with a touch of embarrassment. "That's the first time I've heard *that.*"

"It's the truth, Desi." He reached for her shoulders and pulled her down onto his body, stretching his hands down the length of her back and coming to rest on her backside.

"I'm so big there," she managed to say hesitantly between kisses.

"I'll take a woman with a nice round behind over one who's flat any day. A man likes to have something to hold on to. Shhh." He kissed her again, then rolled over so that he was on top. His hands acquainted themselves with her curves, searching for pleasure points. She squealed when he grazed her hipbone, and he knew he had found one.

That was it for him. Abruptly he broke the kiss and sat up, scrambling to undo the buttons of his shirt. It seemed like it took him less than ten seconds to go from fully clothed to completely naked, his clothes thrown carelessly on the floor.

"I was wondering why I was the only one at this party without clothes," Desirée murmured as he returned to her. Now she felt his arousal against her stomach, thick and heavy, and pressed her palms into his backside, trembling with excitement and anticipation.

Austin nibbled at her throat and collarbone, and when he reached her breasts he inserted a finger of his other hand into the dark cove between her thighs. Her muscles involuntarily constricted around him as she moaned his name. She brought her hands up to rest them on his shoulders and in the process caught a glimpse of shiny gold on the fourth finger of her left hand. She fingered his left hand for his ring. It was an odd but pleasant sensation, being totally naked except for the wedding band.

Austin moved over her so that once again they were face-to-face. His hands threaded her hair as they resumed frenzied kissing, and in their passion they rolled over until she was partially on top of him. She immediately reached for his rigid penis and with a sure hand began rotating the skin up and down, moving faster and faster as her own excitement escalated.

"Desi . . . I can't wait anymore," he said, choking on the words and barely able to get them out, one hand gripping her rear in desperation.

A quick glimpse at his feet revealed his toes were bent backward. "Yes, you can," she whispered soothingly. "Just tell yourself we have all night."

"No." It came out rougher than he intended, but his need was dire. He could hardly bear the thought of leaving her luscious body long enough to apply protection.

He sat up and moved her on her back. "I've got to put on a condom. I'll make it quick, I promise," he said, kissing her for an instant.

Austin cursed himself for not putting a few individually wrapped prophylactics in his wallet. Now he had to go through his bags. He tried to remember where he had put the package he'd bought at the hotel in Abidjan that specialized in brief encounters. He'd been rushing that night; he knew that if Desirée saw what he had, she would put a wall around herself for the remainder of their surveys, especially after what had happened between them in New York. The thought of carrying condoms on the trip hadn't even crossed his mind, but when he'd covered her body with his in that Treichville nightclub and felt her body tell him that she wanted to be close to him as much as he wanted to be close to her, he knew the spark originally ignited in New York had returned at full intensity. He had purchased the condoms after he finished talking to Phil the night of the shooting, wanting to be prepared in case there was another moment like the one on the floor, a more private one when it was just the two of them.

He found the box in the zipped compartment of one of his bags. With frantic hands he tore open a packet and applied the prophylactic. When he stood and faced Desirée his breath caught in his throat.

She had moved up toward the headboard, her head resting on the pillows. The bed had apparently been turned down by housekeeping, but she had slid between the sheets, pulling them up until just above her breasts. But what had him mesmerized was the way her hair was fanned at the sides. Had it only been a few hours ago that he fantasized about seeing her this way?

Desirée's heart was pounding as Austin approached the bed until his body, just an outline through the netting, pushed it aside and suddenly loomed over her. She gasped when he knelt at the foot of the bed, his eyelids heavy, his chest, with its smattering of hair, looking surprisingly massive for a man with such a lean build, and a powerful erection telling her how much he desired her. She was filled with a delicious eagerness that warmed her entire body.

Austin moved with maddening slowness until he was positioned above her, cushioned between her thighs.

They both gasped in pleasure when he slipped inside her after one brief push. They held on to each other, making no efforts to constrain the sounds of pleasure coming from their throats with each plunge. When Austin raised himself so she could no longer embrace his back she wrapped her hands loosely around his neck, met his gaze and held it. She couldn't identify the expression in his dark eyes, but the sheer eroticism of his intense stare coupled with the strength of his thrusts suddenly became too much and she began to tremble uncontrollably, crying out in release.

"I'm sorry I couldn't wait for you," she said when they cuddled in the center of the large bed. "I'm a little embarrassed."

"Don't worry about it. I'll get mine next time."

"You sound like it's going to be a while until the next time."

"Oh, no. I just wanted to let you rest for a minute. Next time starts now." He rolled her on top of him and pulled her down for a kiss before slipping inside her once again.

Desirée fell into an exhausted slumber, but Austin lay awake for nearly an hour, watching her sleep. There was so much he didn't know about her, he thought. The man who had come close to having her as his own always, for instance. Why had they decided against marriage? He freely admitted his jealousy of this faceless man who had, if only for a brief time, captured her heart.

It was two-thirty A.M. when Desirée awoke to the sound of Austin's even breathing next to her. She gazed at him until her eyes adjusted to the light and she was able to see his handsome features clearly. His clean-shaven face looked almost angelic, but she was uneasy nonetheless. It wasn't possible for her to regret what they had shared just a few hours before, but she would be missing a few screws if she didn't question the wisdom of their actions.

She slipped out of bed, picked up his shirt from the floor, put it on and went out on the balcony. It was cold, but all was quiet. The moon was small, a sickle in the sky. It was so beautiful here. She knew that as long as she lived she would never forget this night, and she wanted to savor it for a few moments before the reality of her situation set in.

She had given in to her desires and to Austin's, and wonderful as it was, there were complications. What was going to happen when she went home? Would she and Austin try to arrange to work together, have trysts all around the country and the world, but nothing with depth or meaning?

Her reverie was interrupted by the sound of his voice, which was loud enough in the quiet night to make her jump. "What're you looking so serious about?"

"When did you wake up?" she demanded, her hand on her rapidly beating heart.

"Just now. I reached out to hold you and you were gone. Why don't you come in; it's gotten awfully chilly out here." He had put on his pants, but was barefoot and bare-chested.

"All right." She went in, and he closed the door behind her.

"You look awfully cute in my shirt, but I've got to ask you what's on your mind at"—he turned to glance at the digital clock by the bed—"three o'clock in the morning?"

She looked at him quizzically. "I was just wondering . . . have you ever been in love, Ozzie?"

He shrugged. "Yes, but not since college."

"What happened to her?"

He leaned against the dresser. "I don't know. We did

keep in touch after graduation, at least for a while. I was working in Atlantic City and she lived in upstate New York. Then she took a job in Ohio, and that was the beginning of the end. The distance did us in, I guess. We were both career-oriented. Not that there's anything wrong with that," he added hastily, not wanting to offend her.

Desirée grew quiet. Although his response confirmed that Monique had not been a great love in his life, the last thing she wanted to hear was that distance had been the culprit, especially if it had only been the distance between New Jersey and Ohio, which was much less than the 2000 miles that separated Denver from New York.

They undressed and got back into bed, Austin's hand possessively cupping her breast, but it was a long time before she fell asleep.

Their next destination, an oceanfront resort in The Gambia, was an ideal place for two people who had just become lovers. Its pearly pink beaches and calm waters had justly earned it the nickname "the African Riviera." It was a mecca for well-to-do Europeans who were eager to spend their time in a warmer climate and their money at the gambling tables, as well as African-Americans looking to make pilgrimages to the village where Alex Haley's search for his roots finally ended. It was by far the most primitive of the nations they had visited, from its outdoor customs area at the airport to the informal storefront restaurants, many of which did not even have signs over the doors. To Desirée it all added to the country's charms—that and the client hotel being located right on the shores of the Atlantic. Opening their screened windows afforded them the soothing sound of the rushing tide in the otherwise silent night. It was a setting made for romance, and Desirée and Austin made the most of it, lying in the aftermath of lovemaking listening to the surf before falling asleep wrapped in each other's arms.

In spite of the romantic setting of surf, sailing and sunsets, they knew they were there strictly to do a job, which was not neglected. In this regard there was a bonus—with their new intimacy, there wasn't a smidgen of doubt as to the nature of their relationship on the part of all who served them. None of the hotel staff would have pegged this couple as the dreaded Americans who would be reporting every facet of every contact to management.

"Ozzie, will you look at this?" Desirée asked, pointing to the pillowcases on the bed. "Doesn't it look like someone slept on these already? Look how wrinkled they are."

"They look awful. Let's see what the sheets look like." He pulled the bedspread back. "Hmm. They look crisp enough. Put the pillows back and take a picture."

Desirée did as he suggested, then placed a call to housekeeping. "Our pillowcases are incredibly wrinkled. Can you send up fresh ones, please?"

An hour later someone knocked on the door. Austin answered it. "They brought our pillowcases, fresh from the laundry," he said when he returned.

"Good." Desirée looked up expectantly, then broke out in uncontrollable laughter when he held up two pillowcases that were every bit as wrinkled as the originals. "They've got to be kidding."

"They're dead serious. Get the camera. The head of Accolade will be very interested in what his employees consider is a fresh-looking pillowcase."

Desirée reached for the Polaroid. "All I can say is, I'm sleeping with a towel between me and that pillow."

"Why do they call it *The* Gambia?" Desirée asked as they relaxed on the beach on lounge chairs arranged under an umbrella.

"I don't really know. Some places just have a 'the' in front of them. You know, the Netherlands, the Bahamas, the Philippines, the Bronx."

"It's *the* Bronx?"

"Yes. I know the reason for that one. The family who settled much of that land was named Bronck, and since they lived so far north their friends would say they were going up to 'the Broncks'.' The name stuck; they just changed the spelling."

"Interesting story. You probably know that because you're from New York."

"Just something I read someplace, but I don't think it's a particularly well-known story, even among New Yorkers. Most Manhattanites can't be bothered with anything having to do with Queens, Brooklyn, the Bronx and especially Staten Island." He tapped her shoulder. "Come on; this salt air is making me hungry. Let's get an early dinner. I want to have some more of that soup with the peanuts and rice."

"As long as it doesn't have yams. After I get back to the States it's going to be a long, long time before I can eat another sweet potato or anything that even remotely reminds me of one."

Dakar, Senegal, was the last stop of the African surveys. It was a cosmopolitan city, but Desirée felt like pieces of her heart had been left in The Gambia and at the guest house at the botanical gardens north of Accra, Ghana.

Now that they had landed in Dakar, she found herself feeling a little sad. They would soon return to New York, where the affair they had embarked upon would most likely end, along with their time abroad.

Still, she had no regrets. This was how it felt to truly be in love. What she had felt for Calvin didn't come close to what she felt for Austin. Her relationship with her former fiancé had been easy and unhurried; but her feelings for Austin were intense and fierce. She felt like she came alive when he appeared, and she didn't even want to think about leaving him to return home.

She told herself that the inevitable end of this affair was for the best. There was little chance of their being able to continue together with so much distance between them, and even if they did she would eventually have to meet his family. Austin had said he had grown up poor in Harlem, and although she was sure their circumstances had changed, as Austin's certainly had, she knew better than to think their humble beginnings would make any difference. Her mother often said there were few people on earth more snobbish than black folks who'd made a little money. There was no point in setting herself up to get her feelings hurt, not after what she'd been through. It would be hard enough to cope with not being able to lie at Austin's side at night, feeling his arm rest possessively around her waist, the insistent throbbing of his erection against her backside. It was heaven, but knowing it was coming to an end was hell. If only there was more time . . . what she wouldn't give for three more nights!

The corners of her mouth turned up in a smile. But she *had* three more nights with Austin, and then some. They would be completing two surveys here—that made six nights total. She'd make each one of them memorable.

Thirteen

"Bad news, Ozzie."

Austin tensed. This was the last thing he expected Maddie to say. "What's going on?"

"We got screwed again."

"How could that've happened, what with all the security and checking? Did something slip through?"

"No. Whoever's behind this has really gotten devious. They actually penciled out the original answers on the forms for the Hopkins group and changed them. I've been getting calls all day."

"Not the Hopkins Group!" Austin exclaimed. A management company with 100 franchises ranging from roadside inns—they disliked the term *motel*—to luxury lodgings, the Hopkins Corporation was Wallace and Hughes's biggest client.

"Unfortunately, we didn't notice it until after the GMs started calling about the mistakes."

"Does Phil know?"

"Yes. He checks in every day from Paris. He said he'd like to let everyone go and start fresh with a new crew, but that wouldn't be fair to those who didn't have anything to do with it—not to mention the lawsuits you'd be slapped with for termination without cause. But this has got us at our wits' end."

"Listen, we're fighting to stay alive here," Austin said, his voice steady and confident despite the fear in his belly. "If we don't identify this traitor soon, we'll be out of business. Has anyone been upset about a job-related matter recently? Maybe unhappy with their performance appraisal, or reprimanded for something?"

"I've been going through personnel records. So far I haven't seen anything even remotely applicable. No major blowups—as for performance appraisals . . . well, people are never happy with their raises. Everybody feels they deserve more."

"In other words, everybody's still a suspect."

"You got it."

Austin muttered an oath. "You'll also have to pay extra attention to the way the forms look as you check them. Erasure marks, correction fluid, stuff like that."

"Diane is helping. I've instructed her to put any forms aside that have had original answers changed. I'll have to look at the text to determine the right answer." Maddie, too, swore. "This is getting to be a real pain in the butt, Ozzie. I've already got my hands full. I'm putting in an extra hour a day and still can't get out from under. These reports are all supposed to be shipped within ten days, and we've been late."

"Ship half of them to Elaine. Did Phil say anything else?"

"He said we might be barking up the wrong tree by automatically suspecting the word processors. Someone at a higher level might be behind all this."

"You mean one of the agents?"

"He said an agent would have more reason for sabotage. One of our rivals might be bribing someone to send out reports with errors in them to help clear their own path. Let's face it, if you're going after a sale, it helps a whole lot if the prospective client isn't happy with their present team."

"True. And the timing couldn't be worse. We're coming up on renewal time." All annual contracts expired on

December thirty-first of each year, and renewals had already been put in the mail to clients.

"I know. Whoever's behind this knows exactly what they're doing. Phil wants me to start keeping a log of which agents are in the office on which days. I guess we can automatically rule out anybody who hasn't been around, like Chuck Lowe."

And like Desi, Austin thought. He still resented Phil's comment that Desirée wasn't immune from suspicion.

"What about Bill Sampson?"

"What about him?"

"He's in the office all the time. We all know he's in dire straits because of his latest divorce."

"Yeah, but . . . hasn't he been with you guys since New York?"

"I know. It's an unpleasant possibility, but we have to consider everybody."

"That means Mickey is also a suspect. He's in the office as much as Phil."

Austin frowned. That was a low blow; Maddie knew he and Mickey were close friends. "All right, I get your point. But don't lose faith, Maddie. We'll find whoever's doing this to us."

"Yes, but when?"

Regrettably, he had no answer.

"What was that?" He was remotely aware of Desirée speaking to him.

Desirée blew out her breath in frustration. Austin had been distracted all day. She might as well be having dinner alone. "I *said* . . . oh, never mind. Why don't you tell me what it is you're thinking about? Your body might be sitting across the table from me, but your mind is somewhere else."

"Oh, just a small problem at home. It's nothing."

"Yes, I can tell how minute it is," she replied dryly. She had to face the fact that that the party was winding down. Austin had begun tuning her out. It was clear something was troubling him, and it was just as clear he wasn't going to share his concerns with her. She bit down on her lip to keep her eyes from filling with tears. Somehow she hadn't expected it to hurt this much, even though she should have seen it coming.

Austin realized how lame his assurance sounded in view of his being so out of it all morning. "No, really, Desi, it's all right. I just have a tendency to throw my whole self into a situation and forget everything else, especially where work is concerned."

"Do you want to talk about it? Maybe I can help."

Austin smiled at her across the table, glad she was reassured, but he wasn't ready to tell her about the saboteur—not yet. Phil had been right when he said the fewer people who knew about it, the better, and already too many knew something strange was going on. "Maybe when I have a better handle on it," he replied. "But this is going to occupy a lot of my time when we get back. I hate to ask you this, Desi, but how do you feel about staying on in New York another month or two? It looks like this situation is going to keep me from traveling. You can be Weaver's junior agent. It would mean a lot to me."

Desirée suppressed her happiness at being asked to stay on in New York. It wasn't too hard. Austin hadn't asked her to stay because he wanted to continue what they had started; his reason was for the good of Wallace and Hughes. Still, she was happy to have any excuse to stay in New York. "I can stay," she replied casually, then added, "I didn't know Weaver was a senior agent."

"He's not, at least not when he travels with me. But he's qualified to be one. He knows the business inside out. As our salesperson he has to; not that he's gotten any new clients lately."

"Would you say you do more traveling—excuse me, *did* more traveling—with Weaver or with Phyllis?"

"Probably Phyllis, but I've also worked with other agents based in Boulder; we just leave from our respective home cities. Wallace and Hughes earns a lot of frequent flier miles, as you might imagine. Eve keeps track of them all. That reminds me; I'd better let Kevin know you'll be based in New York for the first half of November before he does the schedule. Eve gets a little crazy when we change bookings at the last minute."

"Do you ever travel with Mickey?"

"Not as often as I'd like to, but since he's the top senior agent after Phil and myself we usually need him to supervise. My preference is to travel with a man, which is what I usually do, since there are only a handful of women."

"Oh? Why is that?"

"A long time ago I was on a survey with Fran Perkins at a hotel in Raleigh, North Carolina. We were going over our notes in her room the morning of our presentation to the GM. We were running a little late, and I had thrown a jacket over my jeans, which I took off when I got to her room. I just had on a T-shirt underneath, and she was in hot curlers and a bathrobe, with some sticky-looking white cream all over her face. Our appointment was in an hour, and I had ordered room service to save time. The clerk, a white dude, college aged, took one look at us and stalked out in a huff."

"He thought you two had spent the night together."

"Yeah. We laughed about it at the time, but it made me uncomfortable. We were in the South, and I couldn't help thinking what might have happened to me if it had been, say, thirty years earlier. This was back when the

O.J. Simpson murder trial was going on, so it was a pretty tense time anyway."

"I remember. But at least you were getting ready to leave the hotel."

"We were going across town to another place, but you can bet on that next assignment we had all our notes together for the presentation the night before." He laughed. "So your being African-American is a good break for us, especially now that Phyllis is gone. Both Mickey and I have noticed that some of the clients seem a little uneasy at the sight of burly black guys traveling with sweet-looking blondes."

"You're not burly, Ozzie."

He chuckled. "I am when I'm traveling with a white woman."

"Doesn't seem fair, does it?"

"It's not. But we're in business to inform our clients, not shock them." Austin watched as Desirée discreetly lowered her food-laden fork and dropped the contents into her plastic-lined purse. "You know, *that* really isn't fair. I have to spend an hour in the workout room every day."

"One of the benefits of being female," she said lightly. "Besides, they usually want that outlet surveyed anyway, and I hate to exercise."

The waiter appeared and offered to take their plates. "May I bring you some dessert?" he asked.

"No, thanks; I'm full," Desirée said.

"But you were saying how you'd love to try that Death by Chocolate," Austin prodded with a hint of a smile. "I'll have the orange pound cake," he said to the waiter.

"Would you like to try our Death by Chocolate, ma'am?" the waiter inquired. "It's very good. A double fudge brownie topped with hot fudge, plus ice cream and whipped cream. It's a bit messy, though."

Desirée knew that was precisely why Austin tried to

order it for her, while selecting an easy-to-dispose-of piece of pound cake for himself. "Nothing for me, thanks." She flashed the waiter a sunny smile, and Austin's expression gave no clue that under the table her foot was connecting with his shin.

"Stinker," she hissed after the waiter was out of earshot.

Desirée fell asleep soon after boarding. "I have a headache," she murmured.

Austin watched her as she slept, reminded of how he had done the same thing on the flight over. So much had changed since then. In the space of a few short weeks his feelings for her had progressed from a strong attraction to what felt like love. Desirée Mack was not going to get away from him, he vowed.

He wanted to wait until they got back to New York to tell her how he felt. A part of him didn't like the idea of waiting, but he thought it would be better if he made his declaration in an everyday setting, not on the exotic assignment in which their relationship had blossomed, lest she think he was being less than sincere. Desirée hadn't expressed any concern about their future, which made him think she believed their affair wouldn't be of any consequence, a fling. She might even think he indulged in this type of behavior all the time. He hated for her to think he could be so callous, but soon she would know the truth.

Austin became concerned when Desirée didn't show any interest in her lunch. "I think you'll feel better if you eat something," he coaxed, holding a forkful of Salisbury steak a few inches from her mouth. It wasn't the tastiest meal in the world, but it was edible, especially when you were hungry. But Desirée merely scowled and shook her head, leaning back into her seat. "All I want is a Tylenol," she mumbled. Eyes closed, she reached for her purse, which was resting on the vacant middle seat. After a few moments of fumbling, she pulled out a small white plastic bottle. "Damn these child-proof bottles," she swore, half grunting as she struggled to pop the top open. "Nobody can open them but the kids."

Austin reached over and took the bottle from her hands. In a matter of seconds he had the cap off. He carefully poured two tablets into her palm, then handed her the orange juice she had requested for a beverage but had not drunk. She didn't look well, he thought. Actually, she looked awful. Her eyes had lost their luster, her forehead glistened with perspiration and the very act of breathing seemed to exhaust her. For the first time it dawned on him that perhaps her problem was more serious than simply not feeling well. It was a long flight across the Atlantic, and this jet was no Concorde.

Austin watched as Desirée swallowed the pills and settled back in her seat, her eyes closed and her hands clutching her upper arms. He stood up and retrieved her jacket from the overhead bin. "Thanks," she murmured as he covered her and tucked the ends around her shoulders.

Impulsively he touched his palm to her forehead. She felt cool, if a bit clammy. At least she didn't have a fever.

Desirée fell asleep. When she opened her eyes again she frowned, as if annoyed at something or someone. Then she abruptly threw the jacket off her. "It's *hot* in here," she complained.

Austin bent to retrieve her jacket, which had landed on the floor. "No, it isn't," he said patiently.

Desirée was busy gulping down the rest of her orange juice. "Are you kidding? It's worse than a jungle!"

He watched as she patted her face and throat with a

napkin, which quickly became damp with her profuse perspiration. Once more he leaned toward her and touched his palm to her forehead.

She was burning up.

Austin immediately pressed the overhead call button. "Where's your Tylenol?" he asked Desirée.

"In my bag. Ozzie . . . I feel terrible. I mean, really bad."

"I know you do." He reached for the bag and fished inside until his hand closed around the bottle.

"Yes, sir?" asked the flight attendant, seemingly appearing out of nowhere.

"My wife is ill," Austin stated without preamble. "Is there a doctor on board?"

The woman glanced at Desirée, who was leaning back limply in her seat. "I checked the passenger list myself, sir. I'm sorry to say there isn't. But it won't be much longer before we land in New York. Perhaps something to drink would help?"

It was another two hours until they were scheduled to land at JFK Airport, a fact Austin didn't bother to point out. Instead he said, "Yes. Ice water, please. And a blanket, if you've got one."

"Certainly, sir." The attendant went off to get the requested items.

Austin scanned the dosage instructions on the bottle. It had barely been two hours since Desirée had swallowed two Tylenol, and technically she shouldn't take any more for another two. He didn't want to overmedicate her, but he had to do something to get her fever down. They were just regular strength; he felt fairly confident two more pills wouldn't hurt her.

The flight attendant returned with the water and blanket.

"Thank you." In his concern Austin was only dimly aware of identifying Desirée as his wife in his rush to help her. He coaxed her into swallowing the two pills, along with the entire glass of ice water, then covered her with the thin blanket despite her protests of already being too warm. "You've got some kind of bug, Desi. Sweating it out will help."

Too weak to put up much of a fight, she relented. Austin pushed her seat as far back as it would go, followed by the empty middle seat, so she could stretch out.

"Mr. Hughes?"

Austin turned from settling Desirée to see a graying man in a navy blazer with bars on the shoulders. His name tag identified him as M. Richfield, copilot. "I understand Mrs. Hughes is ill."

"Yes. It happened suddenly." Austin glanced at Desirée, who was now clutching the blanket around her upper body and shivering.

"Fever and chills?"

Austin nodded. "Just a few minutes ago she was burning up, and now she looks like she's cold. This plane can't get to New York fast enough."

"You know, years ago I was with the Flying Doctor Service. I'm no doctor, of course, but it seems like malaria is a very real possibility."

"Malaria!"

"Did she take prophylactics?"

"Yes, we both did. But my doctor did warn me it wasn't a sure safeguard." Once more he glanced at Desirée, who lay unmoving. "I don't know what else I can do for her." She looked so miserable huddled across the two seats. Austin hated this helpless feeling.

"You've just about covered it, from what I remember. We'll make arrangements to rush you through customs when we land, and have a wheelchair waiting as well. My hunch is Mrs. Hughes isn't going to feel much like walking."

"Are we on time?" He said a silent prayer that there would be no delays.

"We're actually running a few minutes early, barring any backlog at Kennedy. I'm sure she'll be all right. Just get her to a hospital as soon as you can."

At the airport, Austin arranged for their luggage to be held by the airline; then he wheeled Desirée to the exit and hailed a cab. There wasn't time to shuttle to the lot and pick up his car; he wanted her to get medical attention as soon as possible. "Hudson Hospital," he instructed as he got Desirée seated in the back. She still felt warm, but her body was trembling as if she were freezing.

The cab driver, a middle-aged man with a ruddy complexion, whirled around. "She ain't havin' a baby, is she?" he asked suspiciously.

"No, but she's very sick, so step on it." It sounded like dialogue from a B movie, but Austin didn't care. Desirée needed medical attention immediately. He'd thought about bringing her somewhere nearer like Jamaica Hospital right off the Van Wyck expressway, but decided he wanted her to be where someone he trusted could be involved. He only hoped Zack was on duty.

Fourteen

It took forty-five minutes for the cab to reach upper Manhattan. The driver brought the vehicle to a halt in front of the emergency entrance. Austin pulled several bills from his wallet and placed them in the sliding tray that was the only contact between the front and back seats, which were separated by a bulletproof partition.

"C'mon, Desi, we're going to get you the care you need," Austin said, lightly tugging at her arm.

"Uh-uh."

Her refusal caught Austin off guard; then he realized she was too weak to move. "It's all right. Just stay here by the door and I'll come around and help you out."

"Can I give you a hand?" offered the cabbie.

Austin was grateful. Desirée was limp, which added pounds to her slender frame. He could've gotten her inside, but an extra set of hands would mean he wouldn't have the delay of first having to go inside and get a wheelchair.

They hoisted Desirée's arms over each of their shoulders. It wasn't busy in the E.R., and she was immediately checked in and brought to the treatment area. Austin thanked the cab driver and tipped him generously, then asked the triage nurse if Dr. Warner was in.

Zack appeared moments later. "Hey, man, when did you get back?" he asked, his tone conveying his delight at seeing his friend again.

"Just now. Desi's sick. I brought her here right away. Didn't you see her back there?"

"No, but I'll find her right away. I'll check with you as soon as I can."

It seemed a very long time before Zack reappeared. "We took lab tests and cultures, and a consult from infectious disease has been requested. With her symptoms and because we know she just got back from Africa, he suspects malaria."

"That's what the copilot on the plane said."

"Does she have health insurance?"

"Yes. She insisted on being covered immediately because of the travel, instead of waiting ninety days. She's not the first agent to ask for that. Phil and I don't make an issue of it."

"Good. The consult is recommending admission to control her fever, get her rehydrated and to identify which strain she has. Some are more serious than others, though I'd guess she just has ovale, which is the most common in West Africa. She's going to be isolated until she's diagnosed. And she's going to be very weak. Even if they choose to discharge her in a few days—and she won't be going anywhere until her lab results are back—they'll only release her if she has good home care."

Austin didn't hesitate. "She does have good home care. I'll take care of her." Desirée didn't belong in a hospital; she belonged at home with him.

Zack looked at him, curiosity in his blue eyes. "Listen, Ozzie, I don't mean to get into your business, but I'm getting the feeling there's more here than meets the eye. I mean, I know you wouldn't just leave Desirée hanging, but I'm sensing it's more personal. Of course, you might just be worried about a"—he caught himself before saying "wrongful death", feeling that would only upset Austin more—"lawsuit from her for putting her health at risk."

"I don't want anything to happen to her, Zack," Austin emphasized, neither acknowledging nor answering his friend's question. "I'm warning you, don't keep anything from me about her condition."

Zack nodded. Austin probably didn't even realize that in his fierce protectiveness of Desirée he had answered his friend's question. His reply was delivered calmly. "She's a very sick girl, Ozzie. I won't lie about that. But I don't think she's got a life-threatening condition. There really isn't anything you can do now. Why don't you go in and see her for a few minutes and then go home and get some rest? You've just flown across the Atlantic, man. Desirée will probably be here for at least three days. You can bring her some of her own things to make her more comfortable. Just remember, malaria is a draining illness. She should be able to go back to work in about six or eight weeks, but it'll be months before she fully recovers."

Standing alongside the bed that held Desirée's sleeping form, Austin remembered Zack's comment about the long road to a complete recovery. Guilt gnawed at him. He had hoped for a way to keep Desirée in New York as long as possible, yes, but seeing her so weak and helpless, hooked up to an intravenous device for hydration, was not what he would have chosen.

He realized Zack was right. There was nothing he could do for Desi now. A good night's sleep sounded like a good idea.

Then he remembered their luggage, still out at JFK, along with his car. He hadn't given a thought to how he was going to get home; his only purpose was to get Desi to the hospital.

After a conversation with Zack, they agreed that Austin would hang around until the end of Zack's shift;

then they would go to the airport. Austin would retrieve his and Desi's luggage and go home at last.

It was four more days before he was able to bring Desirée home. She was completely rehydrated and her temperature was stable, but she was still weak, a condition her doctor had alerted Austin would linger for several weeks. "When can I go home?" she asked from the reclining passenger seat, the flat monotone of her soft words a subtle accent to her fatigue.

"We're going home now."

"No. I mean *my* home. Denver."

"You won't be able to go anywhere anytime soon. You're too weak to fly."

She unconsciously poked out her lower lip. Was she imagining things, or did Austin sound downright cheerful about her dilemma? She couldn't imagine why he would be. Not only would she be unable to take his place with Weaver for surveys, she was flat on her back and required constant care. There was no way he could be happy with a situation that was wreaking havoc with his plans for his precious company.

At least the African leg of the surveys were completed before she became ill. She had looked forward to spending the time off she had earned after performing so many appraisals shopping, seeing some shows and dining out. Now she didn't have the strength to even pick up the phone and call her mother or Zack's cousin Sydney Chambers, the only female she knew in New York.

Sydney had visited her at the hospital when she learned from Zack that she was a patient. Desirée felt guilty for not having the energy to chat with her new friend, but Sydney assured her it was all right. Instead she worked on Desirée's hair, which had become a tangled mess after days with no attention, managing to brush it out, part it and make six neat corn-rowed plaits from crown to nape while Desirée, too weak to lift her head, simply shifted position while lying down. "I admit I was looking forward to hearing all about Africa, but it looks like we're going to have to put off the girl talk for a while . . . not that you're going anyplace," Sydney had said.

That seemed to be the consensus; she wasn't going anywhere anytime soon. Desirée had commented to Austin on her first full day in the hospital that her mother would be worried if she didn't call, and the next thing she knew, he had whipped a phone charge card out of his wallet and was asking her for the number. Desirée listened as Austin smoothly introduced himself to her mother and explained that they had just gotten in from Senegal the day before. "Desi's feeling a little under the weather, but she's right here waiting to say hello." Then he put the phone to her ear so she could talk without the effort of holding the receiver.

"Hello, sweetheart," Helen said. "I just got the postcard you sent me from Zambia."

"No, Mom, it was from The Gambia."

"Oh, is there a difference?"

In the midst of her sulking, Desirée couldn't help giggling at the memory of Austin wincing at the sound of her mother's shriek when she learned Desirée was hospitalized with malaria. He quickly recovered and took the receiver from her.

"Mrs. Mack, I assure you Desi is not in danger—" He fell silent, obviously listening, and Desirée could hear her mother's agitated voice from her bed. "Malaria is like an extremely bad case of the flu, but she's not in any danger; she's just weak. I should be able to bring her home in a day or two. They want her without fever for a full twenty-four-hour period before they let her go." Again he listened, shaking his head, although of course her mother couldn't see him. "No, Mrs. Mack, you don't have to come out. But I doubt Desi'll be up to doing any traveling. I promise you I'll take good care of her. If you'd like more assurance from a professional, I'll ask the doctor to contact you tomorrow. No, no trouble at all. All right. Try not to worry, Mrs. Mack. Here's Desi again."

He held the receiver to her ear a second time so she could exchange a few more words with her mother. The hysteria in Helen's voice had been replaced by a calm concern, the result of Austin's efforts, Desirée knew. She liked the smooth way he handled the situation. She supposed sometimes that take-charge persona of his that she found so irritating could come in handy.

Reflecting her own thoughts, Austin said, "I promised your mother I'd take care of you, Desi, and I intend to keep my word."

She didn't reply, waiting for him to add something along the lines of how it was the least he could do, reminding her that he was acting out of obligation, not out of genuine caring. That knowledge was what made being with him so difficult. She was constantly reminding herself that she would never have his love. After becoming lovers they had gone through three appraisals in The Gambia and Senegal with all the intimacies of any married couple, and not once had he said anything about what would happen once they returned to the States.

The expected response from Austin did not come, but Desirée refused to allow herself to become optimistic. Instead she gazed out at the passing Westchester County scenery as the Buick sped down the Hutchinson River Parkway under Austin's careful guidance. She wasn't surprised that he didn't try to engage her in conversation; she was still so feeble that the simple act of talking was enough to wear her out.

Once Austin guided the car along the exit ramp and

merged into city traffic Desirée was able to get a better look at the neighborhood, as opposed to trees spectacularly colored with fall foliage and an occasional building. The immaculate streets, reasonably smooth roads, abundance of trees and inconspicuous recessed shopping areas with unobtrusive signs identifying the merchants told her they were in an upper-class neighborhood.

There wasn't much development as they continued on. Austin steered the Buick into an attractive development of white duplex and triplex attached town houses with navy trim. There was a fenced playground at the edge of the property, beyond which Desirée could see the waters of the Long Island Sound sparkling in the sunlight.

Austin's unit was a duplex. He unlocked the front door, then stood back to let her enter. Desirée's first glimpse of the house was of the living room, on the left. It was a rather small room, as she supposed rooms would be in town houses, dominated by a black baby grand piano in the corner by the stairs. A white leather sofa and a chair with an ottoman in the same fabric provided seating, but the room looked like no one ever sat in it. A pastel oriental rug added some subtle color, neatly positioned under a large glass-topped coffee table. There were no end tables, just a sculpted white floor lamp in a twisted pattern. "Nice room," she murmured politely, feeling she had to say something. It wasn't a lie, not exactly. It *was* a beautiful room, just too antiseptic for her taste.

She followed Austin down the hall, getting a glimpse of a formal dining room on the right. The stairs to the second floor faced the living room—and beyond that was an open room with a wide-screen TV, a stereo system and a slightly worn navy velour sectional. A wood-burning fireplace was built into the corner. Now Desirée understood the showroom quality of his living room—it *was* for show. This comfortable room led to a large kitchen. It was in these rooms where he obviously spent most of his time.

"You've got plenty of room here. I thought everything in New York was supposed to be so cramped," Desirée commented.

"But this is the suburbs, remember? I even have grass in my backyard. Of course, it's only slightly bigger than a breadbox."

"What's upstairs?"

"Bedrooms and bathrooms. Pretty boring." Austin watched as she got settled on the sectional, leaning back into the pillowed back. The thick ends of the braids closest to her face fell in front of her shoulders, making her look like an adolescent with pigtails. "I want you to be comfortable, Desi. Don't be afraid to put your feet on the furniture. Just think of this as your home-away-from-home."

"I thought the company condo was my home-away-from-home."

"Yes, but that doesn't have the services you can get here."

"What services?"

"Your own personal butler who'll cook for you and serve you meals in bed."

"Mmm, sounds pretty good." Desirée yawned. She was beginning to tire, although all she'd done beside take the ride from northern Manhattan to Westchester was walk through the downstairs portion of Austin's house. She wondered if she would ever feel like her old self again. "I think I'd better go lie down; I feel real tired all of a sudden."

"Sure. But drink this first." Austin handed her a small glass of orange juice, which she drank in a few gulps. He helped her to her feet, and she leaned on him as they walked to the stairs. Desirée found herself wishing his house was on one level. The stairs might as well have been Mount Everest. Maybe she could simply stretch out on the couch. It was comfortable enough. . . .

They paused, and she saw Austin flip a switch at the base of the banister. The hum of machinery sounded, and she watched in amazement as a chair attached to a railing came into view, coming to a full stop just inches from where she stood. "Madame, your chariot awaits," Austin announced.

"This is incredible," Desirée breathed as he got her settled into the chair. "Austin, where did you get this?"

He flipped the switch again, then followed a few paces behind as the chair ascended. "Much as I'd like to say I had this little contraption installed for your comfort while you were in the hospital, I cannot tell a lie. It came with the house."

"Came with the house? Isn't that unusual?"

"Not really. A retired couple lived here and the chair was used by the wife, who'd had a stroke. They were both killed in a collision with a truck on the way to one of her physical therapy sessions. It was all pretty messy, with a lawsuit filed by their two daughters."

"How awful."

"They were anxious to sell from an emotional standpoint. Real estate is outrageously expensive in Westchester County—it's not unusual for people to commute as much as ninety minutes one way from upstate, where houses are more affordable—and on the advice of the realtor I made a ridiculously low offer, never expecting it to be accepted. But it was, and here I am. A few extra dollars and I bought some of the furnishings as well, like the piano and this little gadget here." He helped her get settled in the chair.

"I hope you didn't take advantage of the daughters' grief."

Austin bristled. "It's not like I held a gun to their heads, Desirée. They didn't *have* to accept my offer." He flipped the switch, and the chair began to ascend the stairs.

She realized she had chosen her words poorly. "I'm sorry, Austin. I know you aren't the type of man to do something like that. It was more like responding to opportunity's knock." She practically had to shout over the rather noisy chair.

When he helped her out of it she said, "This area seems a little on the ritzy side. Are you the only black person living in this development?"

"Sometimes I think I'm the only black person in *town.*"

They shared a laugh. "Here we are," he said, guiding her through double doors at the landing.

Desirée knew right away that this was the master bedroom by the room's large size, the fireplace—an extension of the one in the den directly below—and most of all by the huge bed positioned against a mirror-covered wall. It hadn't occurred to her that he would want her to share his bed. She really hadn't thought about sleeping arrangements, but now she realized it would be silly to go back to separate quarters after sleeping together through three countries.

She wasn't sure how she felt about continuing their affair now that they were back in the States. *I'm too tired to think about it now,* she decided. Besides, it wasn't like she was up to sex now anyway, and she probably wouldn't be for some time yet. Austin pulled the covers down, and Desirée only stopped to remove her shoes before slipping between the cool sheets. "I don't understand it, Austin," she said. "One minute I'm feeling pretty good and the next minute I'm beat."

"Remember, the doctor said it's going to take a long time before you feel like yourself again. You just take it easy and remember I'm here to take care of you."

She smiled weakly as he covered her, then leaned forward and kissed her cheek. "After all, if it wasn't for the company, you wouldn't be in this mess."

Desirée closed her eyes, but the smile remained frozen in place until she heard the door close behind him, when it faded slowly, like the last shot of a movie.

Fifteen

Desirée felt a gentle shake of her shoulder. It had to be Austin. "Mmm?"

"Desi, I'm going to go to the office for a little while. I'll be back by noon, all right?"

She opened her eyes. "Ozzie? You're leaving?"

"Only if you'll be all right for a few hours."

She shifted position and tried to sit up but was only partially successful. "What time is it?"

"Seven-thirty."

"Oh. Yes, I should be okay."

"I left the number to the office by the bed in case you need me for anything before I come back. You sure you're all right?"

"Yes, I'll be fine."

He kissed her on the mouth. "You're beautiful when you wake up."

She grunted a reply, and then he was gone.

Desirée found she was unable to go back to sleep, and after a few minutes she opened her eyes. That was when she noticed the tray beside the bed, which held orange juice, a Danish and a banana, as well as the remote control to the television. How thoughtful of Austin. She'd give him time to arrive at his office and then call him. This was almost enough to make her forget his remark of yesterday . . . but not quite. He felt responsible for her only because she had become ill while working for the company. It had nothing to do with anything else, like what she meant to him.

She sat up, feeling an immediate surge of energy she knew wouldn't last.

The master bath was behind the mirrored wall. It was equipped with a glass-walled shower—big enough for two, she couldn't help noticing with a knowing smile—and his-and-her sinks. There were a few personal items—deodorant, cologne, boar-bristled brush, toothbrush and toothpaste—neatly arranged around the sink Austin had apparently claimed as his own. Austin had left a folded washcloth and towel for her on the counter between the two sinks, but other than that the area around the other sink was bare, and so was the built-in vanity at the far end, near the second of the two walk-in closets. She was sure this was the closet reserved for the lady of the house, since it was only a few feet away from the vanity. She stood in front of it for a moment, pondering the propriety of her proposed action, which could only be called snooping, before curiosity triumphed over the wish to do the right thing and, holding her breath, she opened the door.

She half expected to see some of Monique Oliver's forgotten clothing hanging in the large closet, but it was empty. She let out her breath, not realizing until that moment that she had been holding it.

She washed up, placing her washcloth and towel on the rack inside the shower. Before she left the bathroom she placed her toothbrush in the marble stand next to his. She smiled at the sight of their toothbrushes side by side.

She sat in a chair and ate a leisurely breakfast, kept company by a morning news and information show. She had missed the more harder-edged news stories of the first hour and had little interest in the more frivolous issues of the second. The gleaming chrome of Austin's stationary exercise bike in the corner of the room caught her eye, and the next thing she knew she was on it, putting her feet in the stirrups and rotating the pedals. It had been ages since she'd done any exercise; all she did was lie in bed all day. If she didn't do something soon, she'd get soft and saggy.

But her energy quickly ebbed, and she barely made it back to the bed before collapsing into the sheets. In minutes she was asleep.

Austin called at eleven-thirty. "I was planning on just putting in a half day, but I've got a ton of work to do. We're shorthanded—Valerie resigned—and Elaine is buried under a ton of paper, reports sent from Boulder that need to be double-checked before we send them out. That will get better tomorrow, since we've got a temp coming in."

"Is Elaine usually responsible for checking work out of Boulder? What about Diane Brown and her people?"

"I guess it's okay to tell you: Someone has been tampering with the reports, making us look bad. We're in hot water with some of our clients, including one of the biggest. We don't know who it is, but until we have them identified we'll have to double-check every single form that leaves our office."

"How awful! Are you finding any errors in the reports?"

"Actually, not a one. Whoever's been sabotaging us probably knows how careful we're being and is either waiting for us to slack off or is planning something else. God only knows what they'll try next."

"I hope you catch them soon, whoever they are. But at least now that you're getting a temp to help Elaine, you'll be able to come home earlier."

"Maybe a little earlier. I'm very busy outlining a new

service for us to offer, and I want to present it as soon as possible. The way things are going, we're going to need a backup. But enough about all the problems at Wallace and Hughes. How are you feeling?"

"Oh, I'm all right," she lied.

"There's some leftover pizza in the fridge. Do you think you can make it downstairs?"

"Of course. The chair is there. Don't worry; I'll be fine. Just go ahead and do your work. Then I'll get to see you that much sooner."

But it was seven-thirty before Austin returned home. Desirée had eaten the rest of the pizza for lunch—there had only been two slices left—and there wasn't anything else to eat. She hadn't known a man yet who kept any food in his fridge. She considered calling the office to tell Austin she was hungry but vetoed the idea. He was just trying to finish up. Surely he'd be home soon.

Austin showed up with boxed dinners from KFC. "I'm so sorry, baby," he said, bending to give her a hug. Desirée was curled in a fetal position, her head pounding from not having eaten in nearly eight hours. "It took longer than I expected, but I brought you some dinner."

She wolfed down the chicken, biscuit and corn on the cob. "That was good, but Ozzie, you were so late getting home and there's nothing to eat. Even if there were some cold cuts . . ."

"Yes, you're right. I'll run out now and get some before the deli closes." He got up and picked up his jacket.

"I like ham and Swiss," she said as he moved toward the front door. It would have been nice if he had asked her, but she sensed he would make the decision about what she wanted when he got there, just as he'd decided she wanted KFC without bothering to consult her. Hell, he hadn't even called to say he'd be much later than he'd implied.

* * *

Over the next two days Desirée ate a lot of ham and cheese. Austin left early in the morning and never returned before seven o'clock. He always left breakfast for her and brought dinner home with him, but he never asked her what she felt like eating. One night it was Wendy's, the next Taco Bell. She presumed he typically ate on the run like this, but Desirée's taste buds were craving something more nutritious than all this fast food.

"Ozzie, do you think you might be able to do your work at home instead of in the office?" she asked as she munched on a Mexican pizza.

"I tried that a couple of times, when it snowed. For some reason I just couldn't get my mind to work. Probably nothing more than mind over matter."

"It does seem strange, since you do a lot of work in hotel rooms."

"Yeah, I've written some fabulous summaries at client sites. I think I'm so accustomed to my home being the one place where I can get away from everything that it's impossible for me to do any work here."

"That's probably because it's so comfortable. Maybe you should set up a home office."

"That's actually on my to-do list. Unfortunately, I've never gotten around to it."

When Desirée's mother called later that evening she used her most reassuring tone and told her everything was fine, but in truth she had serious reservations about Austin's ability to care for her. She felt no stronger now than she had when she left the hospital. Sometimes it took a monumental effort to get downstairs, even with the motorized chair; and when she got there what she really wanted to do was go back up.

* * *

The next morning, after having her breakfast, Desirée sat in a chair and watched old episodes of "The Honeymooners," her favorite TV show. No matter how many times she saw them, the episodes still made her laugh out loud. From there she tried the talk shows but quickly lost interest. It amazed her how many people were willing to make absolute fools of themselves in front of all America.

By ten-thirty she was feeling sleepy. She decided to lie down for a while and get dressed when she got up.

"Oh, my; what have we here?"

Desirée stirred. The back of her brain sent her a message, and she groggily wondered if she had left the television on. Then she heard movement in the room, and instantly she awakened.

As she had feared, she was not alone in the room. The intruder wasn't a burglar but a harmless-appearing brown-skinned woman of about sixty with a short, graying natural, who held an oversized wicker basket full of cleaning supplies.

"I'm sorry to have startled you, dear," the woman said, her tone soft and friendly.

"Oh, that's all right," Desirée replied, relaxing. She smiled. "I should have expected you. Somehow I didn't think Austin was keeping this place so clean on his own."

The woman returned the smile, revealing well-preserved teeth with a slight overbite. "He's actually pretty neat, but this is a rather large house for a man to keep up. But they say that's what mothers are for."

Desirée blinked. "You're Austin's *mother?"*

"All his life."

"Oh, Mrs. Hughes. I . . . I didn't know." She abruptly

stopped talking. It was bad enough she had just pegged Austin's mother as a cleaning woman. At least Mrs. Hughes didn't seem upset by her mistake, but making excessive apologies would only make things worse. "I'm Desirée Mack." She let it go at that, not sure how to accurately describe her relationship with Austin. *Employee* seemed ludicrous, but *significant other* was too strong. His mother had just caught her in Austin's bed, for crying out loud. Surely she could figure it out, and probably had already.

"Oh, my! Are you the girl who became ill in Africa?" Mrs. Hughes asked as she approached the bed.

"Actually, I was fine until halfway over the Atlantic on the flight back."

"He told us about you. I asked if you were all right, and Austin told me you would be taken care of. He didn't say he was going to leave you here alone while he's at work."

"Oh, I'm all right, really."

"I might agree if Austin lived close enough to check in on you at lunchtime, but you're nowhere near White Plains." Mrs. Hughes placed her palm on Desirée's forehead.

"I haven't had a fever lately. I just feel very weak."

"Well, what do you do about lunch? I know Austin doesn't keep any food here."

"There's some meat and cheese for a sandwich."

Mrs. Hughes's eyes narrowed. "And what about dinner? He's not home before seven or eight o'clock, is he?"

Desirée looked away. It was true that Austin always worked later than he said he would, and that her stomach was often singing by the time he finally did show up with dinner.

Mrs. Hughes put her hands on her hips. "That son of mine. I'm ashamed of him. How could he leave you here like this all alone?"

"It's all right, really, Mrs. Hughes."

"No, dear, it isn't. I'll be right back."

Mrs. Hughes returned within five minutes. "It's all settled. I want you to get dressed. Take your time; it'll take me a little while to clean the house. You're coming home with me."

Desirée was stunned. "I am? What about Austin?"

"I just called him. I told him he ought to be ashamed of himself, so involved in his company that he doesn't realize you're in no condition to be left alone. What are you, just two or three days out of the hospital?"

"Yes . . . but he's having serious problems at work, Mrs. Hughes. He and his partner have a lot to lose if they go under."

"He'll have a serious problem with *me* if he doesn't care for you properly. I know about his client trouble, but it's no excuse. You're part of his company. If it wasn't for him, you wouldn't have gone over there and gotten sick in the first place. He'll be over to see you after work. Now, you start getting ready, and remember not to rush. I'll be at least an hour. I'll probably go to the store as well."

Desirée nodded. "All right, Mrs. Hughes."

As she soaked in a warm bath, Desirée had to admit that she had a bone to pick with Austin herself. How could he not tell her that his mother would be in to clean his house? Didn't he realize the embarrassing situation he was putting her in? It could have been avoided so easily by her simply using a different room. But at least Mrs. Hughes hadn't seemed shocked to find her—or if she was, she'd covered it well. Surely it wasn't a typical experience for her to find a strange woman in her son's bed. Not that anything sexual was going on; Desirée simply didn't have the energy required for anything vigorous. She did enjoy going to sleep snuggled against Austin's body, his hand resting possessively on her thigh or breast. She felt comfortable here at Austin's, in spite of the far-from-ideal circumstances, and was apprehensive about going to stay with his parents, whom she didn't even know.

By the time Austin's mother finished cleaning, Desirée was all ready, having bathed, dressed and packed a small bag. "Since it's almost noon I went to the store. I thought you might want some lunch, so I fixed you some tomato soup and a BLT sandwich," Mrs. Hughes informed her.

"Oh, thank you. I was a little hungry."

"I figured as much. You have to eat to keep your strength up."

After Desirée ate, she felt stronger than she had all week. She rode the chair upstairs to get her purse and small suitcase but walked back down on her own power.

Outside, Mrs. Hughes unlocked the passenger side door of the car for her and took the suitcase. "I'll put this in the backseat."

"Oh, I'll do it, Mrs. Hughes." Desirée was beginning to feel uncomfortable. She couldn't have Austin's mother waiting on her.

"No problem, dear." The older woman took the bag.

"Do you live near here?" Desirée asked when they were on the Boston Post Road—the very one, Mrs. Hughes informed her, that the colonists had used over 200 years earlier to travel between New York and Boston in horse-drawn carriages.

"In Mount Vernon. Not too far. We live in Austin's building."

"His building?"

The older woman chuckled. "Yes. He and his friend Zack own an apartment house. There are nine apartments on three floors."

"I met Zack."

"He's a charmer, isn't he? And so handsome."

"That he is. I didn't know he and Austin owned an apartment building."

"Austin likes to say it's the bank's building, but it really works quite well for them. They use a real-estate manager to rent out all the apartments and to get repairs made. It's hard to find apartments here in Westchester and they rarely have vacancies, although the couple in one of the upstairs apartments just relocated to Virginia somewhere. Still, it was rented quickly by a young woman who seems very sweet. Of course, both the boys insisted that Paul and I move in as soon as they bought it. That's my husband," she added.

"I guessed as much."

"We were still living in the old place on Amsterdam Avenue and One Fifty-Eighth Street. We'd lived there for years; raised both our children there. We have an older daughter, Charlene. She's married and lives in Rockland County."

"Is that far from here?"

Mrs. Hughes laughed. "That's right, you're from Denver, aren't you? Rockland County is next to Westchester, except it's across the Hudson. You have to take the Tappan Zee Bridge."

"Tappan Zee," Desirée repeated. "There are some strange names for bridges here. We went across the Throg's Neck when we went to the airport."

"I suppose they are strange. I don't know where they get them from, even though I've lived in New York all my life."

Desirée was beginning to feel weak again. Funny how she'd taken her good health for granted. "Mrs. Hughes, do you mind if I put my seat back?" she asked.

"Of course not. The knob is on the side."

Desirée dozed off until they arrived at the Hughes apartment, in a building covered with dark green shingles. "We live on the first floor,'' Mrs. Hughes informed her.

"Good. I don't think I'm up to climbing any more stairs . . . but I know I can carry my bag. It isn't heavy."

The Hughes apartment had a homey feel to it, with a lot of pictures and comfortably worn furniture. As Desirée expected, there were two bedrooms.

"Is Mr. Hughes at home?" she asked after she'd sat down at Mrs. Hughes's invitation.

"No. He's at work. He transferred to the local post office after we moved here. Austin tried to get him to stop working—he and Zack would only accept a token rent from us, well below what they get for the other apartments—but Paul insisted on going 'til he's sixty-five. I, on the other hand, had no problem quitting," she added with a chuckle.

"Did you work at the post office, too?"

"I did housekeeping at one of the downtown hotels. I think that's how Austin first got interested in the hotel business."

"You're very proud of him, aren't you?"

"Oh, yes. Both of my children have done well, and Paul and I couldn't be happier. I'd just like to see them settle down, or in my daughter's case, get more settled. Charlene's almost forty and hasn't had any children yet, and Austin spends too much time with that company, if you ask me."

"That's one of the drawbacks of being your own boss."

"I suppose." Mrs. Hughes looked at Desirée curiously.

She rushed to change the subject, sensing that Mrs. Hughes was about to ask her about her relationship with Austin. "Can I help you with anything?" she offered with a brightness that belied her fatigue, praying the older woman would decline.

"Now, none of that. I just want you to rest."

Sixteen

"D.W., how are you?"

"I've been better, Ozzie."

"Yes, I know the feeling." Austin paused; he and Charles de Wessington, otherwise known as D.W., or Dee Dub, vice president of the Hopkins Group, always had a good rapport, but this was harder than he thought it would be. "I know you're probably feeling the heat from the bad reports, and I'm sorry. I'm sure Phil told you someone in-house is deliberately sabotaging our work. I know that's not your problem," he added quickly, "but we need to use all possible resources to help identify who our traitor is."

"You think I can assist with that?"

"Yes, I do. I'm sure you get solicitation letters from other companies offering to do your QA all the time. I'm thinking whoever is behind this is going to contact you while the memory of our mistakes is still in your mind."

"I see. I don't get any of those letters directly; Kay knows I have no interest. But you're free to talk to her."

"I appreciate it, Dee Dub."

"Good luck. You do know this can never happen again."

Austin nodded, then realized de Wessington couldn't see him. "Yes, I realize that."

"Hold on. I'll tell Roberta to pick up."

The line was retrieved within seconds. "Hi, Ozzie. What's up?"

"Roberta, do you keep pitch letters you receive from our competitors?"

There was a slight hesitation. "Yes. I've started a file."

Probably on D.W.'s recommendation, since the report fiasco. There wasn't a moment to lose. Their company would not be able to survive with the loss of the Hopkins Group. "I'd like to know who sent you letters recently, like in the last month."

"Sure. Can you hold a minute while I get the file?"

"Yes." Roberta, like everyone employed in Hopkins's corporate office, would never simply instruct him to hold on and click off. Those people knew their customer service skills.

"Thanks for waiting," she said upon her return. "Okay, here it is. Most of them are the regulars who write us twice a year. Here's a new one. It's from Roberts and Associates out of New York."

"Is there any way you can fax me a copy of the letter?"

"Sure."

"And that's the only one you've gotten that's not from someone who contacts you regularly?"

"That's it."

"Thanks a million, Roberta. You won't forget about that fax?"

"I'll send it right now."

"You're a doll."

Moments later, Austin had the faxed letter in his hand. It began by asking if they were displeased with the their current QA supplier and issued an invitation to try their "error-free" reporting. It was signed by Raymond Roberts, president. The letterhead reflected an address on West 59th Street in Manhattan.

He immediately dialed the number on the letterhead.

"Raymond Roberts, please," he said to the woman who answered the phone.

"I'm sorry, sir; Mr. Roberts is out of the office. May I take a message?"

"When do you expect him back?"

"I'm not sure, but he calls in for his messages regularly."

Calls in? "Is this an answering service?"

"Well . . ."

Her hesitation was his answer. "Can you tell me if this is really the address of Roberts and Associates?" He read the full address from the letterhead.

"That's actually our address. This is Mailboxes."

"I see. Thanks a lot."

"Did you wish to leave a message?"

"Yes, but I can't remember the name of the fellow I need to leave it for. Maybe if you told me the name of his associates?"

"I'm sorry, sir; I can't do that."

"All right. Why don't we forget it, then." He hung up, then dialed Maddie in Boulder. "Maddie, it's Austin. Has Phil called in yet?"

"Phil's here. He got in from Lisbon yesterday. I'll put him on."

"Hey, man. Tell me something good," Phil greeted.

"I've got some information for you." Austin recounted what he'd learned. "I was expecting her to say someone from Denver was soliciting them. That name doesn't sound familiar, but most of our staff have connections in New York since they used to live here."

"So we're no closer than we were before."

"That's right."

"How did Dee Dub sound?"

"Unhappy, but civil. I think they'll sign for next year, but I wouldn't be surprised if they add a clause that gives them the right to terminate at the end of any quarter. He implied that if this happens again, we're history. Anyway, I've looked up Raymond Roberts in the Internet White Pages. There are dozens of them in the metro area."

"How about a private detective? Tell him we're looking for the Raymond Roberts who just started a QA service. It's their job to find people. I know it'll be expensive, but we've got no choice."

"All right. I'll do it tomorrow. I'm going to leave a little early today."

Once Desirée retreated to the Hughes's extra bedroom she managed to sit up for about fifteen minutes before she gave in to fatigue and went to bed. It was dark outside when she opened her eyes. There was no clock in the room, so she checked the lighted dial of her watch. It was after six.

She got up, not too quickly, and sat on the edge of the double bed for a minute before standing up and venturing into the hall. The apartment was filled with the scent of roast chicken, but it was quiet. Where were the Hugheses?

"Mrs. Hughes?" she called to no avail.

There wasn't a phone extension in her room. She wondered if Austin had called to check on her while she was asleep. Was he on his way to see her?

She sat in the living room and turned on the television with a remote control lying on the coffee table. The local news was on. She watched, not really seeing, with an eerie feeling of abandonment.

A sports segment was followed by a commercial, and when the break ended there was Skye Audsley at the anchor desk, describing a sinkhole somewhere in New Jersey that had swallowed up several cars. Then they cut to film of a reporter on the site.

Skye looked dashing as ever. Funny; she hadn't thought of him since before she'd gone to Africa.

Desirée turned her head at the sound of voices. "Ah, there she is, all awake and ready to eat," Mrs. Hughes said happily. "She must have known you were coming, Austin."

Austin rushed in behind his mother, not stopping until he stood before Desirée with her hand in his, his eyes searching her face anxiously. "Are you all right, Desi?"

"I'm fine."

"You should ask how *he* is," his mother said. "I just read him the riot act for leaving you to fend for yourself in your condition."

"We'll have more after this," Skye said from the television.

"Oh, I'm glad I didn't miss the news," Mrs. Hughes said. "I just love that Skye Audsley. He's such a handsome young man."

Austin looked at the set and then at Desirée, and he released her hand. She didn't like the way his features hardened. She felt she had to say something reassuring. "I was just watching the news, Ozzie." It wasn't like she turned on the set with the distinct hope of seeing Skye Audsley's handsome face; it was merely a coincidence. She wasn't interested in Skye.

"Well, well. This is the young lady. You're not looking too bad."

Desirée knew the short-statured man with the large belly and receding hairline who had just come into the living room was Paul Hughes, Austin's father.

"Dad, this is Desirée Mack. Desi, my father."

Desirée started to rise, but Paul Hughes stopped her. "Now, you stay put. I know you've got to take it easy." He bent to shake her hand. "Welcome. I'm sorry we didn't get to meet you before this."

"Thank you, Mr. Hughes. I'm still on the disabled list, but I'm pretty sure I'll live."

"Yes, you will at that. Sarah, how long 'til dinner?"

"You all can come in now."

At dinner Desirée learned that Mrs. Hughes had made a quick trip to the post office to pick up her husband from work, and that they'd arrived home at the same time Austin did, the earliest he had left work all week. Desirée would rather he had left of his own accord, rather than because his mother had bawled him out, but she was glad to see him anyway, and at least his concern for her seemed genuine.

Over a tasty meal of chicken, mashed potatoes and gravy—which was so good that she even ate the accompanying peas and carrots—Desirée studied the senior Hugheses. She decided Austin looked most like his mother.

"How is everything going at work?" Paul Hughes asked Austin.

"Not that great. We're doing a lot of checking because of past problems. It's very time-consuming, and we're not turning up anything. I'm designing another service to offer to hold the clients we have and to attract new ones. I'm also hitting the sales trail pretty hard."

"What about Weaver?" Desirée asked.

"Weaver's in a slow period, which happens sometimes. He hasn't landed a sale in months, so he's working as an agent. We need him for that anyway. Remember, each survey requires two, and we're one short since we haven't replaced Phyllis, plus you're on the disabled list."

"Oh, that's right."

"Well, I don't want you overdoing it, " Austin's mother cautioned. "Next thing you know, you'll be getting sick, too."

"I'll just have to move in with you, Mom. You can

take care of both Desi and me," Austin replied with a wink Desirée's way.

She pressed her arms in close to her sides to control the tremor that went through her. It had been the same the very first time he had winked at her. It had been too long since she'd been aware of being close to him. Last night and the ones before she'd slept too deeply to even know he was there after the first few minutes. She found it ironic that now she was feeling stronger, she would be sleeping alone.

Desirée offered to do the dishes, a proposal Sarah promptly turned down. "Why don't you and Austin take a ride or something?" she suggested.

"Good idea," Austin said quickly. "Come on, Desi, get your coat. The night air will do you good."

Once outside, Desirée suggested they walk instead, and Austin agreed. "If you're sure you're up to it."

"I can make it to the corner and back without passing out. Seriously, Ozzie, I feel better today than I have since I got sick." It was his mother's care, she knew.

"Good. I was going to suggest we go out for a few minutes. There's not much privacy at my parents'."

"We could have talked in the room I'm staying in."

Austin's dubious expression conveyed without words how little he thought of that idea.

"It's not like we would shut the door, Ozzie. You forget, I was asleep in your bed when your mother showed up this morning, so it's not like we have any secrets from her. But I do wish you had told me that she cleans your apartment. I know we're both grown, but it was rather embarrassing for me."

"I'm sorry, Desi. I was so busy with everything that's going on at work, I completely forgot."

"I know you didn't mean to put me on the spot. It was very strange, though, looking up and seeing a strange woman in your bedroom carrying this huge basket. I thought I'd died and gone to the Four Seasons." Desirée gasped. Why had she said that? Now he would know her initial impression of his mother, for the finest hotels opted for their maids to carry their cleaning supplies in oversize wicker baskets rather than the more convenient but unsightly wheeled steel contraptions used by so many other inns and resorts.

But Austin merely laughed. "You thought Mom was the cleaning woman?"

"Well . . . she was carrying one of those wicker baskets, with all her stuff in it. . . . I don't know what to say, Ozzie."

"It's all right. I know it was an honest mistake, especially since I forgot to tell you." Austin chuckled. "Actually, it was seeing the maids with their baskets that gave me the idea to get my mother one to keep all her supplies in. She uses it at home, and she brings it when she comes to my place. She did housekeeping at a hotel for years."

"Yes, she mentioned that."

"She actually enjoys it, although she certainly prefers cleaning her own home as opposed to other people's hotel rooms. When we were kids it was like being in the army. Charlene—that's my sister—and I had to get our rooms inspected before we could watch TV or go outside. I still say our apartment was the cleanest on the block." Austin met Desirée's eyes with a hint of embarrassment. "In another time my mother would have run one of those Molly Maid places, but in the Sixties things were just starting to change for black people."

"I know what you mean. My mother says when she was in school any black girl who wanted to pursue a career went into either teaching or nursing, because those were about the only fields that were open to them at that time. She jokes that she became a nursing instructor so she could combine the two."

Austin nodded in agreement. "Thirty-five years ago you didn't find a lot of black people working in the offices of Fortune Five Hundred companies. I'm just glad my mother doesn't have to clean rooms anymore." He reached for her hand. "There's something else I need to apologize for. Mom made it clear I wasn't doing right by you by going off to work such long hours and leaving you alone in the house. I can see a difference in you already, and you haven't been with her for even one day. It must be her home cooking."

She laughed. "I can't argue with you there. It's been a while since I had a home-cooked meal, and she's a fabulous cook. I've got to tell you, Ozzie, I was scared to death when your mother insisted I come home with her. I just didn't know what to expect. And it all happened so fast. My own mother couldn't take better care of me, and she's a nurse." She gasped. "My goodness, I forgot! My mother doesn't know where I am. I've got to call and let her know. If she can't reach me, she'll be frantic."

"It's all right. You can call from my parents'. I'll charge it to my phone card. Come on, let's head back."

"When am I going to see you again, Ozzie?"

"Tomorrow. I'm going to miss you tonight, Desi. I'll probably lie awake for hours, wondering if those last two weeks in Africa were just a dream."

"I know what you mean. It was nice, at least until I got bitten by a certain disease-carrying mosquito."

"Yeah, and if I ever run into that bug again, I'm going to stomp it out and then drown it in the toilet."

They laughed, and Desirée was proud of herself for keeping the conversation light. Talking with Austin was always a delight, even if what she really wanted to do was grip his shoulders and demand to know where she stood with him, and what was going to happen when she recovered.

* * *

After three days with the senior Hugheses, Desirée was beginning to feel like herself again. She still tired easily, but she felt she had improved enough so that she no longer required constant supervision.

"Ozzie, do you think I can come back to your house until it's time for me to go home?" she asked him on Sunday. He had watched football with his father while she napped and had come to her room to check on her before dinner.

"I'd like nothing better. I just want to make sure you'll be all right during the day." He stroked her cheek; her skin felt warm and moist against his palm. "You see the doctor tomorrow, don't you?"

"Yes. Your mother is taking me to the hospital outpatient clinic for follow-up."

"Ask the doctor if he thinks you can be in the house by yourself. I think he might suggest you spend another week here with my parents, but at least that will clear it with my mother, who I can tell you right now is not going to want you to leave." Austin desperately wanted Desirée back with him again. He had even thought of bringing her to the corporate condo during the hours he was at work so she would be close enough so he could check on her, but he didn't think it was such a great idea to get her dressed and out of the house early in the morning before she was fully awake. He knew from talking with his mother that Desirée spent a great deal of time napping and often woke up drenched in sweat, and even now her skin and hairline were damp.

"Your mother has been wonderful to me. Your father, too, but she's the one who's been like a private nurse. I'll never be able to thank her enough."

"My mother is a very caring person, and she's grown pretty fond of you."

"It's mutual." Desirée thought of the icy reception she'd received from Calvin Edwards's parents, neither of whom were able to conceal their shock when he presented her to them. It was the bitter memory of that meeting that had made her so leery of meeting Austin's family and, in turn, it was the Hugheses' genuine kindness and compassion that had helped a painful recollection fade. She would miss them when she went home.

"There's something else I need to ask the doctor," she said.

"What's that?"

"I need to get home, Ozzie. Thanksgiving will be here in a couple of weeks. I don't want my mother to be alone for the holiday."

Austin frowned. No, of course she wouldn't want that. Desirée and her mother were close, and he would expect no less, given that she was an only child whose father had died when she was in high school. That was one of the first things she'd told him about herself, when they were first getting acquainted. Had that been just two months ago? So much had happened between them since. The thought of her going back to Colorado was enough to make him feel like someone had driven a stake through his heart. But how could he possibly keep her here?

"It's a long flight between New York and Denver, Desi. I don't think you're up to it. You probably need at least another month before taking a trip that long. You can get back in time to spend Christmas."

"What about my mother?"

"Why don't we bring her here?"

"Here?"

"Has she ever been to New York?"

"No, but—"

"New York is wonderful during the holidays. Store window displays, Rockefeller Center, all that."

"I feel better than I did before, but I'm not going to be up to doing any sightseeing, even by then."

"Let's call her. I'll ask her to think about it. If she says yes, I'll send her a ticket."

"Ozzie, you would do that for me?"

He leaned forward and kissed her mouth. "You'd be surprised what I would do for you, Desi."

She blinked. That was the sweetest thing he'd said to her in a long time. He did care about her; he had to. Could it be possible that he loved her?

But the mood didn't last. Austin was already reaching for his wallet, where he carried his phone card. "You'll have to tell me the number. I'll dial it."

Desirée wanted to scream in frustration. With his swift change from a touch of tenderness to matter-of-factness, he was impossible to read. She watched listlessly as he picked up the telephone extension he had surprised her with the second day she was here, insisting that she shouldn't have to get up and go into another room if he or her mother called while she was resting. She leaned forward when she saw the confused expression on his face after he had dialed, wondering what was wrong.

"Hello . . . May I speak to Mrs. Mack, please?" Austin asked.

Desirée frowned. Her mother lived alone. Who had answered her telephone?

"Hello, Mrs. Mack. It's Austin. No, she's fine. She's sitting right here. I'll put her on in a minute. We were just talking, and she's worried about Thanksgiving coming up, and her doctor saying she's not strong enough yet to fly to Denver. I suggested I send you a plane ticket so you can come and spend the holiday with us here in New York."

Desirée leaned forward, straining to hear her mother's response.

"Oh, I see," Austin said.

"What?" she hissed.

He gestured for her to be quiet. "I just wanted to assure you that it's an open invitation, so if you change your mind, please just let me know. I'm going to put Desi on now. Take care, Mrs. Mack."

He handed Desirée the phone.

"Mom? You don't want to come to New York for Thanksgiving?" She listened as her mother explained, her eyes growing wide in astonishment.

After a brief conversation they said their good-byes.

"That was quick," Austin remarked.

"She had company," Desirée said. "Frank Mitchell. They go out occasionally, but I had no idea they were so close."

"She seems pretty happy, even though she's worried about you."

"I guess that was Frank who answered the phone." Desirée sighed. "I can't imagine it. She's actually going to have dinner with Frank's son and his family on Thanksgiving. She had already arranged for me to join them. It sounds like it might be serious. I'm afraid to ask. I know it really isn't any of my business."

"You sound surprised."

"I *am* surprised. I know she's only fifty-six and my father has been dead for twelve years, but I just never thought of my mother as a, well, as a . . ."

"As a woman?"

Desirée shrugged. "Now you're making me feel foolish."

"I don't mean to, Desi."

"I guess I'd better get ready for dinner."

"All right. And as much as I'd like to sit here and watch you, I'd better go and let you get dressed."

"Oh, the telephone. Why do people always call when I'm about to put dinner on the table?" Mrs. Hughes complained.

"That's why we put an extension in the kitchen," her husband pointed out from his seat across from the living room television.

"And who asked you?" she said playfully as she picked up the receiver. "Hello? Oh . . . hello, Monique. We're well, thanks. How are you? Good, good. Yes, he's back. As a matter of fact, he's here right now. Would you like to speak to him? All right. Just a minute." Mrs. Hughes gingerly placed the receiver on the kitchen counter, facedown. "Austin!"

"Yes, Mom?"

His mother's gaze was locked on the pork chops she was turning. "You have a telephone call."

"Here?" Austin realized who it probably was. "Is it Monique?"

"Yes, it is. You can get it in my room if you'd like."

"I don't have anything to hide, Mom." He picked up the receiver. "Hello, Monique."

"Hi. This is a surprise. I called your mother to see when you were coming back. I didn't expect you'd be there."

"I'm watching the football game with Dad and they invited me to stay for dinner. I'm sorry I haven't called; we're really going crazy at the office."

"How long have you been back?"

"About a week and a half."

"Oh, were you due back that soon?"

Austin frowned. Monique had known how long he was going to be away. Why was she calling him now, anyway? They really had nothing to talk about. "Monique, my mother's about to serve dinner," he said as his mother bent to remove a pan of cornbread from the oven. "Can I call you back later?"

"Yes, I'll be here. I left a pair of earrings at your house and need to pick them up."

"Oh, yes. Gold seashells. I found them. Actually, I've got them in the car."

"Well, I'm at home. Why don't you stop by after you leave?"

"Better yet, why don't you meet me at Smitty's for a drink?" He didn't want to go to her apartment. "All right. Seven o'clock. See you then." He hung up and waited for his mother to comment.

She didn't disappoint him. "Aren't you balancing an awfully heavy plate, Austin?"

He kissed his mother's cheek. "It's all right, Mom. I'm not being a player. I broke it off with Monique before I left for Africa. When I met Desirée, Monique just didn't do it for me anymore."

"So there is something going on between you and Desirée?"

"Yes. It happened while we were in Africa. But that has nothing to do with Monique. It was pretty much over between us before anything started with Desi and me."

"I had a feeling you two were more than colleagues," Sarah replied, tactfully refraining from revealing how she had gotten her impression. "But do you think it's such a good idea for you to be involved with one of your employees?"

"It happens all the time. There's nothing wrong with it. I wouldn't try to take advantage of her; you know that."

"Of course. Well, for what it's worth, Daddy and I both like Desirée very much. I can't say I felt quite the same about Monique. There wasn't anything wrong with her, but she seemed so anxious, like she was trying too hard." Sarah took a tub of margarine out of the refrigerator. "Go and get everybody, will you? I'm ready."

"Okay, Mom. And thanks."

* * *

“Do you have to go, Ozzie? It’s so early.”

“I know, but I’ll see you tomorrow. There’s something I need to take care of. I’ll tell you about it tomorrow.” He put an arm around her as they walked to the door. When he kissed her good-bye he didn’t want to let her go. She was so beautiful, even as ill as she’d been. He hadn’t gotten a good night’s rest since she hadn’t been sleeping beside him, and when he did get her back he wanted her to stay forever.

Seventeen

There wasn't much of a crowd at Smitty's Bar; just the usual Sunday night hangers-on, mostly men who had been watching football and lingered over their drinks now that the game was over. Austin had wanted to get here before Monique, although he was sure she would never arrive before he did . . . and if she did, she'd make sure he never knew it.

He remembered the day he ended it, which was the last time he'd seen her. It had happened at a quiet Italian restaurant in New Rochelle a few days before he left for Africa. When he extended the invitation he told her he had something to discuss with her, using a carefully somber tone lest she think it was a marriage proposal, hoping she would figure out what was coming. But when they were shown their table she sighed dramatically and said, "Oh, Ozzie, I thought this was going to be so easy."

"Just spit it out, Monique." Austin had no patience for her theatrics, but at the same time he had to marvel at her manipulation of the situation, as if it had been *her* idea to have dinner and talk.

"All right." She took a deep breath. "We've had so much fun together since we've been seeing each other, but I think both of us know that we've gone as far as we can. I got very sentimental when we went to Phyllis's wedding. Weddings affect me that way. The way she and Eddie were looking at each other . . . It suddenly hit me that that type of thing is never going to happen between you and me, or else it would already have happened. Do you know what I mean?"

"Yes, you're right. Actually, I'd been thinking the same thing, Monique. We've both known it. I guess it just needed to be said."

She smiled. "Oh, I'm so glad. Did it occur to you at Phyllis's wedding?"

"Around that time, yes."

"Then we agree? From now on we're just friends?"

Austin's first thought was that they had never been anything more than just friends, but he saw no reason to hurt her feelings. If anything, he was relieved. Monique was pretty sharp, and she most likely had picked up the vibes he was sending and decided *she* was going to be the one to break it off, not the other way around. He'd go along with that. What really mattered was that they both had full understanding that they wouldn't be seeing each other anymore.

"Sure," he said.

"Good. I've met someone, you see, and it's moving very nicely. Already more of a bond has formed between us after spending just a little time together than what we've had in over a year." She gave him an embarrassed smile. "You aren't upset with me, are you?"

"No, of course not. It's the best thing for everyone."

She'd never bothered to ask him what he had wanted to talk to her about, which was a dead giveaway that she already knew. He didn't care; he was just happy the breakup went so smoothly. Now he wished she would hurry up and get here so he could give her the earrings, exchange pleasantries and be on his way. He had no interest in catching up or reminiscing about old times.

He took a seat at the bar and ordered a beer. It seemed silly to wait for someone in a bar and not order a drink.

He had been waiting for nearly fifteen minutes before she showed up. "Ozzie! It's so good to see you!"

"Hello, Monique." He rose and dutifully kissed her cheek. As usual, she looked like a million, even in jeans, a sweater and a waist-length leather jacket that was stylish but probably did little to shield her from the cold. He knew from the intimate nature of their previous relationship that cosmetically she had more paintbrushes than Picasso, yet she always emerged from the bathroom looking fresh and natural.

"Thanks for meeting me."

"No problem. I'm sorry I didn't call you about your earrings." He had meant to, but between the issues at Wallace and Hughes and his concern over Desirée's health, he simply hadn't had time. "Here they are." He reached into his pocket and held out the earrings, which he had wrapped in several sheets of bond paper and secured with tape. He was glad he'd come across them in the bathroom before Desirée saw them.

She took the package. "Thanks. It wasn't urgent, but of course I did want to get them back eventually." She smiled at him. "So how was Africa?"

"It was pretty nice. The client seems very happy with our work. And how are you?" She was being quite cordial, and he felt the least he could do was reciprocate.

The bartender interrupted before she could answer. "Can I get you something, miss?"

Monique shrugged. "Why not? I'll have a seabreeze."

Austin paid for her drink when it was delivered; he felt it was the right thing to do. He would drink the rest of his beer slowly and escort her out as soon as she was finished with her seabreeze, which shouldn't take long. "How are things going with you? Your new relationship?" He knew she was dying for him to ask and decided to accommodate her.

"Very well. It's actually become serious."

"That must be the reason for the way you're glowing. I'm happy for you, Monique."

"Thank you. I'm very happy these days."

Austin waited for her to ask if he had found happiness, but she continued to talk only about herself—her job, her plans. He was relieved when she at last drained her drink. "I'll walk you to your car," he offered.

"Thanks."

After seeing her off, he walked to his own car and headed back to the home he had worked so hard to create, the home that had never before felt so empty.

Desirée was waiting when Austin arrived at his parents' apartment the next day. "I've got good news and bad news," she said after hugging him hello.

He kept an arm draped around her shoulders. "Okay. Give me the bad news first."

"The doctor says he wants me to spend at least ten more days with constant care."

Austin grunted. "You're right, that *is* bad news. What's the good news?"

"He says I'll probably be feeling a lot better by that time. I told him I wanted to go back to work as soon as possible."

"I don't think you'll be feeling quite *that* good, Desi. Here, sit down."

They sat on the sofa. "That's what the doctor said," Desirée said. "But I feel guilty about collecting my pay, even though it's only half. I'm not doing anything to earn it."

"You became ill while traveling for the company. Just because it wasn't an accident and you don't qualify for worker's comp doesn't mean you should be left out in the cold. We're not going to cut off your salary. I just wish we could keep you at a hundred percent. I was, uh, overruled."

She knew he meant Phil had vetoed the idea. "Half is fine. My apartment's been sublet, so I don't have to worry about paying the rent. I told the doctor the type of work I do, and he said it's a possibility that I'll be able to return soon, since I can get plenty of rest in between department surveys. There's no physical exertion involved in writing summaries. He just suggests I don't fly until about the second week of December, and then preferably with a companion, because it's such a long flight." She tried to say the words casually, but she would love it if he would suggest he go with her.

Austin looked thoughtful. "Well . . . since you're so anxious to go back to work, suppose we assign you to do the Exeter with me."

"Where's that?"

"It's on the Upper East Side of Manhattan. Small, exclusive, very British. A lot of old-lady decor. You know, doilies and those awful floral prints everywhere, none of them matching."

Desirée chuckled. "I never knew why that type of thing is considered high-class. Can you imagine the reaction a woman would get if she wore a floral print blouse with a different floral print skirt?" They laughed. "Isn't that survey already scheduled?"

"Weaver is supposed to go with me, but we can change easily enough. There's no air travel involved, which will make Eve happy. She's pulling her hair out over the changes we've made already."

Desirée was silent for a moment. She knew most of the changes had to be made because of her illness. "Well, I'd love to go. I can drink a lot of tea."

"Good. Now, about your travel plans. . . . I believe they're doing two hotels in the Tech Center right there in Denver next month. It's always slow in December;

everything stops around the twentieth until after New Year's. And, of course, we're not sure yet what kind of New Year we're going to have."

"Aren't the contracts coming in?"

"Not as fast as they have in the past, and we haven't even raised our rates. Word travels very quickly in this business. Of course, our culprit might be helping it along, spreading rumors that Wallace and Hughes is incompetent while they go after our clientele. But I think my new plan will go over big."

"You haven't told me much about it."

"I'm still working on developing a new service for our clients, an over-the-phone appraisal of their reservationists. I'm going to offer a one-time freebie, and I expect most of the reservationists will do so badly that the bosses will rush like mad to sign them up for the seminars I'll be offering on the proper way to take a reservation . . . and then sign up for monthly, bimonthly or quarterly surveys to make sure they stay on their toes."

"That sounds wonderful, Ozzie."

"I think it'll work very well, but the preparation is a tremendous amount of work. Weaver will have to fly out with you. I won't be able to get away then."

She tried to hide her disappointment behind a smile, but her cheek muscles had an achy feeling.

Desirée brushed out her hair, which had a wavy texture after being removed from the cornrows, though it was strawlike to the touch. It was badly in need of a touch-up and deep conditioning. Good thing her mother couldn't see it. Helen Mack had always stressed the importance of everyday hair care and breakage prevention. This was Wednesday, and Austin was going to pick her up after work on Friday and bring her back to his house. Monday they were to check in to the Hotel Exeter. How could she go anywhere looking like the Bride of Frankenstein?

"What's wrong, Desirée?"

"Oh, Mrs. Hughes, look at my hair. I just took out my braids, and it looks awful." She sniffed. "After all the sweating I've been doing, it doesn't smell any too good either. I've got to get my hair done."

"My goodness, you've got a lot of hair."

"That's why I won't even consider trying to do it myself. It's a hairdresser's nightmare, as well as a mother's. I don't know how Mom managed when I was a little girl. I would have run for the nearest hairdresser and handed them a pair of scissors so they could cut it all off."

"I'm all done with that stuff since I started wearing my hair natural," Mrs. Hughes remarked. "I just go to the barber along with Paul. But there's a girl living upstairs whose hair always looks beautiful. I'll ask her where she gets her hair done."

"I'd appreciate that, Mrs. Hughes. I'd feel better going somewhere that's been recommended, since I don't know any of the hairdressers in the area."

"Sure you do. We're going to miss having you around, Desirée. It's been a real pleasure having you here."

"It was so good of you to have me."

"I've got to take good care of you. You're important to my son."

Desirée had to ask. "Did he tell you that?"

"He didn't have to. I may be getting old, but my eyes still work. I don't know what he's going to do when you go back to Denver. I guess in your line of work you can arrange to work on the same jobs, so you can at least spend some time together until you can work it out."

"I hope so." At least working with him would keep them in contact. It wasn't much, but right now it was all she had.

The thoughts of traveling made her remember something she wanted to do. "Please excuse me, Mrs. Hughes. I just remembered a call I have to make."

She asked the operator to charge the call to her home phone. "Hello, Eve. This is Desirée Mack."

"Desirée! What a nice surprise."

"I wanted to give you a call and apologize to you. I know you had to make a lot of changes to the agent schedule for November when I got sick."

"No, not at all. Most of the changes I made were because we're so shorthanded . . . and because Ozzie isn't traveling this month. We moved Fran Perkins to do the Texas and New Mexico hotels with Weaver, and Sandy Wallace will be going to Chicago and Indianapolis with Phil. You have nothing to feel guilty about."

"Thanks, Eve. I appreciate it. So how's everything with your boyfriend?"

"He's wonderful. I was there for a long weekend a few weeks ago. Just between you and me, I'm seriously considering relocating to New York."

"It sounds serious."

"It is."

After they were done talking, Desirée wondered how willing she would be to pack up and move to New York if Austin asked her to. The way things stood now, no. She would have to have a commitment from him first, a commitment she might not ever receive.

She was still deep in thought when Mrs. Hughes looked out the window at the sound of a car door slamming shut. "Oh, there's Vivian now."

"Who?"

"Our upstairs neighbor, the one I wanted to ask who does her hair." Mrs. Hughes was getting to her feet. She went to the apartment door and opened it, standing in the doorway expectantly. "Hello, Vivian," she said.

Desirée heard a muffled greeting, then an affirmative

response when Mrs. Hughes asked her to come in. She held her hand to her hair, which she had caught at the crown with a coated rubber band, braided and wrapped the braid into a bun of sorts. It looked presentable, but she was still a little self-conscious.

She and the Hugheses' upstairs neighbor exchanged hellos before Mrs. Hughes performed the introductions. Vivian St. James was probably a few years older than Desirée, dark complexioned with luminous brown eyes and a lone dimple on the right. She wore her hair in a short layered cut, fuller on top and tapered in the back and on the sides, with wide, thick bangs that covered her entire forehead.

"Desirée is a friend of Austin's. She's staying with us for a few weeks," Mrs. Hughes explained when Vivian had sat down. "She and Austin went to Africa, and she came down with malaria."

"Malaria! Do people still get that?"

Desirée laughed. "Trust me, it's very much in existence in tropical climates. Just not in the U.S., so you don't have to cancel that trip to Florida or South Carolina."

"Vivian is the manager of personnel for a big company in White Plains," Mrs. Hughes informed Desirée.

"Well, not exactly manager, at least not yet. I'm just an administrator."

"I'm sure you'll be a manager soon."

"I hope so, Mrs. Hughes."

"Anyway, Desirée was saying she wanted to get her hair done before she goes back to work on Monday, and of course with my hair I wouldn't know what to tell her."

"You wanted to know who does good work," Vivian guessed.

"Exactly. Your hair always looks so nice."

Vivian laughed. "Thanks, but I'm definitely overdue for a touch-up. Lucky for me, the way it's cut pretty much hides all the new growth. I'm going on Saturday. I go to a salon in New York." She looked at Desirée. "If you're not familiar with New York you shouldn't go alone, especially if you're recovering from a serious illness. Why don't I call and see if I can get you an appointment around the same time as mine? That way we can take the train down and back together."

"That would really be nice, Vivian. But do you think they can take me on such short notice?"

"I've been going there for years. I'm sure Jean can do me this one favor. She can work on one head, then on the other as soon as the first one is rinsed." Vivian rose. "I'll go upstairs and call her now. I'll let you know what she says."

Eighteen

"Saturday night instead of Friday? How come?"

"Ozzie, my hair is a mess. I can't register at a luxury hotel looking like this. I'm going to the city Saturday to get my hair done. Vivian, your parents' neighbor, was nice enough to offer to bring me with her. She even got me an appointment." Desirée sighed. "I guess this will be a real test. If I can stand five hours at the hairdresser, I'm definitely ready to go back to work."

"Five hours?"

"It usually takes at least that long, sometimes longer."

Austin shook his head. "Makes me glad I'm a man."

"I'm glad you are too, chum," she said with a smile.

"You'll probably be exhausted by the time you get home."

"Probably, but just think of all the work you can get done while I'm getting beautiful."

"But I was looking forward to picking you up Friday night. I was even going to leave work early, believe it or not."

"That's wonderful, but it really doesn't make sense to do that, since Vivian and I have to catch the train for the city early Saturday."

"All right. I guess I'll just keep working on the phone QA project."

"How's it coming?"

"I'm working on the assessment forms. You know,

there are plenty of other services out there who appraise the performance of hotel reservationists. It's the type of business that can be run from your kitchen table, and rumor has it there's one woman out there doing precisely that. Our product has to be better than everyone else's."

She nodded. "I know."

"Part of the problem is the federal regulations regarding unauthorized recordings. We'll have to record the conversations to be able to assess them properly—it's impossible to try to do it while the conversation is taking place; nobody would be able to remember the details of an entire conversation—but afterward we'll have to erase the tapes instead of sending them to the clients with the rest of the package, at least for now. If it's a go, we'll have to get signed consent from anyone who's likely to answer the phone. That can get really sticky, especially if we're doing an eight hundred service. These people aren't known for career longevity—not that taking reservations is a career. Most of them are college students and will move on."

"I guess human resources will have to make a consent form part of the paperwork in the new hire package. I didn't know you were planning to survey the toll-free services."

"They're actually my main target for new business."

Desirée was silent. She knew he and Phil were both worried about the future of their company, and with good reason, but the devotion Austin showed to Wallace and Hughes was difficult for her to deal with. More than once she had felt practically abandoned. She wanted to be number one in his life, even though that seemed impossible.

She chewed on her lower lip. Maybe instead of feeling neglected she should try to help him. Maybe he would make her his assistant or something, and they could launch the new division together. Working side by side with him in an office setting with plenty of time to develop a relationship after hours would be much more enriching than their merely sleeping together all over the country.

"Ozzie, maybe I can help you."

"Maybe you can. A second opinion is always good. I'll show you what I've got. Maybe you can look at it while you're under the dryer or something."

"Well, aren't you the lady executive," Vivian commented as Desirée got into her car for the ride to the train station.

Desirée clutched the wine-colored leather portfolio Austin had given her. "Austin asked me to look at something he's working on. It's probably not the most exciting thing to read, but it beats looking at outdated magazines."

"Amen. I've got a book myself."

"I really appreciate this, Vivian."

"Sure, anytime."

"People are always saying how nasty New Yorkers are, but I've met some really nice people since I've been here. A friend of Austin's came to the hospital and braided my hair when I first got sick, and now you."

"Can I ask you something, Desirée?"

"Sure," she said, her apprehension masked by enthusiasm. She knew that when someone asked permission to ask something it was usually personal.

"Are you and Austin involved?"

"Yes, we are," she answered without hesitation. While she would be reluctant for anyone at Wallace and Hughes to know about the two of them, here in Mount Vernon, it was just fine if the entire city knew. "Why do you ask?"

"I was just curious. That was the first impression I

got, but when you said a friend of his had braided your hair I wondered if I had gotten my signals crossed. I mean, I presume you were talking about a female."

"I was, actually. She's a cousin of Zack's."

"Who?"

"Zack. He co-owns the building you live in with Austin."

"Oh. I don't know him. I dealt with the management company when I got my apartment. I only know Austin because he happened to be visiting his parents when I was moving in. He did say that he was one of the owners and that he hoped I would be happy living there."

"Now it's my turn to be curious, Vivian."

"Go ahead."

"Were you hoping Austin and I weren't involved?"

"I can't really say that, since I was pretty sure you were, but if nothing was going on I wouldn't mind starting something with him myself." Vivian giggled. "Of course, now that I know I'll have to look elsewhere."

"Are you in the market for a boyfriend?"

"I'm in the market for a *husband*. I'm thirty-three."

Desirée found Vivian's honesty about her attraction to Austin refreshing, and she was relieved by her willingness to forget about him. She liked Vivian; she would hate for a promising friendship to falter because of jealousy over Austin.

"Hey, wait a minute," she said. "You need to meet Zack."

"Well, I don't know. What's he look like?"

"He's gorgeous. With a capital *G*."

"You've got my attention."

"He's a doctor."

"When do you want to set this up?"

Desirée laughed at Vivian's haste. "I'll talk to Austin about it. I haven't seen Zack since I was in the hospital.

Maybe the four of us can do dinner and a movie or something."

That night Desirée wore her hair loose, something she always did after a touch-up, because she liked its silky texture, which she knew was only temporary. The moment she washed her hair herself the silkiness would give way to the familiar coarseness.

Dressed and ready to go, she was still fooling with her hair in her room when Austin arrived to take her to dinner at six. He knocked on the partially open bedroom door before entering.

"You look lovely," he said, taking her hands. It was the first time in weeks he had seen her fully dressed and made up. Her lips were their usual brick tint, her nail polish was freshly applied and her cheeks were glowing with a hint of deep red. She was wearing a maroon collarless blouse, gray slacks and a blazer of tiny maroon, gray and navy checks.

"I'm not really dressed up, Ozzie, but I guess it's an improvement over how I've looked lately. You did say I didn't need to get fancy."

"No, you don't. We're just going to a little Italian place near here."

Desirée took a deep breath before plunging on. "Do you mind if we go somewhere else? I'm not really in the mood for Italian." Actually, that type of cuisine was fine, but she had to do something about Austin's attitude. She'd never known a man who was so intent on being in charge.

The surprised look on Austin's face was priceless. "Uh . . . sure. What would you like?"

Desirée suppressed a smile. Too bad she didn't have a tape recorder handy, like the one she used on the job; she might never hear those four words roll off his lips again. "I want a big, juicy burger with melted Swiss cheese and big battered onion rings. And a strawberry milk shake."

He broke into a wide grin. "I've got just the place. Let's go."

"Let me just grab my coat and purse."

In minutes they had said good-bye to Paul and Sarah and were in the car. "We're not going very far," Austin said.

She could tell from the road sign that they had entered the city of New Rochelle. Austin parked near a two-story white stucco building with a sign reading SMITTY'S. "You'll love their burgers. I think they're the best in the county."

"It must be a well-kept secret," Desirée said as they walked in and saw maybe fifteen patrons, most of whom were at the bar. A middle-aged gentleman was just sitting down at a shiny black baby grand piano on a raised platform in the front corner.

"Oh, they do all right. It's early yet." He took her elbow and guided her to a booth, giving a generalized greeting to everyone present and receiving multiple replies.

"Hi there, Ozzie," a jeans-clad waitress greeted, adding, "Hi, Mo—" before stopping abruptly when she got a better look at Desirée. She simply placed laminated single-page menus on the table and disappeared.

Desirée met Austin's gaze. "If she called me Monique, I swear I would have tripped her."

They shared a laugh. "In that case I'm glad she cut herself off before she ended up sprawled out on the floor. And she didn't mean anything by it, Desi. It wasn't anything more than force of habit. But like I told you, no one is going to see me escorting Monique anywhere anymore. It started to end between us the moment I met you."

She felt a tingle as she smiled. "I won't even try to be blasé and make like it doesn't matter to me, because it does. I'm very happy to hear you say that."

"I meant it, Desi."

"I know you did."

"Did you get a chance to look at the assessment forms while you were at the hairdresser?"

"Yes. I thought they looked pretty good, actually. I couldn't think of anything to add, but I'd like to call and make a fictitious reservation myself, just in case there's something I'm overlooking."

"That's a very good idea. Why didn't I think of that?"

"Just think of me as your backup system." Her head turned as the rich sound of a baritone voice filled the room. The music was being provided by the man at the piano, but his lips weren't moving. "Who is that singing?" she asked.

"Lemuel Smith at the bar."

"He's got a beautiful voice, better than most of the people I hear on the radio. But I wonder how he can sing and tend bar at the same time?"

"He can do it now because there aren't a lot of people here. When it's busy there are three people bartending, and sometimes he still manages to sing while he's washing glasses."

"Does he ever stand or sit over by the piano?"

"No. Lemuel's shy. Some people sing in the shower. He only sings behind the bar."

Desirée began humming the melody of the ballad. She closed her eyes and imagined she and Austin were kissing . . .

The scent of food jolted her from her daydream. Her eyes grew wide at the sight of her burger, which she cut in half and still had to hold with both hands. "This is delicious," she said after swallowing the first bite.

"I knew you'd like it."

"Oh, and the onion rings are heavenly. I like this place, Ozzie. That bartender can sing for me anytime."

"Well, he's actually more than just a bartender. He owns the bar."

"Whatever. Ozzie, have you talked to Zack lately?"

"Yeah, a couple of days ago. Why?"

"Well, Vivian is such a nice girl. I thought it might be nice to introduce the two of them."

"Matchmaking, huh?"

"Why not? Zack isn't seeing anyone special, is he?"

"He's having too much fun. Something about him being a doctor makes all you black women go crazy."

Desirée giggled. "I guess it must be because our mothers tell us how happy they would be if we brought home a doctor, even a so-called 'fake' one like a dentist or an optometrist. Shucks, even if he was a vet it would be cause for celebration. It's a status thing." She leaned back, her lips going from upturned to flatline.

"What's wrong?"

"Nothing. I just remembered something unpleasant."

Austin played with his napkin. "Can I ask you something, Desi?"

"You can ask." The implication went unspoken.

"What happened with your engagement?"

Somehow she had known he was going to ask that. She sighed. "Something along the lines of what I was just talking about. Status. His parents felt I didn't have the right image for them."

"Image?"

"They were the first black family in Missoula, Montana. Funny how some people are so proud of being black . . . as long as you're not *too* black, if you catch my drift."

"Oh. That type."

"I'll never forget the shocked looks on their faces when Calvin brought me to meet them. You'd've thought

I had a third eye in the middle of my forehead, like a damn Cyclops."

"I'm curious. How did, uh, Calvin handle it?"

"I don't know. As soon as I realized what time it was, I was out of there."

"Wait a minute. Did this happen in Montana or Denver?"

"They were in Denver. I met them at a restaurant for dinner. Calvin showed up at my apartment not long after I walked out and apologized. He suggested that it could be worked out, but I told him it wouldn't work. I'm not interested in joining any family that doesn't feel I'm good enough for them. I don't care if they live across the street, and I would see them every day, or on the other side of the earth, and I would only see them once every couple of years. Just knowing how they felt would gnaw away at me. Attitudes like that don't change."

"It must have been difficult for you to do, especially if you loved him."

"Of course I loved him. I was going to marry him. I just don't happen to believe love conquers all, that's all. He couldn't help the way his parents were. Sometimes you have to admit you made a mistake and move on, and that's what I've done. I have no regrets." Just some hurt feelings, and even those were fading fast.

The bar began to fill up as they ate, although it was still far from crowded. They lingered about a half-hour after they finished eating, and on their way out Austin introduced Desirée to Lemuel Smith. She told him how much she enjoyed hearing him sing. She had enjoyed his choice of material almost as much as his voice; it was like tuning into a classic soul station during the Quiet Storm.

She relaxed in the passenger seat of the car, her heart

beating with growing anticipation. She was going home with Austin at last.

When he placed his palm on her lower thigh and began to caress her knee a shudder ran through her upper body. Thank heaven they didn't have far to drive.

She studied his profile, trying to memorize every feature, wanting to be able to picture him clearly when she was far away from him. His hair was so close to his head, she realized he'd probably been to the barber that afternoon. His nose was narrow, his mouth wide, with generous lips. He drove easily with one hand, keeping the other firmly planted just above her knee in a hold that was as firm as it was gentle.

"Home at last," he said, poising the control that opened the garage door.

"I missed it."

"It hasn't been the same without you." He accelerated, coming to a stop when the Buick was completely inside the garage.

They alighted at the same time, and she walked over to his side, where the door to the house was. Austin unlocked the door and flipped on the light switch, then stood back so she could enter.

"Welcome home," he whispered into her hair, too softly for her to hear.

Nineteen

"Well, everything looks the same," she remarked as she walked through the first floor.

"You say that like you've been away for years. It's only been a few weeks."

"I know. It must be because I spent most of my time upstairs." She removed her coat and tossed it on a chair, then walked over to the piano and ran her hands over the keys. "Do you play?"

"If I tell you something, promise you won't laugh."

"I promise."

"I always wanted to play the piano, but we didn't have one. When I bought this I started taking lessons, even though I'm a grown man. It's kind of embarrassing, going in for my lesson as some eight-year-old is leaving."

"Well, I think it's wonderful. You shouldn't let being grown interfere with doing something you always want to do. If you take that attitude, you might as well say your life is over. There are things I'd like to learn to do myself."

"Like learning how to speak French?"

She froze. "How did you know I can't speak French?"

"Because that night in Treichville you couldn't tell me what was being said."

"Oh. Well, I did take it in school, but that was a long time ago. I just know those typical tourist things."

He laughed, and she wanted to trace his laugh lines

with her fingertip. "That's all right. I know we hadn't landed the Accolade account when you sent us your résumé. I just couldn't help springing it on you that I knew."

"I've been found out." She stood in front of the piano and pounded out "Chopsticks." A moment later she felt arms encircling her waist from behind. She leaned into him, her head fitting perfectly in the hollow between his shoulder and neck, and tilted her face to one side to allow him to plant kisses along her jaw and throat. His hands moved up to cup her breasts, covering them completely with his large palms. "I missed you so much," he whispered, his lips mere inches from her ear.

"I missed you, too."

In an instant he turned her around and was kissing her hungrily. Desirée returned his urgency, her arms tightening around his back, pulling his shirt out of his belt so she could touch his skin.

Austin began to push her blazer off her shoulders. "You're wearing too many clothes," he murmured between kisses.

"So what're you gonna do about it?" she challenged, her arms going back around his neck. Then she squealed as she felt herself being lifted in the air. She tightened her grip around his shoulders and held on.

Austin headed for the stairs, ascending them quickly. Desirée rested her head on his shoulders and closed her eyes. This was so romantic, being carried up the stairs by her lover, the man of her dreams. Just like in the movies . . .

"Wow. My mother must have fed you five square meals a day. I think you've put on a few pounds."

Her eyes opened in an abrupt reflex action; so much for her fantasy. "Oh, Ozzie, you say the sweetest things." She giggled. No wonder he was moving so fast; he couldn't wait to put her down.

Austin was panting by the time he lowered her onto the bed. "Oh, no, none of that," she admonished. "We haven't even gotten started. You can be short of breath later." She gripped his shoulders and pulled him down on top of her.

They kissed over and over again. Desirée felt lightheaded; it was like she was suspended somewhere between the floor and the ceiling. She loved the way his tongue played with the small space between her front teeth. No man had ever done that before; in fact, one man she dated had asked if she had ever thought about having it fixed with braces.

They broke apart long enough to undress. Austin finished first; it amazed her how quickly he could get out of his clothes. She had slipped off her slacks, socks and underwear and was in the process of unbuttoning her blouse.

"Let me," he said. He began undoing the buttons with deliberate slowness. His long fingers felt warm against her cool skin.

At last the blouse was off, revealing a golden scalloped bra that emphasized the richness of her skin tone, which Desirée promptly unsnapped. She moved happily into Austin's embrace, and together they sank down onto the mattress.

For a few moments they merely lay there, not speaking, content just to be together in intimate silence, enjoying the closeness they had been deprived of during the long weeks of her recuperation.

Desirée's eyes were closed when she felt warm breath on her face. He kissed the niche at the base of her throat, where her pulse had quickened, then moved to tantalize her sensitive nipples with his lips and tongue. Desirée felt his erection brush against her thigh. She reached for it as he moved down her body but couldn't get hold.

Her sigh of frustration was muffled in the back of her

throat when he moved up, turning his attentions to her mouth and kissing her with a sudden fervor that took her off guard.

She raised her parted legs, cocooning him between them, and they both cried out in elation as he joined his body to hers. They quickly fell into a comfortable tempo, their bodies moving in an exquisite harmony, slow and easy at first, then harder and faster until, holding on to each other tightly, the liquid of ultimate fulfillment poured from both of them.

Desirée went on alert the moment she stepped inside the lobby of the Hotel Exeter. A small hotel by Manhattan standards, many of its suites were occupied on a permanent basis by people who preferred hotel living and could afford it. She knew that African-American guests were no longer unusual in luxury hotels, but she had her doubts about this particular place. She doubted these smallish hotels on the tony Upper East Side even employed many black maids.

The uniformed middle-aged man at the front desk looked at her with apprehension. "May I help you?" he offered stiffly.

"I have a reservation. Denise Miller."

The clerk made an entry into the computer without verbal acknowledgment. Desirée glanced at the other clerk, a younger woman, who stood watching her curiously.

"Any luggage?" the clerk inquired tonelessly.

"Of course I have luggage," Desirée snapped. "I'll be here for four days."

"Of course. I meant, would you be needing assistance with your bags?"

No apology, Desirée noticed, just a clarification. "Yes."

"I'll need a credit card."

Desirée had her card ready. Annoyed, she slapped it on the counter. If he wanted it, let him pick it up; damned if she'd hand it to him. Her eyes went to his badge. Joseph Strickland, his name was. Well, Joseph Strickland certainly had a surprise coming. She'd love to be a fly on the wall when the GM called him in and told him about her report. He hadn't addressed her by name, hadn't even called her "ma'am" or "miss." She knew if she had white skin and blond hair it would have been a completely different story.

The moment the door to her room was locked behind the bell person she picked up the phone and called Austin on his cell phone. "Hello, this is Denise Miller. Do you have a figure for me?"

"Yes, I do. It comes to nine hundred and fifteen dollars," he said impersonally.

"Thank you very much. I'll take care of that right away, within the next half-hour." She hung up the phone. Austin had just told her he was in Room 915. He had stressed that she shouldn't call the desk and ask for his room number, and now she knew why. They stood out like sore thumbs among the typical clientele, and he must have feared that the staff would figure out how they were connected, so he'd suggested this alternate method.

Before going to Austin's room Desirée dictated her unpleasant experience at the front desk. She found that making an outline made her summary easier to complete later, and she got started on that also.

"Well, hello there," Austin said when he opened the door to his room. He reached for her hand and pulled her inside. He had her in his arms before the door was completely closed but pulled back when she stood rigid and unyielding. "Baby, what's wrong?"

"Oh, I'm just annoyed. Those people at the front desk were looking at me like they'd never seen a black person before. And I guess when it comes to checking in here, they haven't."

"Ah, yes . . ."

"You knew about this?"

"I suspected. I didn't know for sure. This is my first time here." Wallace and Hughes rotated their agents to prevent them from being recognized; the most anyone could survey the same hotel was once a year. "From its profile it doesn't sound like a place that would have many black patrons. It's too far uptown to get a lot of business travelers, and I think leisure travelers would prefer staying in the business and shopping districts, say between Thirty-fourth and Fifty-ninth, where they're in the thick of things. I know this is the Museum Mile, but that's easily accessible by cab from downtown."

"All I can say is, that man looked like he was afraid my color would rub off on the walls and the sheets. There was a girl there, too, and she was just staring at me like she was trying to figure out whether I was somebody famous."

"She probably figured the only way you could afford to stay here is if you're a celebrity. Maybe she thought you were Naomi Campbell."

"I don't look anything remotely like Naomi Campbell, but that's a pet peeve we'll save for another conversation."

"Fortunately, I'm too short to be an NBA player." Austin laughed. "But as far as Strickland is concerned, he probably resented that you can afford to spend three hundred plus on a hotel room for three nights and pay a bill that's more than what he makes in a week."

"Do you think they'll fire him when they see my report?"

"No, but he'll be called upstairs by personnel and will

be issued a warning. He'll only be terminated if they receive repeat complaints, which, given their standard clientele, isn't likely. Of course, I mentioned Mr. Strickland's lack of warmth myself. The difference was very obvious between the way he treated me and the way he treated the man in front of me. If I'd had a thermostat it would have registered about twenty degrees cooler."

"I can imagine."

"Then, as I was leaving, I heard somebody say—I don't know if it was him or a coworker, 'What lottery did he win?' "

"The nerve!"

"I don't know if it was him or the other guy doing the talking. But that's all right. These are the things they pay us to find out. If everything was hunky dory they wouldn't need us. Fortunately, there's always something that needs work."

"All right, I feel better." She puckered her lips and closed her eyes. "You may kiss me now."

After three nights of being ogled by staff and guests alike, Desirée couldn't be happier when it was finally time to meet with the GM. She took an active part in the interview, ignoring Austin's signals requesting that she keep quiet. The manager, Seamus McTavish—upon learning his name, Desirée had jokingly remarked to Austin that he must be Italian—began to address both of them. Never before had Desirée been made to feel a real part of the interview. Most of the GMs she had encountered talked directly to Austin, with only a glance or two her way, but Mr. McTavish had not met Austin before this. Participating sure beat being window dressing or even an occasional interjection, Desirée thought.

Mr. McTavish shook both their hands and saw them

out. "Well, that went well," Desirée said as they waited for the elevator.

"You were very talkative."

She feigned innocence. "Did I say something wrong?"

"No, but I've always asked you to say as little as possible during these meetings."

"Yes, and I believed the reason was that I was new and it was a first-time client. Neither one applies in this case."

"That's true, but I wish you had discussed this with me beforehand."

The elevator stopped and opened, and they stepped into it before Desirée replied. "Am I being reprimanded?" she asked sharply.

"Very gently. I made a request, and you chose not to comply."

"Well, in that case let me say something very gently to you," she replied. Even though there was no one else around she spoke in a whisper that sounded harsh rather than gentle. "I'm tired of you being so controlling. Everything always has to be your way. You never ask me what I want, even if it's something for me."

"What do you mean?"

"Remember the day I arrived and you got me a pizza? You just assumed that was what I would want. You didn't ask what I liked on my pizza, or even if I ate it. For all you knew, I might hate it."

"Everybody likes pizza, Desirée."

"All right, maybe I couldn't eat tomato or dairy products. I didn't even realize you were getting the pizza for me until we got to the condo."

"I guess I just didn't consider that possibility."

"You do a lot of not considering, Ozzie. When I first got sick you would bring food home but you'd never call and ask what I wanted. *You* made the decision. I had to tell you what kind of cold cuts to get me, because you were ready to decide that for me, too. The only time I get to order for myself is when we're on a job, and I'm surprised you haven't taken that upon yourself, too."

"Why didn't you say something to me earlier? It's clear this has been on your mind for some time."

"I figured that was the way you were. Like I said the other night, some attitudes just don't change."

"I'm sorry, Desi," he said as the elevator door opened.

"It's all right. I just wanted to get that off my chest. And who knows, maybe now that I have, you'll be more aware of it."

"I'll try."

Desirée faced the television, not seeing the various news stories being reported. Something had been gnawing at her ever since she and Austin had been back at his house, but she couldn't identify it. He had certainly been sweet and considerate in the days since her blunt assessment of his behavior, but something wasn't right. She just wished she could figure out why she wasn't as happy as she should be.

She turned when he spoke her name. "What's this?"

"A peace offering. It's the least I can do, now that I know I've been driving you nuts since day one."

They were sitting in his den, having a couch potato dinner of mixed fried rice eaten straight out of the cartons with plastic forks. Desirée put hers down and accepted the envelope he held out.

She unfolded the paper, which appeared to be a certificate of some sort. She soon saw it was personalized with her name in Old English script. "One night at—" she read the name of the hotel and the date of the reservation. "That's Wednesday, isn't it? I don't get it."

"Wednesday happens to be the day before Thanksgiving, and that hotel happens to be right on Central Park

South, which means we can watch the parade from there."

"The Macy's parade I wanted to see?"

"That's the one. It's going to be too cold for you to stand outside for three hours. Even if it was fifty-five degrees and balmy, you're not strong enough. This way you can see the parade in comfort."

"Oh, Austin, I love you!" She gasped, covering her mouth. Where had that come from?

"I guess it's safe to say you want to go." He was smiling, the lines she loved forming on the sides of his handsome face.

"Yes, yes, yes!" As she got up to envelop him in the biggest hug she could muster, Desirée was glad he hadn't acknowledged her outburst.

"Desi."

"Hmm?"

"It's mutual."

She moved her face from his chest and looked up at him. "You're not being fair, Ozzie. I *told* you."

"Then I should tell you. I love you, Desi. I really do."

She brought his face down to hers for a light kiss. It was really going to be all right.

On Thanksgiving morning Austin and Desirée enjoyed a room service breakfast in front of the window of their fifth-floor hotel room on Central Park South, watching the marching bands, performers and giant balloon figures that were the hallmarks of the Macy's Thanksgiving Day Parade.

"This is wonderful, just wonderful," she said, wiping her mouth with her napkin as Santa Claus and his reindeer brought up the rear. "I've never had a nicer Thanksgiving. I just wish my mom could be here."

"I'm sure she's going to enjoy herself where she is."

"Yes, she will."

"Are you ready to go meet the rest of my family?"

"Yes, but it'll be hours before I can eat anything else. We had such a huge breakfast."

"That won't be a problem. Dinner won't be until about four or four-thirty, and it's only noon. By that time you'll be ready to eat again. It's going to take close to an hour just to get there from here."

They spent an enjoyable afternoon at the home of Austin's sister Charlene and her husband, Irwin Harris, who were just as friendly and welcoming to Desirée as Sarah and Paul Hughes had been. Charlene was an excellent cook, and Desirée even helped herself to the candied yams, despite her declaration that it would be a long time before she consumed any more.

She was surprised when Charlene informed Austin that he had a phone call. "It must be Zack," he said as he put his napkin on the table. "He's the only one who knew where I was."

"How about going to a movie later?" he asked Desirée when he returned to the table, where they were all having dessert.

"Sounds fine. Is Zack coming with us?"

"Yes. He's over at his parents' in the Bronx. I told him to give me a call after dinner if he wanted to do something."

"Gee, I wish you'd told me. I would have asked Vivian if she could join us."

"I didn't think about it. Where's Vivian today, anyway?"

"She told me her family lives in Connecticut someplace. You did mention to Zack that I wanted to introduce him to someone, didn't you?"

Austin hedged before telling the truth. "I, uh . . . no, I didn't."

"It's all right. I'll ask him how he feels about it when I see him later."

"Oh, are you planning to introduce Vivian to Zack?" Sarah asked.

"Yes. Don't you think they'll make a cute couple?"

"Yes, I do. Someone like Vivian is just what Zack needs. He's getting a little old to be gallivanting around with the companion of the week. His mama's probably as anxious for grandchildren as I am."

"You don't have to be married to reproduce, Mom," Austin said slyly.

"Any child of *mine* has to, Austin Hughes," Sarah shot back.

Charlene and Irwin exchanged glances, and Desirée thought she saw him nod to her.

"Mom, Dad, speaking of grandchildren . . ." Charlene began, but she was drowned out by Sarah's shriek of joy. When the excitement died down they learned Charlene's baby was due in June.

Desirée felt a twinge of envy toward Charlene. She and Irwin were clearly happily married and were now making the transition from two people in love to becoming a family. Would those lovely things ever happen for her and Austin?

"Zack, are you involved with anyone special?" Desirée asked. The three of them were sitting in the center of an upper row in the theater, she in the middle. They had arrived early to get good seats, and the theater was filling up before their eyes in the minutes before the lights would dim and the feature would begin.

"No, not really. Why? You wanna fix me up?"

"How did you guess?"

"Well, I knew you weren't asking about my love life because *you* were interested."

"Got that right," Austin interjected with such force that Desirée giggled. It was flattering. She placed a reassuring hand on his forearm.

"Besides," Zack continued, "people are always wanting me to meet their daughters, sisters, cousins, friends and so forth. I must be considered a real catch."

Zack's blatantly high appraisal of himself also made Desirée chuckle. "Well, I don't know about all that, but I do know a very nice girl. She's actually one of your tenants. But tell me, do you have a certain type of female you prefer?"

"Yes. Good-looking and intelligent."

"Is that all? I mean, no specifics?"

"I presume you mean with regard to looks, since intelligence is pretty much all-inclusive. Desirée, I've dated all kinds of women. Plump, thin, light, dark, tall, short—"

"Remember Sally Stokes?" Austin interrupted.

"I'll never forget her, all six feet, one inch of her. The girl was taller than me. Definitely the most statuesque woman I've ever gone out with. But there was one thing they all had in common; they were all fine."

"Good. She qualifies. So what are you doing the rest of the weekend? Next weekend is my last one here."

"I'm working all weekend. I'm sorry I couldn't meet her tonight."

"Me, too. Maybe next weekend."

"Okay, you two. Here come the previews," Austin said, reaching for Desirée's hand as the theater lights dimmed.

"Surprise!"

Desirée clutched her chest. She opened her mouth but no sound came out.

"She's stunned," Austin said, and everyone laughed.

"I'm speechless," Desirée said when she found her

voice. "Ozzie, when did you do this?" She turned to Sydney Chambers, whom she had been out with all afternoon. "And you! You needed a new couch, huh?"

Sydney shrugged. "I wanted to pick something that required a lot of looking. I was told to keep you out for six or seven hours."

Desirée turned to the group. "We went to every furniture store in Southern Westchester," she said with a laugh.

"Well, I couldn't let you go back to Colorado with no fanfare," Austin said.

Desirée looked around the room. Austin's secretary Elaine was there with a tall, thin man Desirée presumed was her husband. Charlene and Irwin Harris were there, and so was Vivian and a man she didn't recognize. Had Vivian brought a date? She hoped not; this was the ideal time for her to meet Zack.

She learned that wasn't the case when Sydney greeted the stranger. "Jonathan! I see you made it." She turned to Desirée. "This is Jonathan McIntyre. Jon, Desirée Mack."

"Good to meet you, Desirée."

"Likewise," she said, shaking his hand. At the first opportunity she caught Syd's eye and silently gestured that she was quite impressed. In response Syd flashed a discreet thumbs-up.

Desirée greeted Charlene and Irwin and jokingly made sure Charlene's glass held a nonalcoholic beverage. Then she moved on to Elaine, who introduced her husband, Nick Long.

She greeted Vivian with a hug. "I'm so glad you could come and be part of my surprise."

"I wouldn't have missed it, Desirée."

"That reminds me . . . where's Zack?"

"I was afraid to ask. Maybe he had to work, like he did last weekend."

"His schedule rotates, so I don't know. I'll find out."

Austin, talking with his sister and brother-in-law, saw her approach. "I know what you want to ask me," he said.

"What's that?"

"You want to know where Zack is."

"Yes."

"He escorted one of the nurses at the hospital to a wedding."

"Is he dating her?"

"No, they're just friends. She just didn't want to go by herself. He said he'd be over later. It's early yet."

"Good. Ozzie, it was really sweet of you to invite people over just to say good-bye to me."

"I can't believe you're leaving in three days. What am I going to do?"

"Come to see me as soon as possible, I hope."

"I'll have to do that." He kissed her lightly on the mouth.

"I'm going to let Vivian know Zack will be over later."

On the way Desirée was intercepted by Elaine. "You know, I was wondering why Monique hasn't been calling Ozzie lately. Now I know."

Desirée realized Elaine had seen Austin kiss her. She pulled the other woman aside and spoke in a low voice. "I need a favor, Elaine. I don't want anyone at Wallace and Hughes to know about us. It happened during our trip, and I don't know where it's going. . . . It's very confusing at times. The whole thing has been very unconventional, almost like a dream."

"I guess it's hard to separate what's real from what isn't when you're pretending to the outside world that you're married." Elaine grasped Desirée's shoulder. "Don't worry; I understand how you feel. I won't say a word."

Desirée could only smile and nod; Elaine's simple words contained the equally simple answer to what had been troubling her.

Twenty

"You want to go back to the condo? Why? Are you upset about something?"

"No, Ozzie. You've been wonderful, actually."

"Then why do you want to leave? I don't get it."

"It's because I don't really belong here, Ozzie. I'm starting to get confused over this whole fantasy/reality thing. When we were on assignment we were playing. Now I'm practically living with you. It's too quick. I feel like I've jumped from the frying pan into the fire. I don't know what to make of it."

"I'll tell you. You're staying with me because that's what we both want."

"I'm not denying that, Ozzie; that would be foolish. But it's not working for me like this. I don't want you to take it personally. It will be better this way for me."

"Desi, you've stayed with me the whole time you've been in New York, except when you first got here and when you were at my parents'. You leave in three days. Why not just stay here? I mean, what difference can three days possibly make?"

"It will help clear my head." She tried again. "Look, Ozzie, I'm not trying to give you a hard time here, nor do I want to seem ungrateful. I'm asking you to believe me when I say this is best."

* * *

"Thanks so much for listening, Vivian. I really needed an ear."

"I can understand your being concerned, but I don't think it's that bad, Desirée."

"You didn't see Austin's face. He barely spoke to me last night or this morning."

"Well, maybe you should have told him what you were planning this morning instead of after the party."

"That seems dishonest somehow. I made the decision, and I thought telling him right away was the only decent thing to do, not pretend everything was fine when it wasn't. I knew that meant I was going to put a damper on what should have been a happy moment, but I didn't see any other way." Desirée tried not to think of last night. The space they kept between each other in bed was vast, as if they were afraid to touch each other, even accidentally. It was even worse than the time they'd had to share a bed in Ghana, before they had declared their feelings for each other. Whoever had said never go to bed mad was a very wise soul.

"Anyway," Desirée continued, "I was glad we brought the car Wallace and Hughes leases to Austin's so I could use it once I felt well enough. I was able to just load up my clothes and drive off this morning."

"Well, I understand how you feel, but I'm not surprised that Austin didn't get it. He's a man. That says it all."

"I guess I could have explained it better. Staying with him in real life right after staying with him under pretense is too much for me. No wonder I'm confused. I'm always right there, anytime he wants me. There's no courtship. Once in a while I'd like to say I've got other plans, not to be making it up but because it's the truth. Ozzie and I aren't married; we've just been acting like we are, and because of that we're both missing out on something special. Besides, I still don't have the slightest idea if we're going to be able to sustain our relationship after I go home." She sighed. "This has got to be the weirdest relationship I've ever been in."

"Don't knock it. At least you're in one. I'll probably never get to meet the famous Zack."

Desirée nodded. She, too, had been disappointed when Zack didn't show up last night. "I thought you said he and this nurse were just friends," she hissed to Austin at midnight, who said he honestly didn't know what was going on. Desirée had spoken to Zack when he called earlier that morning to apologize for missing the party. It turned out that he and the nurse *were* just friends, but he met someone at the wedding and ended up spending several hours with her after the reception. Desirée had smiled in spite of feeling let down. She visualized all the single women at the wedding making a play for the handsome doctor who was escorting a female friend. A real catch, Zack had described himself. He was probably right.

Now she had an idea. "You know, if you want I can give him your number. That way he can call you and the two of you can set up a meeting yourselves."

"Thanks, but no thanks. I've met so many jerks over the years that I can't shake, I've learned to keep my phone number almost as sacred as my Social Security number when it comes to not giving it out. I guess it just wasn't meant to be."

"Hello."

"Hi, Desi, it's me."

"Hi, Ozzie!" Desirée was happy to hear from him, but she found herself holding her breath. He had barely said good-bye to her when she left his place that morning. What was he calling to tell her?

"Did you have a good day today?"

"Yeah, it was real nice. I had some shopping to do. Vivian drove up, and we had lunch, then went shopping together."

"Good. Uh . . . have you eaten dinner yet?"

"No, it's only five o'clock. Probably in another hour or so."

"Would you like to have dinner with me? There are plenty of restaurants in White Plains, so we won't have to go far."

She broke into a grin. "You want to take me to dinner?"

"Yes. Do you want to come?"

"Yes."

"Six o'clock all right?"

"That's fine."

As she replaced the receiver she smiled and wondered if he was going to bring her flowers.

Desirée's spirits were low as the jet became airborne. She was going home, leaving Austin behind, after what had been the happiest period of her life. If she weren't on a crowded airplane she would curl up in a corner and cry her heart out.

"You all right, Dez?" Weaver asked.

She forced a tight little smile. "I'm all right." *And don't call me Dez,* she thought crankily. Austin's name for her was special, but it irritated her when people she wasn't friendly with shortened her name like that, like it would really wear them out to say three syllables.

She knew she was especially grouchy because it was Weaver sitting next to her and not Austin. Weaver was a pleasant enough fellow, and he kept to himself, which was fine—the last thing she wanted was a lot of meaningless small talk. The female flight attendant certainly found him handsome, with his dark red hair and matching neat beard, judging from her sweet tone when she offered him refreshments. Desirée resented the way the attendant looked at her, as if she was trying to figure out what their connection was. Of course she and Weaver weren't a couple, but it was none of the woman's business.

"You're tired, aren't you?"

"A little," she admitted. "This flight seems endless, and these doggone seats feel smaller every time."

"We're almost there. It's a good thing they flew us out a day early. You'd be too tired to start work this afternoon."

"I'm glad, too." That had been Austin's idea; he had instructed Eve to make the travel arrangements for the day before the survey. She was looking forward to spending some time with her mother. "But I'm curious about something, Weaver. I live in Denver, but where are you going to stay tonight? Do Wallace and Hughes have company-owned property in Colorado?"

"Not that I know of, but I have friends here. I'll be bunking with them tonight. I'll see you at the hotel tomorrow."

"Mom!"

As Desirée embraced her mother, her unhappiness over being separated from Austin was momentarily forgotten. The emotional impact of seeing the very first person she had known in her life after a prolonged separation was too much for her, and she began to cry.

"Baby, what's wrong?"

She could barely get the words out. "I guess I just realized how much I missed you."

Helen's arms tightened around her daughter. "Yes, I know, sweetheart. I missed you, too. And I've been worried about you. I don't care what Austin said about how well you were doing."

"I'm fine, Mom. Honest. I still get tired easily, but the doctor says I'm going to feel that way for a couple of months yet."

"You look wonderful, that's for sure." Helen stroked her daughter's hair. "Are you taking care of your ends?"

Desirée giggled; it was so like her mother to ask if she was following her hair care regimen. "It was braided most of the time. I had it touched up, and I've been going in for washes and sets every week since I've been feeling better. I'm still not up to doing it myself. Besides, it comes out so much nicer when they do it."

"It does look nice. Just don't use a curling iron unless you absolutely have to; it'll break your hair off."

"Under the dryer, Mom. I blow dry only occasionally."

"That's my girl." Arm in arm, they fell into step along the long hall that led to the main terminal. "Your friends have been calling to see when you're coming back; Alisha, Eva, Lorna. They were all shocked when I told them you had malaria."

"I got get-well cards from them. I'll call them tomorrow, before I start my assignment."

"And where is your companion? You said someone was traveling with you."

"He's probably already at the baggage claim by now. He's meeting a friend. I'll see him at the hotel we'll be working at tomorrow. I'll be doing two hotels, both of them in the Tech Center."

"You don't look to me like you're ready to go back to work, Desirée."

"It's the flight. I worked in New York and it went fine. I just took a few catnaps during the day. I shouldn't even have to do that too much anymore."

"Well, at least you can work without having to drive all the way to Boulder."

"Oh, Mom, it's only twenty-five miles. And I will be driving up there eventually, after these two surveys. I'll be working in the office, at least part-time, while work is slow over the holidays. It'll be nice to see everyone again. But I'll see Mickey at the second survey in the Tech Center. He's going to be my senior agent, and Weaver—he's the one who flew out with me—will work with someone else; one of the fellows, he said."

"Who's Mickey?"

"He's the one who trained me and supervised me on my first assignments."

"Oh, yes, I remember. The one you said was real good-looking. Tell me, what does Austin look like?"

"He's handsome. Not like Mickey, though. Mickey is both beautiful and rugged at the same time, with a great build. Ozzie's not as large, but he looks pretty good. I've got some pictures of him that I can show you." It was part of the job to photograph their rooms, as well as their room service trays, which they were able to do in privacy; and they had cheated with the Polaroid and taken some photos of each other—"test shots," Austin had called them.

"And will I get to meet him anytime soon? You've been pretty mum where he's concerned, but I can tell he cares about you very much."

"The feeling's mutual, Mom, but right now we're just going with the flow. I don't even know when I'll see him again."

"Well, surely he said something when he took you to the airport."

"He didn't take me to the airport."

"He didn't!"

"I know it sounds bad, Mom, but it's okay. They've been having some problems with someone on their staff who's been sabotaging their work and sullying their corporate reputation. He's been very busy working to counter that, since if it keeps up, it could put them out of business. He came to the condo where I've been staying and said good-bye. All he said was that it wouldn't be long before we were together again, which is pretty damn vague." She sighed. "Right now I just want to get my luggage and go home."

"All right. We won't talk about it anymore."

The hotel was full of business types, half wearing traditional business suits and the other half sporting more casual attire, blazers over jeans and moccasins. It was easy to blend in. It had been raining in Denver for two days. Fortunately the temperature was in the forties and fifties, too warm for snow.

As she had done in other surveys since her illness, Desirée made sure she got plenty of rest in between outlets. A twenty-minute catnap was usually sufficient to refresh her energy level.

Still, working with Weaver was different from working with Austin or Mickey. The two of them had virtually no contact, and she felt quite alone. She found herself relieved when it was time to check out of this hotel and check into the one nearby, also in the Denver Tech Center, where she would be working with Mickey again.

When she checked out she stopped and had lunch, then went to the next hotel, which was less than a half mile away. She smiled at the front desk clerk. "Denise Miller. I have a reservation. I know I'm a little early . . ."

"I'm sure we have a room ready for you, Ms. Miller. Welcome to the Charlton."

"Thank you."

She'd been in her room for three hours when the phone rang. "Hey, Niecy!" came Mickey's familiar voice.

"Hey, yourself. I wanted to see if you were in yet, but

I thought I'd wait a little longer before placing a call to your room."

"Good girl. You always want to be low key about contacting your senior agent, and if you're in a small hotel it's best to arrange to meet somewhere beforehand. You don't want to tip off the front desk. I'm in room ten eighteen, so you can call me direct from now on. What's your room number?"

"Five twenty. So tell me, how are things up in the high-rent district?"

"Ah, they're all right. I won't be getting any chocolates on my bed. This hotel isn't exactly the crème de la crème, you know."

"Since you don't mind slumming, why don't you come down?"

"Sure. I'll be right there."

When Mickey arrived minutes later they hugged like the good friends they had become. "Well, you don't look too bad," he said afterward. "In fact, you look like you've gained weight."

"That's what Austin says. I feel pretty good, but not quite like my old self. But I'm getting there, a little bit closer each day." She took a seat at the desk.

"No, sit here," Mickey said, patting the back of the more comfortable black upholstered chair in the corner.

"Why, Mickey! Are you actually being a gentleman?"

"I'm not all that bad."

"Tell me about South America."

"Brazil was great. But a couple of poolside bartenders have found themselves out of work, since I alerted management they were making change from their own pockets."

"That was bold."

"No, bold is the bellhop who gives you a free bag of marijuana because he's trying to drum up some drug business. That happened to me in Philly. I don't know why people try this stuff. They've got to realize that sooner or later the party's going to end. So, I understand Austin's mother nursed you back to health."

"Yes, and she couldn't have been nicer. My own mother couldn't have done more for me."

"Yeah, Mrs. Hughes is good people. Mr. Hughes, too. Tell me all about Africa."

She had just finished telling him about the pain of visiting the slave house on Goreé Island in Senegal when a bulletin came on the television. "The Williston Hotel in the Denver Tech Center has been evacuated after a member of the housekeeping staff discovered what looked like a bomb under a bed."

"Did you hear that? Isn't that where Weaver is?" Desirée asked.

"Yeah, him and Ernie King. It's Ernie's last survey. He resigned, you know."

"No, I didn't know. I really didn't know him well."

"Well, he might be going out with a bang. I'll bet he'll never forget this, being forced to leave a nice warm room to go out in a drenching rain."

"Ozzie, it's Phil on two. He says it's urgent."

"All right. Hold my calls, will you, Elaine?" Austin picked up the phone. "Phil, what's up?"

"I've got bad news, Oz."

Austin tensed. "All right, spill it."

"They had to evacuate the Williston this afternoon, all three hundred and fifty rooms. The maid found what looked and sounded like a bomb under the nightstand. It was in Ernie's room."

"Oh, no!"

"He swears he doesn't know anything about it. It wasn't real, by the way."

"That'll save his ass from serious criminal charges, but it won't do much for us."

"The GM is ready to strangle us. He's already threatened legal action."

Austin took a moment to vocalize his frustration with a choice phrase, slamming his palm onto the desk for emphasis.

"Yeah, I know just how you feel. I'm waiting to get the call from Fieldcrest, telling us to forget about next year. Do you realize that they're the second largest client we've got after Hopkins?"

"Ernie," Austin said angrily. "He has to be the one. He's been responsible for all the problems we've been having. And he's turned in his resignation, too? He wanted to foul us up one more time so he'd have a shot at Fieldcrest. What'd he tell us, that his wife wanted him home more? Bull."

"He insists it's the truth. He even told me the name of the restaurant he'll be managing. I called over there and asked for him. They said he won't be starting until the first of the year and offered me the present manager."

"All right, so he's not starting his own service, but somebody who is could be paying him to sabotage us."

"Like Raymond Roberts, the phantom? The detective says he doesn't think this man even exists, except on paper. Someone probably invented him to use as a front so they won't have to use their own name."

"That just means anyone could have set up that phony address and answering service. Our man hung out for a week, waiting for someone to check the mail, but no one did. We're right back to square one."

"Wait a minute, Ozzie."

Austin listened as Phil talked to someone in the background.

"Maddie started a log of agents who were in the office

in case we had another problem in the future, but she tells me she also made a list of who was in the office the times we had trouble. Now, she can't be a hundred percent sure, because she had to put it together after the fact . . ."

"All right, I get it. Just tell me if Ernie's on it."

"Yes. So are Jared, Kevin, Mickey and Bill Sampson. Everyone else was either here during one time but not the other, or not here at all."

"And Ernie is the only one of the four who was at the site of this fiasco. Like Jared, Kevin, Mickey and Bill, he came out here from New York when you did. Any of his family members or friends back home could have set up that mailbox. Add all of it together and what do you get, Phil?"

"He insists he doesn't know anything about anyone plotting against the company."

"Well, he's not going to say, 'Yeah, I'm the one.' "

"Not likely, but I've told him he's through, and that means we shouldn't have any more problems."

"No, we shouldn't. Who was with him, anyway?"

"Weaver."

"It's safe to rule him out. He was either here in New York or out on the road while everything was going on out there. Damn! If I'd known all this was going to happen, I would have gone out there."

"I'm sure Desirée would have liked that. So would I."

"Have you seen her yet?"

"She's at the Charlton with Mickey. Good thing, too. It's raining here, and pretty hard. Half the people at the Williston didn't have umbrellas and got soaked."

Austin couldn't stand thinking about Desirée being so far away from him, especially now, with Christmas so close. "I want to come out. Let me talk to Eve." He could finish up what was imperative in a matter of days. Elaine could take it from there, looking up the names, titles and addresses of everyone he was making a pitch to. She could now sign his name so well that probably only a handwriting expert could tell the difference.

Twenty-one

The mood in the office was tense. Everyone knew that Ernie King had been identified as the traitor and about the fiasco at the Williston Hotel and its possible repercussions on their jobs. There was little conversation among the usually chatty data operators, and no laughter. Desirée found the atmosphere uncomfortable.

Now that the surveys had slowed down for the holiday season she was working half-days in the office, reporting to Phil's secretary Maddie, who set her up proofreading reports line for line. It was tedious work, but Desirée was glad for it; it kept her mind occupied. The only time she was aware of the tension in the office was when she went to make coffee or use the rest room.

"How is it looking for next year?" she asked Maddie, who was opening the mail.

"We've gotten some of the larger management companies and chains, but the Hopkins Group only signed for six months, one set of surveys for all their hotels instead of two. That's scary enough by itself, since they're one of the larger clients, but what makes it worse is that we haven't heard from Fieldcrest at all, and after what happened at their hotel they probably won't, no matter what Phil says to them," Maddie replied in a whisper.

"What'll happen if they don't sign?"

"Layoffs."

"Sounds like I'd better rent my apartment for another few months and keep staying with my mother. I think I'm about to experience the last-hired, first-fired blues."

"Maybe not."

Desirée looked at the secretary sharply. "What do you mean?"

"I know they paid you while you were out sick. I mailed your direct-deposit notices to you, remember?"

"Oh, that's right."

"Bill said Ozzie insisted on it, and that means you've got him in your corner. I also know there are other agents they aren't that happy with. Like Weaver Mobley, who's supposed to be bringing in sales and doesn't. The only reason he's still here is because they never replaced Phyllis, you've been out sick and now Ernie is leaving. They're short-handed, and for the time being they still have a full workload.

"Then there's Fran Perkins, who's been described by several clients as 'loud' and 'unprofessional.' She's not thought of too highly, either. My hunch is that those two will get their walking papers before you do."

Desirée shrugged. She realized part of Maddie's job was to be a go-between for Phil Wallace and Bill Sampson. Nothing probably happened in the office without her knowing about it. "Maddie, what about Bill?"

"What about him?"

"He's in the office every day, and he's got very expensive child-support payments."

"Phil and I considered him, too, but there's really no way he could have done it. He's got a pretty heavy schedule since he's been working that second job. He rolls in here every day at around nine-thirty and is gone by five, and when he is here, he's always holed up in his office. He's never near the reports."

"I guess that makes sense."

"You almost sound sorry that it's Ernie and not him."

"No. I don't even know anything about Ernie."

"Well, you might get mad at me for saying this, but I thought it was Mickey."

"Mickey?"

"Yeah. He's asked to become a partner, you know. Phil and Ozzie turned him down. He's very knowledgable and very ambitious. But I'm glad it wasn't him. Phil and Ozzie would have been heartbroken."

"I'm glad it wasn't him either, but I never would have suspected him. I'm not upset that you did, though." Desirée patted the stack in front of her. "These are done, and it's only eleven o'clock. Do you have any more?"

"Not right now, actually, but I'm sure Diane could use some help editing, now that we've determined that everything leaving this office has to be perfect. Don't worry. Once we get to the last date Ernie was in the office we're in the clear, and then we can get things back to normal."

"Sure. I'll take these over to her and volunteer."

"I've already edited these," Diane explained to Desirée, handing her a large stack of printed documents with proofreader's marks scrawled in red ink. "What I need help with is getting them made on the computer. Jennifer is on vacation this week, and we're swamped."

"I can handle that."

"Do you know how to use the network?"

"No, but I'm sure I'll catch on quickly once you show me how."

"Confidence. I love it!" Diane pulled up a chair next to Desirée.

Within ten minutes Desirée was bringing up reports on screen and making the changes and corrections Diane had indicated on the draft copies.

"Oh, I'd better get a pen so I can write this down. Be right back."

"You won't find any pens in the supply closet."

Desirée remained standing. "I won't? Why not?"

Diane chuckled. "Because Phil Wallace doesn't believe in providing employees with pens that he feels will end up at their homes. There are yellow legal pads in there, correction fluid, letterhead, envelopes and folders for completed client packages, but no pens or pencils. This company is run on a shoestring, didn't you know?"

"I guess I didn't."

"Here, use my pen."

Desirée took the pen Diane offered and sat down. "Thanks."

As each set of documents was completed, Desirée did a mass print. When the last set was sent she went over to the printer to collect her work.

There was a single printer used for the entire office, and someone—probably Maddie—had taped down a typed note on the table, requesting that all documents being picked up be looked at carefully to avoid anyone inadvertently taking someone else's work, as print jobs were often mixed together, depending on the order in which they had been sent to the spool.

Eve, the travel agent, was at the printer going through the paper in the output tray.

"You're looking very pretty today," Desirée told her. Eve was wearing an emerald green dress with a turtleneck and a pleated skirt. It was quite attractive with her red hair, and she appeared to have lost more weight.

"Thanks. I've got a date tonight. You know, I'm just looking for two lousy pieces of paper," she said. "There's a lot of stuff belonging to operator nine-seven-eight. Who's that, anyway? Did they hire someone new?"

"That's me. I've been helping Diane."

"Well, I hope my sister's treating you right. I know she's frantic, with one of her assistants on vacation."

"Are you two sisters? I never would have guessed." They had the same last name, but she'd never thought much of that, since there were a lot of people named Brown. As Desirée studied Eve, she realized that the freckled, curly-haired redhead with a tendency to overweight shared the same saucer-blue eyes as her slim, blond, straight-haired sister, who had no freckles. Their eyes were their sole common trait. "You two don't really look alike."

Eve's smile was sad and ironic, almost a nonsmile. "I know. She's prettier than I am."

Desirée was speechless. She certainly hadn't been thinking any such thing; she simply had been a little slow to recognize any similarities between them. Had there been anything in her words that could have been taken out of context, something unwittingly callous? What was it she'd said . . . "You two don't really look alike."

No, she decided, there was nothing wrong with that. The resignation in Eve's voice was rooted somewhere else, perhaps from a lifetime of having overheard insensitive adults compare her unfavorably to her sister. She probably made it a point to point out Diane's more significant attractiveness before anyone else did, feeling it wouldn't hurt as much if it came from her. How could anyone have any self-esteem with that kind of attitude?

Desirée smiled, trying to be cheerful. "Since you've got a date tonight it sounds like you've said good-bye to your New York love."

"Oh, no." Eve's expression brightened, but she spoke in a whisper. "He's here in town."

"He is? How wonderful!"

"Yes. We've been spending just about every minute together."

"Desirée, I know you'll be leaving soon, but can you pick up the phones for me?" Maddie asked. "I'm going to lunch now."

"Sure. Can I do it from the editing room?"

"Oh, yeah. There's a phone in there. Thanks a lot."

The phones were quiet as more of the staff left for lunch. Desirée was working to insert the reprinted pages with the ones that hadn't been altered and was glad for the silence.

She reached for the phone when the line began to ring. "Good afternoon, Wallace and Hughes. Desirée speaking."

"Hello, beautiful." Austin's melodious voice filled her ear.

"Ozzie, hi!"

"Miss me?"

"You first."

"More than I can tell you."

She closed her eyes and spoke from the heart, forgetting she was sitting in an office at Wallace and Hughes. "I miss you, too." She opened her eyes and chose her next words carefully, not wanting to sound overeager. "I hope it won't be too long before I see you again." Maybe he was calling to tell her that he was coming, she thought hopefully.

"Soon, Desi, I promise. But right now I need to talk to Phil."

She tried to keep the hurt out of her voice. "Sure. I'll get him for you."

"Desirée, Frank is coming by for dinner."

"I was wondering when I'd get to see ol' Frank."

"He was here while you were on your assignments. He'll be here any minute."

"Any minute?"

"You forget, you were sleeping. It's almost six-thirty."

"Oh, that's right."

Frank Mitchell was a heavyset, dark-skinned man in his late fifties with a booming voice that perfectly suited his position as circuit-court judge. He asked about her trip and seemed genuinely interested. "I've always wanted to go to Africa," he said. "Perhaps I can convince your mother to come with me."

"After dinner you'll have to look at Desirée's pictures, Frank," Helen said. "She's got beautiful shots of the markets and of the schoolchildren in their cute little blue-and-white uniforms."

"I'd love to see them."

After dinner Desirée returned to the spare bedroom of her mother's two-bedroom bungalow, where she had been staying, to get her photographs. She picked up the phone when it rang, knowing her mother was entertaining Frank in the living room. "Hello."

"Hi, Desi."

Her spirits lifted right away at the sound of Austin's voice. "Hi!"

"I just wanted to let you know I'll see you the day after tomorrow."

"You will?"

"I'm coming out. Everything's in play, now that we know it was Ernie, and Phil and I need to plot out damage control. There won't be much else happening between now and January." He paused. "God, I miss you."

"I miss you, too, Ozzie. I'll be so happy to see you. Will you be close by?"

"Phil offered his house, but he lives all the way out in Golden. I'm going to stay with Mickey, who's right there in Boulder. I'm looking forward to seeing you again, too. How are you feeling?"

"Pretty good. I worked in the office today until one without a problem. What time do you land?"

"Noon."

"I'll meet your plane."

"What about work?"

"I'll work in the afternoon instead of the morning. I'm a lot closer to DIA than I am to Boulder."

"Wonderful. It feels so good to tell you I'll see you soon."

Austin's call, so much different from their rushed conversation at the office, did wonders for Desirée's energy level, as well as her mood. She immediately began going through her things, trying to decide what to wear. Her wardrobe had been so limited during their African stay, and then in New York; she could only fit so much into two suitcases and a garment bag.

It wasn't until she was falling asleep that it suddenly occurred to her, from somewhere in her subconscious, that it was rather odd for Eve Brown, the company's travel agent, to know that her typist ID code was newly assigned.

Twenty-two

"Guess what, Desirée?" Maddie said. "Phil landed another client. It's a cruise line."

"A cruise line? That's great news. I didn't know he was going after sales."

"Oh, yes. He also approached a chain of movie theaters."

"Movie theaters?"

"Yes. There are plenty of things to check out. Gooey seats, cloudy screens, stuff like that. But we haven't heard from them yet. Ozzie can't do everything by himself, you know; and he's been so busy preparing that phone reservation QA. But get this: The cruise line has eight ships they want us to survey, and Phil told me I might be able to take a cruise if they're short of agents. Can you imagine, me and Jared Fisher on a cruise together?"

Jared Fisher was an agent in his early thirties, the very embodiment of tall, dark and handsome. He reminded Desirée of a young Gregory Peck. "I didn't know you had a crush on Jared."

"Are you kidding? Any woman with a pulse would have a crush on him."

"Didn't Karen used to date him?"

Maddie rolled her eyes. "Karen's dated everybody."

Desirée laughed. "I'm out of here. Don't forget, I

won't be in tomorrow until about one-thirty. I told Austin I would pick him up at the airport."

Desirée stood at the gate, waiting for the passengers to disembark. She hoped Austin wouldn't be the last one to get off.

There he was. He looked exhausted. She wondered if he had been up all night.

He held out his arms, and she happily walked into them. "You look great, Desi," he said, pulling her close.

"Thanks."

"What was it somebody said in that Eddie Murphy movie, *Coming to America*—'Somebody ought to put you on a plate and sop you up with a biscuit.' "

She laughed. "I remember that line. And I hate to tell you this after such a wonderful compliment, but you look beat."

"It's been a rough couple of days, but I had to get as much done as I could. All Elaine has to do now is get addresses and mail out the packages. At least I had the news of landing our first cruise line to give me a boost. You heard about that, didn't you?"

"Yes, Maddie told me. I think it's wonderful."

"I'm sorry I didn't get a chance to call. Between working and getting packed, there wasn't a minute to spare, and I didn't want to ask to speak with you directly at the office. We did agree to keep under wraps as long as we can."

She wished she could be under wraps with him right now. "That's all right; I knew you were busy. But how long will you be here?"

"Until the twenty-eighth. I need a break. I've been working like a dog."

"So you'll be here for Christmas!"

"Yeah. I guess I'll be able to wangle an invitation for dinner with, uh, somebody."

She linked her arm with his. "You know, I always wanted to be 'somebody.' "

"Welcome to Denver, birthplace of the cheeseburger," Desirée said with a wave of her hand as they left the terminal building after Austin had claimed his luggage.

"I didn't know that. I thought this was just the Napa Valley of beer."

"We have that claim to fame, too."

"One of Phil's neighbors is an executive at Coors, I think. Then again, maybe it's one of the others. Most of the breweries seem to have plants out here."

At her car she handed him the keys. "You've got to tell me how to get out of here," he said. "I'll be okay once I get to I-Twenty-five."

"At the parking exit the signs direct you to the highway. Are you sure you don't want me to drive?"

"I'm tired, Desi, but not where I can't drive thirty minutes."

"You've been working too hard. Maybe you ought to take a nice cruise to relax," she hinted.

He laughed. "I intend to. They leave from Florida, so you know Kevin will schedule area hotels in conjunction with the cruises. Weaver has asked if he can go, too."

"Wait a minute. Would you take him with you instead of me? I'd love to go to Florida and take a cruise during the winter."

"Actually, they won't be starting until the spring, after high season."

"I can wait. So, is Weaver holding down the fort in White Plains?"

"Elaine is holding down the fort. Weaver is still out here someplace."

"He is? His work is finished, isn't it?"

"Yes, but he's got some time off, so he asked Eve to make his return after the holidays so he can celebrate with his friends here."

"Oh, yes, I remember. He stayed with them the night before we checked in at the Tech Center. But how did he know about the cruise line if he's off?"

"He called to check in, and we talked then."

"Oh. You know, Ozzie, I noticed something kind of strange yesterday."

"What was that?"

She recounted the incident with Eve at the printer. "Why would she know all the operators' ID numbers? Her work has nothing to do with theirs."

"She wouldn't, unless she's up to something. Like botching our reports."

"Do you suppose she could be in league with Ernie?"

Austin's gaze became steely. "I don't know, but I intend to find out."

When they arrived at Wallace and Hughes, Austin immediately went into Phil's office for a closed-door conference, while Desirée sat in for Maddie, who left for lunch. She wondered what was going on in there.

"Damn it, I feel like an idiot. She makes her own hours and often comes in early, before anyone else is here. She had every opportunity to change the original answers or go on the network and alter what had already been printed and make a switch. Yet I didn't even think of her."

"Don't beat yourself up, Phil. It never occurred to me that Ernie had an accomplice. But do you think Diane is involved, too? They *are* sisters, after all."

"My guess would be no. I think Eve might be a little jealous of her sister's good looks. You've got to admit, Diane does make her look awfully dumpy."

"Think we should ask her? Sometimes if you catch people off guard they say more."

"Let's do it."

Diane greeted Austin warmly, then took a seat at Phil's request. "I'm so glad all the problems are over," she remarked. "Now things can get back to normal around here."

"Diane, I'm going to be very direct with you. We have reason to believe Eve was involved in altering the reports," Phil said.

"Eve? Oh, come on. Eve doesn't think about anyone except her new boyfriend."

"What new boyfriend?" Austin asked.

"This guy she's seeing. I haven't met him. He lives in New York, so they don't see each other very often."

"Well, what's his name?"

"She hasn't said. She's been awfully closemouthed about the whole thing, but that's just how she is. She's always been a little paranoid, like she's afraid I'll try and steal him from her or something."

Austin and Phil exchanged glances, and Phil said, "Thanks, Diane. It looks like we were wrong. I'd appreciate it if you didn't say anything to Eve about this. No point in getting her upset."

"All right." She left, closing the door behind her.

"Nice touch," Austin said. "I know you don't think Eve is innocent. If anything, this New York boyfriend is probably Raymond Roberts."

"Yes. But I don't think Diane is involved." Phil hit the intercom. "Desirée, would you tell Eve I need to see her?"

"She's not in today."

"I'll need her home number, then. No, never mind, I have it." He hung up, then rummaged around in his desk. "I forgot about the employee directory. Here it is."

"Don't call her, Phil."

"Why not?"

"Let's show up on her doorstep. The surprise factor, like you said. We might get more out of her."

"All right. Let's roll."

Eve hummed a show tune as she put away her groceries. She had never been so happy. The love of her life was with her. It would be the best Christmas ever. She couldn't wait to see the look on her family's faces when she showed up for Christmas dinner at their parents' home with a man on her arm. No one else made her feel the way he did. She would show everyone who said she would never get a husband. Not only would she get married, but she would do it before Diane.

She was still working when the doorbell rang. "Would you get that for me, sweetie?" she called out. "It's probably the mailman."

Austin and Phil waited for someone to ask who it was before opening the door, but the door simply opened without a word. When Weaver Mobley saw the two of them standing there, he attempted to slam the door in their faces, but Austin intercepted with his foot.

"It's too late, Weaver. We're on to you, you piece of crap," Austin spat out. "But whatever you tried to do to us, it's all over and you've lost. Come on, Phil. We've got what we need."

"Thanks for making it so easy for us," Phil said before turning away.

They got into Phil's car and drove off. "Damn," Austin said under his breath. "Weaver. It was him all along. He's doing business under the name of Raymond Roberts, right from New York, while we're scrutinizing everyone in Boulder and considering him above suspicion because he wasn't around."

"We looked at everyone but Eve Brown, who was doing all his dirty work. Damn. He probably gave her some line about being in love with her."

"And he had the nerve to ask to survey the cruise line. He wanted to botch that for us so he could go after them himself."

"I'd like to kill him," Phil said through gritted teeth.

"We'll take care of him. He's violated the noncompete agreement he signed, so as soon as I'm back in New York I'll be paying a visit to Mike Overton." Michael Overton was Wallace and Hughes's attorney. "But for now we need to work on salvaging our clients."

"It's got to be handled delicately," Phil agreed. "We don't want to sound like idiots by saying that one of our own set out to do us in."

"You're the expert at handing sticky situations around here," Austin said. "In the meantime I'd like to take a look at Eve's agreement. It might not be as easy to get rid of her."

"Shouldn't be too hard. We'll just withdraw our business and move it elsewhere. We'll still retain all the frequent flier miles we've earned. But I want a locksmith to change the locks on the door that connects her office with ours. Let her get her own damn printer. I don't want her in our office at all. See how long her agency stays operational after she loses our business."

Twenty-three

Desirée was bursting with curiosity. She had barely seen Austin since he'd gotten into town. From the moment they'd arrived at Wallace and Hughes and he disappeared behind Phil's closed office door for a conference, everything had been a blur. Right after calling Diane Brown in, he and Phil had gone rushing out of the office with nothing more than a "Be back later."

She waited to hear from him, hoping he would want to come to her mother's house, but he didn't call until after nine P.M. "It's all over," he said tonelessly.

"What happened, Ozzie?"

"It wasn't Ernie, it was Weaver."

"Weaver! But he was in New York or traveling when all the problems occurred. How could he be responsible for what was going on in Boulder?"

"He had an accomplice: Eve Brown. And Phil and I both want to thank you, Desi. We never would have figured it out if you hadn't mentioned Eve knowing all the girls' ID numbers. That was what made us take a closer look at her."

"Eve! That's just incredible, Ozzie. She seems like such a nice girl, sweet and shy. She told me she has a new boyfriend, someone who lives in New York. It must be Weaver."

"It was. He answered the door when we went to talk to her. And he's not as devoted as she might have thought. Phil and I just met with both of them, and Weaver insisted that sabotaging the reports was Eve's idea."

"And she denied it."

"Yes, and we both believed her. The look of anguish on her face was genuine. It affected her entire body. She was clearly too upset to drive. Diane had to take her home."

"Poor Eve. She probably thought he really loved her. She's even managed to lose a few pounds. And in turn he offers her up as a sacrificial lamb the first chance he gets. She was used."

"Well, I can't feel too sorry for her. She did help him steal clients from us. She even admitted to planting the fake bomb under Ernie King's bed at the Williston."

"She admitted that?"

"Yes, after Weaver pointed the finger at her."

"That was really a bad move on her part. How did she get in?"

"I'm sure Weaver gave her his room number. She probably convinced the maid she was Ernie's wife and got her to let her in."

"Are you going to prosecute her?"

"We're not going to. Phil thinks it wouldn't be worth the trouble, and I'm inclined to agree with him. But the Williston isn't likely to be so charitable. She's the one, after all, who caused a panic and an evacuation. Weaver was the mastermind behind it all, but when it comes to measuring the actions actually taken at the hotel, legally he'd only be considered an accomplice."

"He must have planned it that way," Desirée said bitterly.

"Well, that's Eve's misfortune. Phil and I just want her out of here. Unfortunately, we can't get rid of her, since she's not an employee; but I do think we can make her life miserable enough that she'll want to leave. We're pulling all our travel business from her effective immediately, and that's a big chunk of her income. We had a locksmith come in this afternoon and change the lock on the door connecting her office to ours."

"But her office is part of the Wallace and Hughes suite. She doesn't even have a bathroom in it."

"Like I said, we can probably make her miserable. Not having a bathroom should do it. And if she's late paying her portion of the rent, we'll be able to force her out."

"My guess is, she won't be around that long. It would be best if she changes locations or even closes up, since she'll need money for legal counsel."

"She shouldn't want to stick around, given the circumstances, but some people have unbelievable nerve."

"What about Weaver?" Desirée found it extremely distasteful that Austin had recruited the man who was behind the scheme to topple Wallace and Hughes to escort her back to Denver, although, of course, there was no way any of them could have known that. Her heart ached for Eve, who didn't know that no man who truly loved her would ask her to do anything so despicable.

"No way are we letting him get away with this, but that will be handled in New York, since he works from that office. Eve already told us she'll testify against him."

"What about Diane? Was she involved in it at all? She seems so dedicated to her work."

"She is, and she had no idea what was going on. Eve confessed that she nosed around Diane's office and swiped her list of operator ID numbers. Diane feels pretty bad about the whole thing. She was the one who recommended Eve to be our in-house travel agent. She asked Phil not to be too hard on her, that there's a reason for Eve's behavior." Austin snorted.

"Diane is right, Ozzie. Eve has very little self-confidence." Desirée recounted Eve's comment about her sister being prettier.

"Listen, I'm sorry she's suffered emotional trauma, but she's getting a break from us as it is. Maybe she'll get some therapy, but it's not my problem, Desi."

"I know."

"Right now we're going after Hopkins and Fieldcrest. Hopkins only signed for six months, and after what happened at the Williston, Fieldcrest is probably shopping around for a new service. I've spoken with Dee Dub at Hopkins—"

"Does he really allow people to call him that?"

"He encourages it. Actually it's D.W., short for de Wessington. Anyway, I think they'll sign up for the rest of the year by June, and Dee Dub was also very interested in the new phone program and the seminars that we're launching. Phil has always had good rapport with one of the bigwigs at Fieldcrest. He's out of the office until after New Year's, but Phil will be flying to Dallas to see him the first week in January. I'm betting he'll come back with a contract."

"I've got my fingers crossed for you."

"I know you do, baby. I'm sorry I called so late; I know you still go to bed early. I figured you would want to know what was going on."

"There's something you didn't mention. What happened to Ernie?"

"Phil and I are going to meet with him in the morning. He'll be paid through the thirty-first, the original effective date of his resignation."

"You two have quite a busy day tomorrow. I won't try to talk to you at the office. I know you'll come see me when you can. By the way, my mother wants to meet you."

"I'm looking forward to meeting her. I like your

mother; she's so down-to-earth and no-nonsense. Especially when her baby girl is concerned."

"Her one and only baby girl."

Austin yawned. "Excuse me," he said quickly.

"I know you're tired." A yawn escaped from her own mouth. "Oh, look what you've started. I guess we'd both better get some sleep."

"I'm sleeping on Mickey's couch. It's not very comfortable, but I'm so tired I don't care."

"Sweet dreams, Ozzie."

"I wish you the same. And Desi . . ."

"Yes?"

"I love you."

Desirée was surprised at how easy it was for her to fall asleep.

Epilogue

The party being held at the West Side apartment of a friend of Austin's was lively, with a spirited discussion going on about the latest political storm that practically drowned out the music. "I can tell I'm getting old," Desirée whispered to Austin, "when I go to a party and debate the issues rather than dance. I'm depressed enough, being about to turn thirty."

Austin gave the back of her hand a reassuring pat. "Your birthday isn't until May, and this is only Valentine's weekend. Besides, you don't want to stay twenty-nine if I'm getting a little bit older every year; you'll too young for me."

"No, I guess I don't." Desirée looked over at Zack Warner, who stood by the window cozying up to a sophisticated type with a short bobbed haircut. "I just wish Vivian wasn't on a ski trip this weekend. My last chance to introduce her to Zack, and she's on the slopes in the Poconos somewhere."

"You make it sound like you'll never be in New York again."

"With me running the new call center, it sounds like my travel days will be over after we take the cruise and do those Florida resorts next month."

"I wouldn't say that. I probably won't be doing much traveling, now that my concentration will be on sales. But when I do, I'll pick the more interesting places.

That's what Phil does. You'd never catch him somewhere like Pittsburgh or Kansas City. But we'll probably need extra agents from time to time, and that's where you and Sandy come in."

"At least where I come in. Didn't you say Sandy is pregnant?"

"Oh, that's right. Phil insists the baby was conceived at the Accolade Hotel in Rome."

"And who will manage the call center if I have to go out of town?"

"Between Maddie and Elaine, there won't be a problem. You don't regret taking the job, do you?"

"No. I think it's definitely a good thing for both of us to stop traveling so much and spend time in the same city." That was the only way for them to explore the feelings they had for each other, which were still so new, and see if they would hold fast or weaken. She felt fortunate that such an opportunity had presented itself, especially with Wallace and Hughes closing its New York office and Austin relocating to Colorado. He was selling his place to his sister and brother-in-law, whose move would put them much closer to the senior Hugheses in Mount Vernon. Sarah would be caring for her new grandchild when Charlene returned to work.

Even Austin's secretary, Elaine, would be moving to Colorado, where she would continue to assist him in preparing packages for prospective clients, as well as provide backup for Maddie as office manager. The brokerage firm her husband worked for had offices all over the country, and they had given him a transfer. Elaine was ecstatic. "Maybe now we'll be able to afford a decent house," she'd told Desirée. "Our house now is practically falling down around us. Even the kids are excited." It was great how well things had worked out.

Desirée thought she glimpsed a familiar face in the crowd, and she drew in her breath when she recognized her old nemesis, Monique Oliver. It hadn't occurred to her that Monique would be at this party, but perhaps it should have, since Zack was here also. They apparently knew a lot of the same people.

Monique looked well, but then again, from what she knew of Monique, she wouldn't have it any other way. She watched as Monique moved through the room, greeting people. Her eyes shone as she approached them. "Hello there, how are you," she greeted, and if Desirée didn't know better, she would have sworn Monique was genuinely happy to see them.

She rolled her eyes as Austin got to his feet to kiss Monique's cheek. She resisted the urge to take his arm, to send a signal for Monique that he was hers. She should be above such childish behavior, and she was annoyed at herself for even *thinking* about doing it.

"Nice to see you," she said to Monique with a polite nod.

"You, too. You're looking well. Oh, I want to introduce the two of you to my fiancé."

Both Austin and Desirée were taken aback. It had been less than four months since they had taken off for the Ivory Coast; how had Monique managed to get engaged so quickly?

"Here he is," Monique was saying, and air stuck in Desirée's throat. It was, of all people, Skye Audsley.

"I think you all might have met at Zack's house, but just in case . . ." Monique performed the introductions, and this time it was Desirée's turn to be kissed on the cheek.

"Desirée and I are old friends," Skye said. "You're certainly looking well."

"Thank you. So are you. The bloom of love, no doubt." It was all she could do to keep a straight face, and Austin made a choking sound she suspected was a feeble attempt at covering a laugh.

"You two actually look pretty radiant yourselves. I see Monique has given you the good news," Skye said as he shook Austin's hand.

"She did. When's the wedding?"

"June. Out at my summer place in Sag Harbor."

Monique named a specific date in June. "I hope you both can make it."

"I'm afraid we'll miss it," Austin said, explaining, "I'm in the process of moving to Colorado. I'll be gone as soon as I can find a house."

From the way Monique lost color, it was clear this was the last thing she expected to hear.

"Well, that's wonderful," Skye was saying. "I've skied out there, and it's beautiful. Have you been here in New York all these months, Desirée?"

"No, only until early December; then I went home. I'm just here now for a few days. We're leaving for Puerto Rico tomorrow on a job."

"Good place to be in February."

Monique, who hadn't said a word since Austin informed her of his plans to relocate, nudged her intended. "Oh, look, Skye. There's Bester and Sharon. We should say hello."

The happy couple said their good-byes and moved on. Austin and Desirée looked at each other and broke out into carefully muffled laughter.

"What was that corny line about being in the 'bloom of love'?" Austin asked.

"I'm sorry. It just slipped out. My goodness, Monique and Skye. I can't imagine it. I just hope she genuinely loves him. She strikes me as the type who's more attracted to status than anything else. And his money won't hurt, either."

"I'm sure it'll be okay. I doubt she's so anxious to get married she'll do it without love."

Desirée hoped not, for Skye's sake. Still, she thought, love would come a lot easier to a woman like Monique with what Skye could offer. And a lot quicker.

"I just don't get why she looked so funny when I told her I was leaving New York," Austin said.

Desirée laughed. Men were so dense sometimes. "Let me explain. If it was me moving to New York, it wouldn't be a big deal. She'd merely think I was following you around like some lovesick puppy dog. But you're not supposed to move to where I am; that changes everything. That suggests I'm more than just a fling; that we might actually be serious."

"We *are* serious."

"I know that. And now she knows it, too. It just came as a shock, so much that she couldn't hide it."

"Sounds like a female thing to me. Skye had no trouble recognizing we have something special." He shook his head at the mystifying conduct of the female species. "So tell me, Desi, do you think you and I will ever do the marriage thing?"

She laughed. "You ask that like we've been going together for ten years instead of a few months."

"You didn't answer the question."

"Are you trying to get an idea of what I would say if you asked me? You can be a little sneaky that way, you know."

"Stop answering a question with a question. It's not fair."

"Well, I'm going to do it again. What do *you* think?"

"I'd say if the route to marriage is a road, then we're on it."

Desirée recalled Austin's statement when they were back in Colorado and he told her he had something to show her. He maneuvered her Honda CRV up a picturesque mountain road. His Buick was in New York, and he'd made a deal with the furniture mover to put it on the truck with the rest of his belongings, at a cost much lower than the quotes he'd gotten from the car movers. His car wouldn't be of much use out here in the winter months. The city of Evergreen, Colorado, approximately a mile and a half above sea level, was like being on top of the world. The house Austin brought her to look at was a split level, well spaced from the homes neighboring it on each side. She imagined how beautiful it would look covered with snow.

"You'll have to keep yourself well stocked up here," she said. "When it snows you might not be able to get anywhere for a day or two."

"You'll have to promise to drive over the minute the snow starts. As long as you're with me, I'll have everything I need."

She went inside with him. The rooms were large, and there were plenty of windows. She liked the layout. She couldn't find a thing wrong with it.

"What do you think?"

"I like it, Ozzie."

"Okay. I'm going to make an offer."

"Just like that?"

"You said you liked it. What else do I need to know?"

"But it's your house."

"I love it, Desi. But I wouldn't want to buy a house you didn't like. I wouldn't want to buy a piece of furniture unless you say you like it."

"And why's that?"

"You went to college. I'll let you figure that one out."

"So you value my opinion, do you?" Desirée asked as they were leaving.

"Yes, I do."

"I've just got one more question."

"What's that?"

"Now that you've found a house, when do we go car shopping? You've got to get rid of that Buick."

Dear Reader,

Thank you for going along with Austin and Desirée on their travels and the sometimes bumpy road to true love, and I hope you enjoyed the trip!

In my first book, *At Long Last Love,* I wrote about a woman on the cusp of middle age who had never experienced love and who was plagued by self-doubt. In my second, *A Love of Her Own,* I wrote about a woman whose infertility overshadowed all other details of her existence. After such heavy issues I felt it was time to lighten up a bit.

In case you're wondering, those elusive singles Vivian and Zack do eventually meet, not with the help of matchmakers Ozzie and Desi, but quite by accident (and the accidents keep right on happening!) in my next book, scheduled to be released in December 2001. It's tentatively titled *Reeling in Mr. Right* while I search for a title that makes Mr. Right sound more like the man of one's dreams and less like Charlie the Tuna.

Keep romance alive!

Bettye

Bettye Griffin
bunderw170@aol.com
or
P.O. Box 20354 (new!)
Jacksonville, FL 32255
(Please include a SASE for a response.)

About the Author

Bettye Griffin wrote two dozen romantic short stories during the 1980s and early 1990s, most of them published by the Sterling/McFadden group of "confession" magazines, often getting ideas for stories like "I Married an Illegal Alien for Money," from advice columns. She spent four years Frustrated in Florida herself before getting her first book published in 1998. When not writing, Bettye works as a freelance home-based medical transcriptionist. Originally from Yonkers, New York, she now makes her home in Jacksonville, Florida, with her husband and is stepmother to three children. *Love Affair* is her third Arabesque title.